THE VOICE IN ALL

BOOKS BY AUDREY AUDEN

The Path of Mysteries (2023)

The Voice in All (2022)

Realms Unreel (2011)

For author news and release updates, please visit
audreyauden.com

THE ARTIFEX AND THE MUSE
BOOK ONE

THE VOICE IN ALL

AUDREY AUDEN

LOVE THAT BOOK
An imprint of Love That Labs
Independent Publisher Since 2022
Bethlehem, New Hampshire

THE VOICE IN ALL
Version 3.0.6
Copyright © 2022 by Audrey Auden
All rights reserved

Cover design by Audrey Auden in collaboration with DALL·E 2

Published by Love That Book, an imprint of Love That Labs LLC

ebook ISBN: 978-1-937262-10-5
paperback ISBN: 978-1-937262-11-2
hardcover ISBN: 978-1-937262-12-9
audiobook ISBN: 978-1-937262-13-6

Many scenes from *The Voice in All*
have author-suggested music pairings.

Listen to the story soundtrack at
audreyauden.com

For my existence friend

It's queer how out of touch with truth women are. They live in a world of their own, and there has never been anything like it, and never can be. It is too beautiful altogether, and if they were to set it up it would go to pieces before the first sunset. Some confounded fact we men have been living contentedly with ever since the day of creation would start up and knock the whole thing over.

— Charlie Marlow, *Heart of Darkness* (1899) by Joseph Conrad

Is life so dear, or peace so sweet, as to be purchased at the price of chains and slavery? Forbid it, Almighty God! I know not what course others may take; but as for me, give me liberty or give me death!

— Patrick Henry, rally speech to the Second Convention of the American Revolution (1775)

AVA

I CROUCH MOTIONLESS beside my mother at the edge of the cedar forest. We peer out at the high stone wall of the temple city through a screen of ferns. Our mud-smeared faces and dust-covered hoods should be enough to conceal us from the watchful eyes of the gatekeeper atop the wall. But my mother said there could be other Mohirai watching from anywhere, so we've had to keep still and silent all through this long hot afternoon. I'm desperate to move my legs. Thank the spirits that sunset's approaching, and with it the protective cover of darkness.

My mother's fingers sign, *Ava, look.*

I follow her gaze, searching for whatever she's spotted.

Ahead of us, the relative safety of the forest gives way to an exposed meadow that slopes a long way down toward the sea. About a dozen boys and girls around my age swim near the small crescent beach beside the city docks.

Above the beach looms the great wall enclosing the temple city. The wall stretches from the shore to the forest edge, and the bronze-clad gate at its center stands closed.

Ah, there it is: a flash of movement atop the wall, backlit by the sinking sun. I squint against the glare. A lone Mohira passes behind the narrow gap of a crenellation. The gatekeeper is on the move.

I tap my mother's rough, sun-reddened hand, which looks massive beside my own small brown one. She watches my fingers as I sign, *Is this the expected time?*

She glances at the sun's position and signs, *Yes. Perfect silence now.*

The city gate swings slowly inward. Three Mohirai step out onto the rutted dirt road, dressed in identical dark cloaks over sky blue robes. They follow the road a short distance across the meadow before turning onto a narrower footpath that climbs uphill toward the forest.

Despite the hoods obscuring their faces, I think that's the High Priestess Serapen walking in front, flanked by the other two women. I've never seen anyone else with this gliding gait and peculiar way of clasping her hands as she walks, like she can't swing her arms.

I glance at my mother. Her square, muscular jaw twitches. She signs, *That's Serapen and two of her healer initiates. Three more healers remain inside the wall.*

I repeat the message back to confirm I understand, then sign, *I await your command.*

My mother signals for me to continue waiting.

Serapen and her healers enter the woods about a hundred paces west of our lookout spot. The forest now hides them from us as well as it hides us from them, so we've lost one of our advantages. It's a calculated risk. The only way we could be absolutely sure Serapen is out of the city is to see her leave, and the safest place for us to watch the gate is here at the forest edge.

My mother closes her eyes and draws back her hood just enough to expose her ears. She listens, and I know she hears the three women's footsteps passing somewhere through the woods behind us. When she inhales silently, I know she detects their scent in the air. Those Mohirai could hear us, too, if we made the slightest sound in the underbrush. They could even smell us, if we hadn't thoroughly masked our scent with soil and forest debris.

I wish I could perceive everything like my mother and the Mohirai, whose senses are enhanced by the arts of pharmaka. Unfortunately, with my unaided perception, I hear nothing but sea breeze in the canopy and smell nothing but sweet bracken ferns, spicy cedar needles, and the occasional pungent whiff of low tide.

Despite all my mother has taught me about the risks that accompany the use of pharmaka, I can't help but envy her powers of perception, her size, and her strength. Her body has so many advantages over mine because of pharmaka. At least once per moon, I plead with her to teach me the basics of these arts, enough at least that I might protect myself if I ever have the misfortune to encounter a Mohira without my mother beside me.

But no argument I've tried on this subject has ever moved her. She always says, *Abstinence from pharmaka gives you an essential advantage over all the Mohirai: freedom from the Voice in all.* I don't understand how this is an advantage, though. I've heard the Voice a few times, and to me it seems like nothing more than a disembodied whisper in my mind, insubstantial as a daydream. The Voice can't possibly be as dangerous as facing an initiate Mohira on my own.

The forest shadows lengthen as I wait for my mother's signal. I distract myself from my restless impulse to move by watching the boys and girls playing together in the waves. As sunset approaches, they swim ashore, dispersing in little groups of two and three and four, disappearing into the orchards and gardens outside the wall. One boy lingers behind on the beach, watching the fiery glow of sky and sea as the sun dips toward the horizon.

Inside the temple city, the bells for the evening silence toll, a sweet chord of three notes repeated three times. My gaze drifts toward the magnificent bronze dome of the Children's Temple at the city center, one of the few buildings visible over the wall. The sound of the bells and sight of the dome recall memories of a more innocent time, when this temple city was the only home I knew and I looked forward to nothing more than becoming an initiate Mohira myself.

The girls who had scattered across the grounds gather promptly at the sound of the bells. They converge on the meadow outside the temple city. The bronze gate opens to admit them. As the girls pass through the gate in a silent line, I wonder whether my two former trio sisters are among them. Neither would remember me now, I suppose. The Mohirai probably took those memories from them after my mother escaped the sisterhood with me.

The gate swings shut, cutting off my view of the girls, so I turn to watching the boys instead. They're reappearing slowly from the orchards and the gardens, making their way in little groups toward the rambling stone house of boys on the far side of the meadow, outside the city wall. I glance toward the beach and see the lone boy still standing there, watching the last of the sunset.

My mother opens her eyes, and my attention snaps back to her. She looks at me and signs, *It's time. Serapen is past hearing. Be careful.*

Unable to suppress the excitement I always feel at the

start of a job, I grin at my mother and sign, *Next stop, freedom!*

Her thin lips press into a stern line, and her ice blue eyes bore into mine. *Don't get cocky*, she signs.

We've done this job so many times before that I'm inclined to wave away her warning. There's nothing much different about this time, except that it's the last time. But my mother's grim expression is sobering, so I sign, *I'll be careful.*

DOM

I SIT AT THE BEACH on the last day of summer, distracting myself from thoughts of tomorrow with a final sketch before I lose the light.

Today was hot—too hot for clothes—and this little crescent of sand between the rocky tide pools and the docks is the best place to swim within an easy walk of the city gate. About a dozen of the sixteenth summer boys and girls splash and dunk each other, their naked bodies rising and falling together in the gentle swells. Shouts of laughter merge with the shrill cries of the gulls fishing for their evening meal and the throaty barks of the seals lazing on the rocks.

I glance from the scene before me to the scrap of oak plank I balance on my knees as a makeshift drawing board. In my left hand, I grip a tiny nub of charcoal pencil I found in the meadow after one of the younger girls tossed it aside during her drawing instruction. I smooth my free hand over the wrinkled surface of my parchment, a sour-smelling cheese wrapper I salvaged during kitchen chores a few days ago. Sometimes I wonder what it might be like to draw on new parchment like the girls do, but this piece actually isn't too bad. With my bold charcoal lines now covering its surface from edge to edge, I hardly notice the grease marks.

As I focus on the sea, my shoddy materials fade from my awareness. The steady inhale and exhale of the waves leads my hand in a gentle rhythm, stroke after charcoal stroke over parchment.

I love the sea in any of her moods, from the rage of a winter storm to the calm of a windless summer day, from cheerful mornings to melancholy sunsets. I can almost always lose myself and any troubled thoughts in her presence. Now I study how she transforms at the edge where day approaches night, wave approaches shore, boy approaches calling.

My hand jerks to a stop. I've managed to evade most thoughts of my calling for the past moon, but it's impossible now that tomorrow's the day.

I try to resume sketching, but I've slipped out of the flow. My hand feels stuck. Resigned, I set down my drawing board on the sand beside me.

I study the faces of the boys out there enjoying the waves on our last day together. Not one of them seems to share my dread of tomorrow. If anything, the approach of our Calling Day has stirred them into a frenzy. Each boy knows today is his last opportunity to seize the easy pleasure of our lives here among the Mohirai. The sailors who deliver supplies to the temple city often visit the house of boys, and they make no secret of the rougher conditions in the villages where we'll spend the rest of our lives among the men.

Two of my friends, Balashi and Hanu, break away from the rest of the swimmers and ride a wave back to the beach. Hanu picks up a towel from the sand, shakes it clean, and dries herself. Balashi bounds after her like an energetic puppy but doesn't bother with a towel. He shakes his wet hair, spraying her with seawater. She swats his arm lightly, and he inclines his head in apology. She gestures for him to follow her. They turn in my direction.

Hanu spots me and waves. "Dom!" she calls. "I was wondering where you'd gone." She walks up the beach toward me, Balashi close at her side. Hastily, I pull my tunic from the pile of discarded clothes beside me and drape it over my drawing board, concealing my sketch from view.

She stops before me, a naked silhouette against the sunset. Her eyes rest a moment on my hand, which hovers nervously at the edge of my tunic. I know she knows what I'm hiding, but she won't force me to show the sketch to her, not in front of Balashi. Instead, she wraps her towel around her waist and sits beside me, stretching her long legs out in the sand and leaning back on her hands. The coppery light glistens on the warm brown skin of her smooth shoulders, generous breasts, and gently rounded belly.

Balashi, entirely naked, flops down on my other side and slings his damp arm around me companionably. Despite his fair complexion, he's managed to retain the faintest bronzing after a long afternoon in the sun. His handsome face and indomitable confidence make him a favorite among the girls. They've kept him busy today, but it's clear from the way he eyes Hanu that he's hungry for more.

"What are you thinking, spending today alone, brother?" says Balashi, shaking me by the shoulders as if to wake me from sleep.

"Do you want to come with us?" says Hanu, looking at my unclothed body with frank interest. Balashi's expression clouds at her invitation, but the decision is hers, not his.

"I'm all right," I say. "You two should go ahead."

Balashi shoots me a grateful look, then offers some brotherly advice. "Better make a proposition before the bell rings and the girls are all locked up inside the city again."

"Go," I insist, waving him off.

He shakes his head in bewilderment. "I'll never understand you, Dom."

"Some find as much pleasure in the mind as the body, Bala," says Hanu.

"Easy for you to say." Balashi laughs and claps me on the shoulder. "We men have to get what pleasure we can while we still can."

"You boys, you mean," Hanu says mildly. "Well, come and get it then."

Hanu stands, and her towel slips off. She wraps it back around her hips, taking her time. Concealment only adds to the attraction of her figure, and I can see that she knows it. She catches my gaze, making clear that her offer still stands. I lower my eyes, grateful she's not being as aggressive as some of the other girls have been toward me over the last few days.

I enjoy Hanu's company most of the time. But lately, with her growing excitement at the approach of Calling Day, I've found it impossible to forget the chasm between us. It's not that she flaunts her advantage, not exactly. The Mohirai teach the girls from an early age to be kind to boys and men. And most of them are. At least, most of them try. And Hanu is better than most.

But even Hanu takes for granted things that are forever out of my reach. Her unconsciousness of this is sometimes unbearable. I would give anything for just the basic instruction every girl receives from the Mohirai. Reading and writing, historia and poetika, tekhnologia and pharmaka—all of these and so much more will remain among the mysteries for me. And the sixteenth summer girls haven't even started their novice training in the higher mysteries, which will be followed by centuries of deepening practice through their service to the Voice as initiate Mohirai. So of course Hanu is excited about her path ahead, especially now, on the eve of our Calling Day. But her excitement amplifies my dread.

Hanu pulls Balashi up by the hand and leads him along the beach toward the orchard path. Their laughter drifts back to me as I remain sitting, watching the crimson and gold melting into the west and the deep purple rising in the east.

A little while later, Hanu returns to the beach alone. She searches for the clothes she left on the sand earlier this afternoon and dresses herself. She comes to sit beside me again and looks out at the waves.

I can't help myself from asking. It's always more interesting to hear this story from a girl's perspective, especially Hanu's. I say, "How was he today?"

Hanu chooses her words carefully, savoring each. "Like a summer sunshower. Lovely, invigorating, over almost before he's begun."

I chuckle. Hanu tips her head to the side and looks at me, the corner of her mouth curving in a hint of a smile. She rests her warm hand on my bare thigh and says, "You're another thing entirely, Dom."

I study Hanu's familiar face, committing her to memory —her thoughtful brow, her kind eyes, her sensuous mouth. I may never see her again after tomorrow, but there's still enough time to learn what words she might choose for me today. Clearly she's willing. But I'm not in the mood.

When I make no move toward her, she lifts her hand

from my leg and taps the tunic concealing my drawing board. "May I see?" she says.

She waits, curious but not insistent. It's demoralizing to show my work to a girl who's had so much instruction in the arts. But perhaps Hanu will teach me something useful, even though strictly speaking the girls aren't supposed to share instruction with boys. I pull back the tunic and hand her the sketch. She examines it for a long time. When she looks up at me, her brow is furrowed and her eyes are troubled.

"What's wrong?" I say.

She's probably thinking this is an utterly useless way for a boy to spend his time. But what she says is, "I wonder why the Voice has given you such gifts. You would have been better off as a girl."

I try to laugh, but it sounds hollow. I say, "Wouldn't we all have been?"

"Not all of you, I think," she says. She gestures toward the boys coming ashore with other girls. They split off in twos and threes and fours to seek their pleasure, making their way toward the forest, or the orchards, or the gardens. "None of them have the inclination toward the arts and mysteries. They'll live out their days as happily in the villages as they've grown up here in the house of boys. The Voice will give them all the sense of purpose they need, and pharmaka will give them all the courage they need to make the journey into Death."

My heart sinks at her words. It's not that I'm afraid of Death. I've known since I was a small boy that Death is where all uninitiated creatures go after we've served our purpose to the Voice. And I've seen firsthand that the lives of the creatures we care for are pleasant. Of course I've also seen the awful flash of knowing in the eyes of the countless sheep and rabbits I've slaughtered, in that brief moment before the fall of my knife. But their deaths are as painless as it's possible for us to make them, and their fear is over in an instant. The Mohirai handle boys and men with even greater care than we give our animals, so I can't really fear Death.

It's the prospect of what happens before Death—or, rather, what won't happen—that saddens me. It's the sense of loss, knowing all I might have done as a Mohira. The life of an initiate continues for as long as the Voice requires the initiate's service—centuries, even millennia. Spirits, what a life that would be! But training in the arts and mysteries is wasted on lives as short as men's, and the Voice requires a different service from us. We must pay with our hands, our sweat, and our lives the debt incurred by men who came long before us, the men who brought about the destruction.

Seeing my expression, Hanu takes my hand, her long brown fingers soft and smooth against my work-hardened palm. "Don't be troubled, brother. The Mohirai teach that all find purpose in their callings, men as well as women. The Voice works through you with purpose, as it does through us all, whatever our paths."

Hanu's words reawaken the one bit of genuine excitement I feel as I face tomorrow. Calling Day is the one day in my life when I'll hear the Voice in all for myself, like the Mohirai do. The Mohirai teach that hearing the Voice brings the clarity, contentedness, and courage each man needs to walk his path. I take comfort in this teaching as Hanu and I watch the last of the sunset together.

Inside the temple city, the bells for the evening silence toll, a sweet chord of three notes repeated three times, summoning the girls to return to their dormitory. Hanu stands, pulls me up by the hand, and kisses me lightly on the cheek. "Good night, Dom. Safe passage on your journey tomorrow. I'll miss you."

THE LAST JOB

I REMAIN AT THE BEACH, and Hanu departs. I watch her walk back up to the meadow, where she rejoins the other girls returning from their dalliances here and there about the grounds. Their chattering ceases as they enter the temple city, passing through a gate that will remain locked to me forever.

I look down at my sketch one last time before crumpling it into a ball and burying it in the sand. There's no point keeping it, since I can't take anything with me to the ceremony tomorrow. I pick up my tunic, breeches, belt, and shoes and dress myself, preparing to return to the house of boys.

A creak, splash, and thump catches my attention, and I look toward the docks. A small fishing boat slows to a stop alongside the outermost mooring slip. A tall, slim man hops out of the boat with a line and ties it loosely around a cleat on the dock while a burly man onboard lowers the foresail. It's late for a boat to arrive. Perhaps they've had some mishap out at sea.

"Good evening, brothers," I call as I walk toward them. "Do you need help? I can take a message to Hedi Mohira at the house of boys if you need assistance."

The slim man and the burly man both look toward the boat's stern, where I notice a third man with a thick, dark beard seated at the tiller. All three men wear caps low over their foreheads, so I can't make out any of their faces in the fading light. The bearded man murmurs something to the burly man, who calls back to me in a lilting accent I don't recognize, "Tanks kindly, lil' brother. We'll just sleep te night and be on our way. No need to trouble a priestess."

"I'm sure it's no trouble," I say. "Hedi loves to welcome any man who returns to the house for a visit. Wouldn't you rather come up for a meal and a proper bed?"

The burly man says, "We make an early start. And we heard te bell ring already. Should'na you be abed, yourself?"

His question puzzles me. He can't possibly think I'm as young as that. There's no curfew for boys my age. Perhaps the rules have changed since this man grew up here. Although, in my experience, the Mohirai don't tend to change their rules about much, especially not Hedi Mohira, who has run the house of boys for centuries.

I shrug off my confusion and say, "I'm just heading back to the house now. Are you sure you don't need anything?"

"Not a ting," he says.

"Well … Good night, then."

"G'night."

I walk back to the house of boys from the docks. The first evening stars appear as I cross the meadow. I follow the worn footpath along the split-rail fence of the paddocks, continuing past the stone animal enclosures. The path passes through rows of trellises and terraces and raised garden beds luxuriant with summer growth, soon to be harvested. I have a thousand memories of hauling and sweating, weeding and pruning, milking and shearing in every corner of these grounds outside the city.

Ahead of me stands the house of boys. The house backs into the steep hillside just below the edge of the cedar forest, and its wide arching windows and front door face a magnificent view of the sea. The dormitory windows on the upper two floors are dark. The younger boys on those floors are already in bed, sleeping the pharmaka-deepened sleep of the newly unbound. But golden light flickers from many windows on the lower two floors, where the older boys, our unbindings years behind us, are mostly still awake.

Three lit candles stand on the windowsill of the ground floor bedroom I share with my trio brothers, Balashi and Kuri. Our window's open, and as I pass by on my way to the front door, I hear Balashi speaking in an animated undertone punctuated by Kuri's occasional deep chuckle. This is our last night together as a trio after eight years in the house of boys. I'm sure we'll be up talking half the night, between speculating about what calling each of us will receive from the Voice tomorrow and hearing Balashi rehash his exploits from today.

I don't particularly relish the thought of discussing either right now. If I can delay my return to our room just a bit longer, maybe Balashi will be nearing the end of a tale I've heard a hundred times before with minor variations.

I waver at the front steps of the house. A breeze stirs, and I inhale the sweet and spicy scent of the cedar forest, redolent of childhood memories. An overwhelming desire strikes me to visit my special place in the woods one last time before tomorrow. So I turn away from the front door and walk around to the back of the house, up the steep hillside, into the ferns that grow at the edge of the forest.

A faint animal track through the ferns leads me to the ancient cedar at the forest edge west of the house. It's not obvious from here, but this cedar's massive trunk is hollow. I've always found it strange that, despite so many clear memories of playing around this tree, I don't remember how I discovered that it's hollow. The opening in the trunk is completely hidden by the underbrush. But when I was small, I used to climb up through the heart of this cedar and step out through the top of the hole onto a high branch. The view of the sea is amazing up there, and you can even see a bit over the city wall.

I'm far too big to climb up through the trunk any more, but I still enjoy sitting here when I want to be alone. I pull myself up onto a low, broad branch and lean against the trunk, breathing in the scent of its bark and needles, listening to the familiar nighttime sounds of the forest insects and the more distant sound of waves rolling ashore.

These sounds have lulled me to sleep for as long as I can remember, and this perch is surprisingly comfortable. I've almost nodded off before I realize with a start that I should return to the house. The Calling Day ceremony starts before dawn, and I don't want to fall asleep in the woods and miss Hedi's wake-up call. I hop down from the branch.

I've taken only one step when I hear something unfamiliar amidst the usual nighttime sounds. I pause to listen. There it is again: shallow, panting breaths. Another lover's tryst, most likely. Perhaps some pair failed to hear the bell or lingered behind on purpose. Either way, I have no interest in disturbing them, so I resume my walk back to the house.

There's an abrupt crunch and snap of branches. I turn slowly toward the sound, reconsidering what I heard. Perhaps it's an animal moving through the underbrush. I listen more closely. There's a soft rustle, a light thud, a hissing intake of breath, and a whimper. I feel a protective instinct, like I do whenever a lamb or kid goes missing from the herd. Maybe one of the younger boys wandered off into the woods.

"Hello?" I call out to the shadows.

△▽△

I'll be careful, I sign to my mother.

Still crouching, I creep back into the forest. My mother remains in our lookout spot in the ferns, so she can create a distraction for me if she detects Serapen or the other healers returning to the city earlier than expected.

Once I'm deep enough in the woods that I can't be seen by any Mohira who might look this way from the wall, I stand. I unlace and roll up my dirt-encrusted cloak and stuff it into the bottom of the small leather pack I'm carrying. The linen shirt and riding breeches I'm wearing don't provide any camouflage, but they're less likely than my cloak to catch branches if I need to hide up in the trees.

Barefoot, I follow a faint deer track upslope through the underbrush until it joins a wider footpath. It's just past sunset, but the dense canopy in this part of the forest blocks almost all of the twilight. Fortunately, my feet know each twist and turn of this path, and I find the darkness relaxing. Darkness is a thief's best friend.

I know I'm approaching my destination when cedar gives way to beech. Beech leaves rustle in their branches at a lower pitch than cedar needles and feel softer underfoot. The path disappears into a patch of young beeches, and I push my way through the pliable saplings, feeling my way forward in the darkness until my fingertips brush the cool face of a high boulder. I slide my hands in both directions along the boulder until I find the cave opening.

I kneel before a loose pile of leaves beside the cave entrance and uncover the two bundles I buried here in daylight. The first bundle contains my worn leather riding boots, and I stuff them into my pack for later.

The second bundle contains my disguise. I unroll this bundle on the ground, stand up, and strip off my shirt, belt, and riding breeches. I take the little waterskin from the bundle and pour out just enough to wash the mud off my hands and face. To the Mohirai, dirtiness would be a conspicuous sign of something amiss. I gulp down the rest of the water. It's been a hot day, even in the shade of the woods, although the night air is cooling fast.

I change quickly into the undyed cream-colored wool tunic, roughspun breeches, and cloth shoes that all the girls and boys wear. I rake my fingers through the dark tangle of my unbound curls, plaiting my hair in a single long braid like the girls inside the temple city often wear. A braid can be quickly stuffed inside my tunic to keep it out of the way, or to make me look like a boy from a distance. If all goes well, the disguise won't matter because I won't be seen at all, but looking like just another girl or boy could be decent camouflage in a pinch.

I re-buckle my belt around my waist to keep my tools handy, stuff my riding clothes and the empty waterskin into my pack, sling the pack over both shoulders, and spread the leaf pile around to erase the signs of my presence here. I double-check my mental inventory of what's in my pack and what's in my belt. I think that's everything. Taking one last breath of the sweet forest air, I enter the cave.

I keep my hand above my head to avoid hitting the low cave ceiling, feeling my way forward with my feet as best I can despite the cloth shoes muffling the sensation in my toes. Although it was quite dark outside already, about ten paces inside the cave I enter total darkness. I close my eyes, since I know from experience they're good for nothing beyond this point but catching cobwebs, dust, and—if I'm unlucky— panicking bats. I keep walking forward until the soft soil beneath my shoes gives way to a rough-hewn but level stone floor.

I've reached the start of a long tunnel bored through the hillside. I sweep both hands around me in the pitch darkness, tracing the rounded shape of the tunnel from its high point above my head to the walls beside me. There's about half an arm's length of clearance around me on all sides. Most Mohirai would struggle to move through such a small space; that's why I always do this part of the job.

The cool stone beneath my fingertips is my only guide through the darkness as I walk the steep downward slope in this first section of the tunnel. My hand slides over hundreds of ancient chisel marks with each step. The slope flattens out after a few dozen paces, and then I run. I prefer to move fast through these tunnels. It helps me shake off the feeling that I'm walking into a trap.

The echoes of my running footsteps change as I approach the intersection, and I slow to a walk. My fingertips slide off the wall, grasping nothing but air. If I tripped or turned or became disoriented here at the five-way intersection, I would be in real trouble. I only know where two of these tunnels lead. I rein in the unhelpful thought and walk steadily forward, keeping my hand outstretched. I seem to float through a void without an anchor, with only my heartbeat and my breath for company in what's otherwise complete silence and utter darkness. In ten heartbeats, the fingers of my right hand catch the chiseled stone wall on the other side of the intersection. I allow myself a tiny sigh of relief. The storerooms aren't much farther now.

I walk the rest of the way with my left hand out ahead of me, until my palm lands on a rough wooden door. I grin. Almost halfway done, and I'm making great time.

I fish out a leather drawstring bag that I keep in a buckled pouch on my belt. Carefully, muffling any sound of jingling, I pull out two bronze rings. Each holds a collection of long iron pins. By touch, I locate the pins I need, then kneel before the door. Another ten heartbeats is all I need to pick this lock. The tunnel door swings open, and I step into an unlit storeroom.

I make my way across the dark room by memory. I reach its front door without crashing into anything, and I press my ear to the doorframe. Hearing nothing, I lift the latch and push gently. To my relief, the olive oil I rubbed into the hinges last time pays off now as the door swings silently open. I step out into the dim, flickering light of the corridor and shut the door behind me, double-checking that it remains unlocked for my return.

I glance left and right, double-checking my mental map

of my exits while I'm free from distraction. Three locked doors stand to the left of my exit door, and beyond them the wider central corridor that connects a warren of storerooms beneath the Children's Temple. Five locked doors stand to my right, and beyond them a dead end. I face eight locked doors on the opposite wall.

Satisfied that I'm properly oriented, I hurry to the fourth door from the left on the opposite wall. Picks in hand, I kneel before the lock and set to work. I've never entered this particular storeroom before, but the lock sounds about the same as all the others, and my mother has described what the room looked like the last time she went inside seven years ago. The Mohirai tend to make changes on a timescale of centuries, so I'm hoping to find everything within basically unchanged.

Padding footsteps echo softly to my left, coming from somewhere in the central corridor. *Three more healers remain inside the wall*, I remember, and my mouth goes dry. Perhaps my mother misjudged, and the pharmaka preparations for tomorrow's Calling Day ceremony aren't complete after all. Maybe one of the healers forgot some ingredient and she's coming back here now. I close my eyes, forcing back the distracting thoughts, blocking out all sensation other than the sound of my picks inside this lock. Almost there.

Snick. My door unlocks just as the padding footsteps stop. A door in the main corridor creaks open. Relief washes away some of my nerves. That must be some Mohira visiting a food storeroom. I'm safe here, at least for now. I risk lingering in the corridor a moment longer to light a candle stub from my pack at the nearest oil lamp. Then I slip into the storeroom and lock the door behind me.

I'm exultant, having reached my destination without a hitch and gained the advantage of light, which should speed things up considerably.

The urgent need to sneeze nearly blows out my advantage. I clap my free hand over my nose and mouth, squeezing hard. Tears stream from my watering eyes, blurring my vision. My mother warned me about the smell, but the powerful melange of aromas emanating from the pharmaka ingredients in this room is more pungent than I'd expected. I switch to breathing through my mouth like a swimmer, which seems appropriate because my head is starting to swim. I need to move fast. Even the raw ingredients of pharmaka can have powerful effects on the uninitiated, like me.

I hold up my candle to examine the room. Four large barrels stand in the four corners of the room. Wooden shelves mounted on iron brackets line the stone walls from floor to ceiling. Large clay jars fill the shelves. Each bears a wax label neatly lettered in cuneiform with a description of the jar's contents. My mother explained the organization system: jars grouped chronologically by moon of harvest, then by moon phase. I skim the labels shelf by shelf. Ah, here they are: ingredients harvested near the first full moon after the summer solstice.

I can't suppress an indignant grumble when I spot the jar I need—dried amanitai—on a top shelf. Of course my mother wouldn't have anticipated this problem. That shelf would be well within her reach, within reach for almost anyone but me. Children raised by the Mohirai grow up eating a rich diet laced with many forms of pharmaka, which generally produces tall bodies, long arms, long legs. Not for the first time, I curse my mother's adamant stance on raising me without pharmaka.

I scan the room for possible solutions. The shelves appear solidly built, and they're already carrying considerable weight. It's possible I could step up onto a lower shelf to reach the top one. But I imagine the difficulty of hopping down with such a large jar and the risk of upsetting a whole shelf full of jars. I'm an excellent climber, but the risk seems too great. There must be a better option.

I could try to use a jar from a lower shelf as a step stool. I'm not confident one of these jars could bear my entire weight, though. If there were a plank, perhaps I could safely spread my weight across several jars and use that as a step, but I don't see anything like a plank.

There's that large barrel in the corner beside the shelf, though. I approach and examine it, wondering whether the barrel might be safe to stand on. I slip my fingers into the grooves carved into the barrel's circular top and discover to my delight that the top lifts off. I'm now holding the bit of plank I need for my step stool.

I glance inside the open barrel. It's about half full of what appears to be pure water. Seems odd to store water all the way down here in the storerooms. Healers usually require fresh spring water to prepare pharmaka. I risk a tentative sniff over the barrel. I still think it's water, but I really can't be sure with all the other bizarre smells confusing my nose.

I shake my head to clear it. All this pharmaka in the air must be getting to me. Of course it doesn't matter what's in this barrel; I need to focus on getting the amanitai and getting out of here.

I quickly construct a makeshift tripod stool from three jars and the barrel top. I step up, pull down the jar I need, set it carefully on the floor, and pry off the wax-sealed lid. The mushroom powder inside appears just as my mother described: rust in color, almost as fine as dust.

The jar's nearly full—over a bushel of powder, easily twice what we've agreed to pay the free men in exchange for our westward passage. Usually, I take only what we need, to minimize the risk of the Mohirai noticing what we've taken. But we're never coming back here again, so it seems foolish to leave behind something that could be so useful for bribes. I rummage through my pack and withdraw an empty linen-lined leather sack. I slip the sack over the mouth of the jar and upend the jar's entire contents into it.

A little cloud of mushroom dust rises as I set the empty jar back down. Holding my breath to avoid inhaling any of the airborne amanitai, I knot the sack closed and shove it into my pack. The overfilled sack is a little too big to fit entirely inside my pack, unfortunately. I hadn't accounted for the extra volume. Maybe I should empty some of the amanitai back into the jar so I'll be more streamlined for the run back out through the tunnels.

Unfortunately, I've run out of time for that. I hear footsteps again: two sets. My stomach churns, but I keep calm. It could be more visitors to the food storerooms.

But no, I realize with dismay—these footsteps are too loud to be in the adjacent corridor. They're coming this way, along with the voices of two women chatting.

The first woman says, "Do you need anything while I'm in here, sister?"

The second says, "A handful of withania root should do it."

I curse inwardly. I recognize this ingredient name, because I just saw it on a shelf in this room.

"More withania?" Something jingles like a hundred keys on a ring. The jingling pauses, and the first woman calls out, like she's now separated from her companion. "Did something go wrong with the preparation of the unbinding pharmaka?"

The second woman calls back, "No, but Serapen told me before she left for the clearing that we need more doses."

The jingling stops. The first woman says, "Spirits, it would have been nice for the Voice to tell her that a bit earlier, wouldn't it? We'll be up all night making a second batch."

"Ah, well," says the second. "The Voice works in mysterious ways."

A chuckle, then the first says, "Did she say why? Is it possible there'll be a novice Artifex called tomorrow?"

"She didn't say, though I can't think of another reason."

The first woman says, "Can you imagine a boy in the house of novices?"

Laughter from both of them, then the second woman says, "Hard to say whether that's good fortune or bad for the boy, but the girls will enjoy it, I'm sure. I certainly would have."

The first woman says, "I can't even remember when the last one was called. What do you think? Over a century?

Maybe two?"

To my relief, the women seem to be in no hurry to conclude their chat about the novice Artifex, whatever that means. I have a moment to consider my options. I still have the advantage of surprise. If I burst out of this room, I can escape through the door I left unlocked across the hall. There's little chance these women can catch me in the corridor, and I can move much faster than they can through the tunnels. Even though my pack is now a bit unwieldy, the amanitai powder is light and won't slow me down much.

Unfortunately, I'll be seen if I step out into the corridor. Once I'm seen, the Mohirai will send out an alarm. With an alarm out, my mother and I can still escape through the woods, but that's not where we need to go this time. We need to get to the docks, where the boat is waiting to carry us far from here. Getting to the docks was going to be tricky enough without an alarm, but with an alarm out it will be nearly impossible. Even if we did get to the docks, there's almost no possibility our boat would wait for us after an alarm. No sailor would be foolish enough to cross the Mohirai openly by helping runaways.

And once that boat leaves, it won't be easy to find another. It took my mother years of careful preparation to arrange this departure for us. It could take years to arrange it all a second time.

Think, Ava, think.

If only there were somewhere to hide in here, I could stay put, let this Mohira gather what she needs, then slip out after she's gone. No one would be the wiser until someone notices all the amanitai is missing. By then, my mother and I will be safely out at sea.

I like this plan far better than the first. The only problem is that there's nothing in here large enough to conceal a whole person.

Except … there is a perfect hiding place for someone as small as I am. I spring into action, swift and silent as I return the storeroom to the condition I found it. It's no good hiding if it's obvious I was here.

The keys jingle outside the door again. There's a scrape of metal on metal as a key enters the lock. My stomach drops. I still need to get into my hiding place, but she'll be in here in three heartbeats. She's going to catch me. I get ready to run for it.

There's a faint crunching sound in the lock. Relief washes over me. She tried the wrong key. The jingling resumes.

Her mistake gives me just enough extra time. I lick my fingers and put out my candle, plunging the room into darkness. Stepping toward the opened barrel in the corner, I grasp the lip of the opening with both hands, swing my legs over the edge, and lower myself carefully inside. I gasp involuntarily at the shock of icy water rising up my legs. I bite my lip hard—too hard—to silence myself. I taste blood.

I lean over to pick up my pack and the barrel lid from the floor. Holding my pack tight over my head with one arm and balancing the barrel lid above me with my other hand, I sink quickly until I'm sitting on the bottom of the barrel. The bone-chilling water rises to my neck as I pin my knees to my chest. I try and fail several times to close the barrel lid above my pack. It would be easy if I could just let the pack get wet, but I'm pretty sure a bag of wet amanitai will be worthless to us. At last I manage to close the lid by dropping my head so far forward that my bleeding lip is submerged in the water.

The storeroom door creaks open.

THE VOICE IN ALL

Hiding inside the barrel, with frigid water rising all the way up over my mouth, I breathe as silently as possible through my nose, trying not to blow bubbles. I listen as the Mohira steps into the storeroom and bustles about for what seems to be an impossibly long time, opening and closing at least half a dozen jars as she mutters to herself.

I'm losing sensation in the arm holding the pack above my head at this awkward angle, so I make a minuscule adjustment. To my horror, something powdery spills from the top of my pack into the water. The overfilled bag of amanitai has come untied. How could I have forgotten to double-check that knot?

A scent like dark forest soil floats toward me across the surface of the water. I press my lips tightly shut, but not before a taste of something bitter, sweet, and musky slips over my tongue. The cut on my lip where I bit myself tingles strangely.

I stew in amanitai for I don't know how long, until at last the Mohira departs. The door closes and locks. Footsteps retreat down the corridor. I'm relieved that my plan worked, but I'm worried because I don't know how much of the amanitai I've spilled into the water.

I climb out of the barrel in the pitch dark, dripping everywhere, but there's no help for that or for the amanitai I'm leaving behind in the barrel. My soaked clothes cling to me, and I wedge my tongue between my teeth to stop them from chattering with cold. I feel my way across the room toward the door. Fortunately, this lock only prevents someone from coming in, so I don't have to pick the lock to get out while I'm shivering.

I open the creaky door and step into the corridor. There's no point trying to re-lock the door with my picks. The wet mess I'm leaving behind is an unmistakable sign I was here.

By the light of the oil lamps, I quickly check the contents of my pack. My riding boots at the bottom are wet. But to my relief, the leather sack containing the amanitai remains dry. About a third of the amanitai spilled into the water while I was in the barrel, though. I suppose it's good that I took so much extra, after all. What remains is still more than we need. I retie the top of the sack quickly, triple-checking my knot this time.

I cross the hall, take my exit, and hurry across the unlit storeroom. Chilly air pours over me as I open the back door into the tunnel. Despite my soaked clothes and shivering, my skin tingles with a strange warmth. Probably just nerves. Quickly, I step into the tunnel and pull the door closed behind me.

The rough tunnel wall slides faster and faster beneath my fingertips as I race ahead. Unfortunately, I can't outrun the inner voice, which sounds like my mother, chastising me for my mistake. It's not my narrow escape that bothers me—that Mohira's unexpected appearance in my storeroom was no fault of mine. But the failed knot and lost amanitai were entirely my fault. It's been years since I've made a mistake like that on a job.

I cross the intersection, running at full speed all the way

until I reach the last little rise in the tunnel. A smudge of dark grey appears in the void ahead of me: the cave opening. I've made it.

I pause just inside the opening. The forest outside sounds unusually loud for this time of night, full of animal calls and hums and chirps, some of which I recognize, but many of which I've never heard before. The unfamiliar noises make me uneasy, but there are definitely no human sounds, so I step outside cautiously. I'm surprised by how bright it seems beneath the canopy. It's almost as if dawn's approaching.

My breath comes in short, panting gasps, and I sway on my feet, lightheaded. Sprinting such a short distance shouldn't have winded me like this. Instinctively, I drop to a crouch, pressing my hands to the ground to steady myself. My wet palms tingle where they touch the soil.

As I struggle to catch my breath, an icy understanding washes over me. That taste in the barrel—maybe I swallowed some of the amanitai that spilled into the water. Or that smell —maybe I breathed in too much of that pungent aroma floating around the storeroom.

Stay calm, Ava. Whatever it was, I couldn't have swallowed or breathed in very much of it. I was in the storeroom longer than planned, but not that long. At least, I don't think it was that long. I'm struggling with my sense of how much time has passed. The forest does seem oddly bright for this time of night. How long have I been crouching here?

Confusing impressions swirl through my head. The trees seem to grow taller. Or am I shrinking? Wait, are my arms growing longer? I hold up my hands—dirty again—and stare at them, momentarily awed by the sight of these familiar, wonderful, strange instruments. I wiggle my fingers. They're so far away. All of my body feels far away. I touch my face tentatively to make sure it's still there, and cool mud smears my cheeks.

Focus, Ava. I need to keep moving. I need to find my mother before this gets any worse. She'll know what to do.

The strange distortions of my sight and hearing do nothing to help my rapidly worsening balance. I remove my soaked cloth shoes. Feeling the forest floor under my bare feet again anchors me somewhat better to my surroundings. I know I should bury the shoes, but I'm not sure whether I'll be able to stand up again if I lean over, so I simply throw them as far away from the path as I can.

I walk, much more slowly and carefully than before, back the way I came. If I just keep going downslope, I'll reach the lookout spot. I narrow my focus to the step ahead. But step by step, I'm slowing down. Slower and slower. I try to remember where I'm going and why I'm going and how I'm supposed to get there.

At last I stop, rooted to the path. My throat goes dry. I tremble. A tingling warmth rises up through my feet. My awareness sinks down into the ground, spreading slowly out toward the trees. A profound calm settles over me, and though a small voice inside of me cries out, it's swallowed up by stillness. I've lost myself. All I can do now is listen.

So I listen.

I listen.

I listen.

And I hear the Voice in all. The Voice speaks inside of

me, but also in the rustle of leaves and needles above me, in the touch of the strange breeze stirring around me, in the wink of stars peeking down at me through the canopy. The Voice conveys pure meaning, speaking the language within language.

We are the bridge joining light to darkness. We are the wheel turning season to season. We are the threads binding realm to realm.

No, no, no. I slam my hands over my ears. But the Voice in all can't be shut out. It is inexorable.

We are creator, preserver, destroyer of worlds.

"No!" I cry, trying to drown out the Voice with my own voice. "No, no, no." I somehow tear one foot from the ground and take a step, then another, then another.

Together you shall seek us, find us, know us.

Together you shall amplify us.

"Mama!" I call. I know I'm far from the lookout spot, but maybe she can hear me. Maybe she'll come to me.

Together you shall weave us through the many worlds.

The dark forest around me disappears in a flash of blinding light.

I stand before a smooth wall of reflective glass. The glass wall rises straight up from the hard, flat surface beneath my feet. I recognize myself in the reflection, although I look so strange, wearing clothes I've never seen before, the upper half of my face and my eyes entirely covered by a shiny mask. The glass wall rises all the way up into the clear blue sky, like a bridge to the sun.

It's the glass tower. I've seen this tower before, but only in dreams—never before in such vivid detail.

I rise up slowly through the air like I'm floating to the surface through deep water. I rise faster and faster, until I'm not just floating but flying. I look down and see my strange shoes, striped in brightest blue, white, and green. Between my feet, I see the tops of many glass towers rising from the heart of a beautiful unwalled city. The city sprawls over many hills, bounded only by a vast ocean to the west and a sparkling bay to the east. It's larger than any city I've ever seen in all my years of roaming with my mother through Dulai.

My awareness flows through every part of the city, inside and outside its buildings, above and below broad avenues, over bridges, across the bay, up into the hills beyond. Everywhere, I see strange creatures speeding through the streets. No, they're carts, or some kind of machines, rolling on shiny wheels, though there are no horses or oxen pulling them.

And the people—so many people! I never knew there could be so many people, and here they are all gathered in one place. So many colors and styles of clothes and hair. So many eyes concealed, like mine, behind shiny masks. Even the Mohirai from the most distant temple cities don't look so strange.

But the strangest thing of all is seeing men and women and children of many ages together in one city. I see from the way they speak to each other and look at each other and touch each other that these people belong to each other. I recognize what I'm seeing from what my mother has taught me. These people are bound in kinship, a bond forbidden since the time of destruction, forbidden by the Mohirai, forbidden—I thought—by the Voice in all.

I'm stunned by what the Voice has shown me. The vision fades. The Voice says, *Together you shall answer our call.*

When the Voice departs from me, I find myself lying face down in the dirt, tangled in the underbrush. I open my eyes, and the dark forest spins in my peripheral vision, nauseating me. It feels like I've broken half my ribs, and there's a stabbing sensation below my heart. I whimper involuntarily at the pain in my chest, then bite my lip to silence myself, then wince when my teeth dig deeper into the cut already there. I taste mud and blood.

I need to calm down. Anyone could hear me crashing about the woods and moaning like this. I raise my head a little to scan my surroundings. To my relief, I see the footpath not far behind me. I'll retrace my tracks from there. Maybe I haven't wandered too far from the lookout spot.

I push myself up. Even this tiny exertion makes me start panting again, and the panting rapidly worsens the pain in my chest. I take a tentative step forward, but a root catches my foot, and my balance deserts me. I fall hard onto my knees and try to suppress a cry at the agonizing pain that shoots out from my heart.

"Hello?" calls a voice.

I freeze. It's not the Voice in all, and it's not my mother.

△▽△

"Hello?" I call out a second time, peering into the forest shadows, searching for the source of that last whimper.

Silence. If it is a lost boy, he should answer my call. But

he might be hesitant to show himself, since it's past the younger boys' curfew. A scolding from Hedi can be intimidating, even to me.

"It's all right, little brother," I say, speaking loud enough that he can hear I'm not Hedi or one of the other Mohirai. "You can come out."

No answer.

"It's all right," I say again, in the voice I use to soothe skittish horses. "I'm coming to get you. We can go back to the house together. I'll tell Hedi I kept you out late for chores."

The forest ahead is quite dark, but I should be able to find him. The sound wasn't far away. I walk forward, listening carefully. The rapid shallow breathing resumes, closer than before. I sense eyes on me but can't see anyone.

The breathing stops again, but it was coming from the dense patch of leafy underbrush directly ahead of me. I extend my hand, saying, "It's all right. Don't be afraid."

The leaves burst into motion as a shape springs away from me. It's a small figure, clad in the undyed wool tunic all of the children wear. So it is one of the younger boys from the house, though I have no idea why he'd run from me. I call out, "Wait!"

The boy doesn't stop, so I jog after him. He's unsteady on his feet, and he doesn't get far before he trips and falls flat on his belly. He gasps in pain.

I hurry toward the fallen boy and put my hand on his shoulder. He flinches. His tunic is sopping wet and ice cold to my touch, and there's a strange smell about him that reminds me of mixed wine, although I don't smell alcohol.

I piece together what might have happened. Hedi keeps

the storerooms in the house kitchen locked, but even with the ever-watchful eyes of the house Mohirai, certain bottles have a tendency to go missing. This boy will probably have an awful headache tomorrow, but he'll have learned his lesson. Meddling with pharmaka never ends well.

"Are you hurt, little brother?" I ask. Again there's no answer. With both hands, I turn him gently onto his side to take a look at him.

A curtain of dark curls obscures his face. His lips, rather full and feminine for a boy, are smeared with blood. He pants rapidly through his mouth. A long, wet braid matted with cedar needles and twigs lies across his chest. That's when I realize he's not a little boy. She's a little girl. I brush her hair back from her eyes. Actually, maybe she's not so little. It's hard for me to tell her age. She's no taller than a twelfth summer girl, but her face is closer to a woman's.

"Stay … away … from …" She speaks in gasps. Her face contorts in a grimace, and she shivers so hard her teeth chatter. She's soaked head to toe and clearly in pain, although her only obvious injury is her bleeding lip. As I lean over her, that pharmaka smell gets stronger, but I can't identify exactly what kind of pharmaka it is. The scent is woodsy, maybe floral, but with a musky undertone that's almost animal. I wonder what she's gotten into. Nothing good, from the look of her.

Maybe I should leave her here and come back with help. But she seems very disoriented. She might try to run off again and hurt herself even worse before I can return. I could easily carry her back to the house of boys, though. Hedi Mohira will know what to do.

"Easy there, little sister," I say. "I'm taking you to a healer."

She moans softly, "No … don't … I …"

I slip my arm under her shoulders and raise her to a sitting position. She resists, wincing with every movement, so I try to be gentle. I scoop my other arm under her knees and stand up. She's even lighter than I expected. She's cold against my chest, and her wet clothes soak into mine. The pharmaka scent intensifies, filling my lungs.

Her shaking right hand reaches for her belt. I look down to see what she's doing, and her hand flashes swiftly toward my neck.

The edge of a blade digs into my throat. Every muscle in my body tenses at once. She continues to shiver in my arms, her face so close to mine that I taste her breath on my lips. With a strange sense of detachment, I notice there's no scent of pharmaka on her breath, only a sweetness like spring water. I wonder where that strange smell is coming from, then.

"I don't want … to hurt you …" She's still gasping, but her words come more easily than before. The cold point of her knife quivers on my skin as her hand trembles, tracing a wandering line toward the pulsing artery just below my jaw. "Let me go."

Her eyes and tone are fierce, despite her apparent weakness. My mouth is dry, and I try to swallow, but it's difficult with the knife's pressure against the sinews of my neck. My entire awareness seems to shrink down to the edge of her blade.

"All right," I say, trying to stay calm, hoping this will calm her, too. "All right. I'm putting you down."

She doesn't lower her blade as I lower her feet carefully to the ground. She tries but fails to keep her balance, then pitches toward me, her raised knife hand swinging erratically. I catch her without thinking, and for a moment we're locked in a dangerous embrace, the length of her body pressed against me, her clothes soaking even more into mine, her blade pressed to my throat. Her heart races against my chest, or perhaps that's my heart racing against hers.

I'm afraid to hold on to her because she might try to kill me, but I'm afraid to let her go because with another stumble like that she might still kill me accidentally. I compromise and step back from her, holding her by the shoulders at arm's length. Her knife is still extended toward me, but at least my neck is beyond slashing distance of her hand.

"Careful," I say, as much to myself as to her, as I realize with shock what a near miss I've had. I might not be afraid of Death, but I have no desire to go there yet.

She stares at me, her eyes flickering over my face. She leans back slightly, losing her balance again. I tighten my grip on her shoulders so she won't fall. She glances down at my hands and back up at me. The fierce look fades from her eyes.

"Let me go," she says softly, wincing as she speaks, like her chest hurts her. Maybe she's broken a rib.

"How about this," I propose, doing my best to sound completely non-threatening. "You sheath your knife, then I'll let you go."

"No," she counters, her voice growing stronger. "You let me go. Then I'll go."

I doubt this will work. She's clearly in no condition to go anywhere. But I'm not in the best position to negotiate, because she still holds the knife.

"Fine," I concede. "I'm letting go."

I slowly let go of her shoulders. She slowly lowers her knife. Shivers wrack her small frame again, and the knife falls from her hand, plunging into the soil beside her bare foot. We both look down at it for a heartbeat, then grab for it.

She drops to a crouch, moving with incredible speed considering her unsteadiness a moment ago. Her right hand closes tight around the handle. I grab her wrist, squeezing hard until she winces and releases her grip on the knife. She tries to grab for it again with her left hand, but I see this coming and catch that wrist too.

"Let me go," she growls. But my negotiating position is rather improved, so I don't let go this time. Instead, I haul her by the wrists away from the knife and push her down onto her back. I've never handled anyone, boy or girl, so roughly before. My stomach turns at the sickening thud of her body against the ground. She's simultaneously furious and gasping in pain, thrashing and kicking and even trying to bite me until I splay her arms out beside her so my arms are clear of her teeth. She's stronger than she looks, but not nearly as strong as I am, and she's wearing herself out without managing to inflict much damage on me. I climb on top of her, straddling her thrashing legs.

"Stop," I say firmly. "Calm down."

"You're hurting me," she gasps through clenched teeth. I loosen my crushing hold on her wrists and take some of my weight off her. But when her knees take aim at my groin, I reverse course quickly and pin her legs even tighter between mine.

We're both panting shallowly now, and that pharmaka scent seems to be coming from everywhere at once. Whether it's residual shock from my near miss with the blade or something else, I'm not quite sure, but my vision swims. A sea breeze sweeps through the trees, chilling the wet front of my tunic, and I shiver.

I focus on the girl beneath me, trying to ignore the forest around us, which is slowly spinning. She stops shivering, even though she's more soaked than I am. For the first time, I get a clear look at her face. She glares up at me, her dark eyes fiery, fearless, and calculating. Her cheeks are dirty, and she bares her teeth at me, her bleeding lips quivering with fury. Her expression would be terrifying if she weren't so clearly in pain.

Despite the blood and mud obscuring her face, she looks familiar. Of course I should know her, since I know every girl in the temple city. My mind skims over the names and faces of them all, from the youngest girls in their eighth summer to the girls my age in their sixteenth. But she is none of them. There's a fog in my mind as I try to remember her.

"Who are you?" I ask at last, mystified.

Her expression softens. The look she gives me is resigned, almost pitying, as she says, "Have they taken that from you, too, Dom?"

The question disorients me, but the sound of her voice saying my name cuts through the fog. I struggle harder to remember. A tingling sensation spreads through my palms where they dig in to her bare wrists. She turns her head from side to side, looking at my hands pressing hers into the dirt.

"What are you doing?" she says.

Fragments of memory gather before me. A little girl with a scarlet ribbon at the end of her long dark braid, smiling down at me from a high cedar branch, her bare toes tracing circles in the air. Climbing up through the hollow trunk, learning from her the handholds and footholds on the way to the top. Her animated hands gesticulating in storytelling. Her fingers laced through mine, pulling me along a forest path, pointing the way toward some special place she wants to show me. Her spicy sweet scent of cedar, ferns, and sea salt. Her voice in my ear, whispering secrets, giggling, saying my name.

I stare down at her, stunned. It can't be. "Ava?"

She looks surprised.

"But ..." Confused, I shake my head. This turns out to be a bad move, because it worsens the spinning at the edge of my vision. "Where have you been?"

She hesitates, then says slowly, "I've been with my mother."

"Your what?" I say. Whatever is affecting my vision must be affecting my hearing, too.

"Never mind. Get off me."

Her imitation of the trained voice of a priestess is near perfect, and I almost comply without thinking. Boys learn to obey the Mohirai from an early age, and my deeply ingrained habit of obedience extends even to the uninitiated girls much of the time.

But the skin at my throat prickles in warning. It's been years since I last saw Ava. I have no idea what's happened to her or what she might do to me. Even though we were friends when we were little—at least, that's the memory inexplicably trickling back to me—I'd be mad to trust her now.

"Are you going to kill me?" I ask. The question sounds foolish even to me, but I want to hear her answer before I decide what to do next.

She glances over at the knife, then back up at me. "Not tonight," she says.

Not exactly reassuring, and I'm not going to take her word for it. But it also feels ridiculous sitting here on top of her while she's not fighting back.

"All right," I say. "I'll get off, but hold still or we're going to end up right back here."

I reposition her wrists and pin them over her head with one hand. I retrieve her knife with my free hand and slip it into my belt. I pat down the front and sides of her tunic and examine each pouch on her belt. She doesn't appear to have any other weapons. Except for her hands, her feet, her knees, her teeth … Well, at least she doesn't appear to have any other blades.

Keeping a hold on the knife handle with my left hand, I carefully climb off her. My peripheral vision is still spinning, and my balance is unsteady, so I remain in a crouch, one hand pressed to the ground. She sits up and massages her wrists.

"Sorry about that," I say, gesturing to her wrists. I didn't mean to hurt her, but she didn't leave me many options.

"I'm fine," she says, to herself more than to me, tugging down her wet sleeves over what will likely be some ugly bruises. She looks at me warily and says, "But what was that?"

"What was what?" I say.

She reaches for my right hand and taps my palm with her

forefinger. "That tingling. Did you do that?"

I'm surprised she felt that too. "I don't know," I say. I'm confused by everything that just happened. "I was trying to remember your name, and then my hands felt … strange … and I remembered …" I trail off as more bits and pieces of memory float through my mind in a jumble.

She looks like she's about to ask another question, but she shakes her head quickly and says, "I have to go."

This cuts through my confusion, and I refocus on her. "Ava, you can't. You're—I don't know what exactly. But you're barely able to stand. You're hurt. You need a healer."

"I'm fine," she says again. She climbs to her feet, much steadier now than she was a few moments ago. She searches the nearby underbrush and picks up a leather pack she must have dropped when she fell. She inspects its contents carefully and slings it over her shoulder, preparing to leave.

"Wait!" I can't believe this. She can't leave. I have so many questions. I rise from crouching to standing too fast. The ground seems to lurch to the left, and I stagger to the right. Ava's eyes widen as she watches me struggle to keep my balance.

"Are you all right?" she asks, putting her hand on my chest to steady me, her voice sounding farther away than it should. She looks from me to the footpath behind her and back to me. With a wordless sound of frustration, she grabs my hand. "Come on. I'll take you back to your house first. Listen to me, Dom. Tell Hedi you were exposed to amanitai. Do you hear me? Amanitai."

She looks at me, waiting for me to respond. I'm vaguely aware I should answer, but it's hard to remember what she just said. She pulls me in the direction of the forest edge. I wish she'd slow down. How can she walk so easily now while I'm barely able to stand? And why is she in such a hurry? If she'd just wait a moment, maybe my head would stop spinning.

But she hauls me forward. I follow only a few paces before I sway. In a blur of motion, she darts back to my side, wedges her shoulder under my arm, and wraps her arm around my waist. She tries to hold me up, but she's much smaller than I am. As my legs give way, my weight overwhelms her. We both fall hard to our knees.

I'm vaguely aware of her colorful cursing as I stare up through the little gaps in the canopy that reveal the stars winking down at us. My mind wanders. It's getting late. What a strange way to spend the last night before my Calling Day. It's nice to see Ava, again, though. I've been missing her, even though I didn't remember she existed until just now. Where did she say she was all these years? I try to remember, but it slips away like water through my fingers.

THE DOUBLE BIND

Damn the Voice, curse the sisters, and spirits blast it all. This job has gone badly sideways.

Dom's a dead weight around my shoulders, and when he stumbles, he pulls both of us down hard. I swear under my breath continuously as I heave up with all my remaining strength. The powerful arms and long legs he used to wrestle me to the ground are somehow useless now. I'm not nearly strong enough to lift him, and there's no way I can drag him all the way through the underbrush back to the edge of the forest so he can be found by the Mohirai.

But I can't leave him here. Even though it's been years since I last saw him, as soon as I recognized Dom all I could think of was that sweet little boy trailing me around the grounds for the year I lived here in the temple city, before my mother took me on the run. Somehow I've exposed him to this pharmaka, and it looks like he's starting to go through the same sequence of side effects I was having earlier. He's apparently not feeling the stabs in his chest yet, but I can't bear the thought of him lost and alone in the woods, writhing in pain on the ground like I was before he found me.

Dom's head tips back, and I worry he's lost consciousness. But his eyes are open as he says in a wandering, delighted voice, "Look at the stars. Do you hear them? Don't they sound beautiful?"

I remember the strange things the Voice said to me when I first emerged from the cave, and how I seemed to see in vivid detail the city of glass towers where I often find myself in dreams. Somehow even in that dreamlike state I managed to wander far past the lookout spot where I'm supposed to be meeting my mother. So even if Dom is having some similarly weird experience, maybe he can walk while it's happening, too.

I ease his heavy arm off my shoulders and stand to face him. To my relief, he stays upright, though he's still on his knees. I take one of his hands. His rough, strong palm feels nothing like the soft child's hand I remember holding when we were small. I set my other hand on his cheek and steer his gaze back down from the patch of starry sky he's staring at. He refocuses on me, his expression peaceful and open, more like the boy I remember now that we're not grappling with a knife between us. His deep-set eyes sparkle in the shadows, framed by level brows and long lashes. He's changed a lot, but I recognized him by these eyes, which look out at the world with such intensity—far more curious and perceptive than other boys' eyes, even now, veiled in a haze of pharmaka.

"Come with me," I say firmly, doing my best to imitate the priestess voice my mother uses when she needs me to obey without asking questions. It must be a poor imitation, though, because Dom immediately starts asking questions in that same wandering voice.

"Where are we going?" he says.

"I'm taking you back to the house of boys, to Hedi, so you can get help," I say, pulling on his hand. To my enormous relief, he stands. We haven't made it three paces, though, when he stops.

"But ... where are you going?" he says.

This is too complicated to explain to him, especially in his confused state, and anyway of course I can't tell him where I'm going. So all I say is, "I'm going away from here."

I pull on his hand, but now he won't budge. A deep crease forms between his eyebrows as he searches my face. His voice is clearer, more insistent, his words coming faster as he asks, "Why don't you stay here? Tomorrow is our Calling Day, remember? You've always wanted to be a Mohira."

I was surprised that Dom had remembered even my name, but it seems he's remembered far more. This was all we used to talk about, in long afternoons playing together in the forest. I dreamed of being a Mohira, skilled in the arts, initiated into the mysteries so frustratingly locked away from children. He dreamed of being a Mohira, too, at first, until the reality of every boy's fate became impossible for either of us to ignore, even in play.

I don't understand how he could be remembering any of this, though. My mother told me that unbound memories can't be recovered. And Dom's memory of me was definitely removed by unbinding pharmaka. He didn't recognize me, not at first.

Of course we've both changed a lot in the last seven years, but his lack of recognition was deeper than that. He had that foggy look and those flickering eye movements of someone trying to recall an unbound memory. I'd anticipated that look. When troubling things happen, especially when they happen to children, the Mohirai often use unbinding pharmaka to smooth away the difficult memories. My disappearance would certainly have been troubling to some of the other children, especially to Dom, who was my closest friend while I lived here.

I'll have to discuss this with my mother when this wretched job concludes. Maybe this means I could someday recover my memories of her, from the years before my unbinding. But this is irrelevant right now. We'll have moons of leisure time to talk this all over once I leave Dom somewhere safe and she and I are on the boat.

"Where are you going on a boat?" Dom asks, tilting his head, his eyes widening, his fingers tightening around mine.

Did I just say that aloud? I shouldn't have told him that. I must still be in a haze of pharmaka myself.

Dom watches me with intense interest, awaiting my answer, and there's that tingling again where my hand touches his. My thoughts rush on, strangely difficult to stop.

The boat will take us to the land on the far side of the ocean, far beyond the reach of the Mohirai and the control of the Voice in all. It's a circuitous route, and we'll sail for many moons.

My mother has described the journey to me many times over the last seven years. She knows more about the route than the destination, though. In the absence of better information, I've constructed my own picture of what lies beyond the ocean from bits and pieces of my mother's teachings and my own imagination. I know it's little more than a dream, but the city of glass towers is what I always see when I imagine the place where she's promised we'll be safe, where we can be a family, where people live in freedom from the Voice and the Mohirai who enforce its will. The breathtaking vision of the city that I saw shortly after hearing the Voice flashes in my mind again. For a fleeting instant, I'm flying over the towers.

"Beautiful," Dom says, staring at me in wonder.

I stare back at him in disbelief. He's certainly not talking about me. Somehow, I know he's talking about the city of glass towers. With a sinking feeling, I look down at my tingling fingers entwined in his, my wet sleeve dripping water into our palms. Oh, spirits. This is not good.

I drop Dom's hand and step away from him. I hurriedly strip off my wet wool tunic and breeches, running my hands over my naked body. Everywhere I touch is covered in a slightly gritty, sticky residue of amanitai. I hadn't felt how much of it was on my skin, with my clothes so wet. I have no water to rinse with, so I tear handfuls of leaves from the underbrush and try to scrub off the mushroom dust. It doesn't work; I'm only moving the sticky grit around.

Dom's gaze travels up and down the length of me while I do this. Nakedness is utterly routine among the Mohirai, but he is a teenage boy, after all.

I'm thankful for the little breeze stirring through the trees that slowly dries my skin, though it makes me shiver again, which stirs the ache in my chest again, which makes everything harder again. I clench my teeth and work through the discomfort. To my relief, as my skin dries, brushing my hands over myself causes some of the amanitai powder to crumble away. I clean off as much as I can, until I'm too cold to bear it any longer. I kneel before my pack, my hands shaking badly as I rummage for my riding clothes. I change into them quickly. Dry clothes are a major improvement, but every part of my skin still feels gritty. I'll need to wash myself as soon as my mother and I are on the boat.

"Come on," I say to Dom. "Arms up."

"Why?" he asks. He looks at me with the same wondering expression he had while staring up at the stars. The pharmaka must be hitting him pretty hard now.

"I think there's pharmaka absorbing through our skin," I say slowly and clearly, uncertain whether he's already too far gone to understand me. "You need to take off these wet clothes."

Dom doesn't resist as I pull his tunic off over his head. Bare-chested, he looks as strong as an ox. The Mohirai have clearly prepared him well for the life of manual labor that lies ahead of him. I run my hand over his ribs where the tunic had absorbed the most water. My palm tingles where it touches him, but I don't feel any mushroom residue on his skin apart from what's rubbing off onto him from me.

Dom leans down and whispers, "Ava—"

Just as my mother's voice booms right behind me, "Ava!"

△▽△

Ava's face was a blur while I was having the strange sensation of overhearing her thoughts, but my vision sharpens when she strips off all her clothes.

I've studied a lot of girls' figures as I've taught myself to draw. Most of the sixteenth summer girls are long-limbed, curvaceous, beautiful in a decidedly feminine way. Ava's body is different. She's lean, muscular, small-breasted, narrow-hipped. Every line of her is diminutive and delicate. Her fascinating beauty is more feral than feminine, and it's amplified in motion. She's graceful like the Mohiran dancers, and she moves with precision and speed like a hunting falcon, especially now that she's so focused on whatever she's doing with all these leaves, which is a complete mystery to me.

It's a shame she clothes herself so quickly, but she recaptures my attention when she says, "Come on. Arms up."

I have no objection to her undressing me, but still I ask, "Why?"

"I think there's pharmaka absorbing through our skin," she says, tracing the damp imprints she left on my tunic during our scuffle. "You need to take off these wet clothes."

Before I can sort through the implications of either statement, her hands are at my waist. In a rush of panic, I grab for the knife at my belt and raise it high over my head, out of her reach. But she doesn't even seem to notice the knife. She's too intent on unbuckling my belt and pulling off my mud-smeared tunic. Keeping a firm grip on the knife, I lean forward and let the tunic slide over my head.

She tosses my tunic aside and runs her hand over my chest. Her palm is slightly gritty, which isn't surprising after all our grappling in the dirt. That tingling sensation follows the movement of her hand over my bare skin.

Over her shoulder, something looms in the shadows. Startled, I tighten my grip on the knife.

"Ava—" I whisper in warning.

A massive cloaked woman steps toward us, her eyes locked on the knife raised high in my hand. Her deep voice calls out in warning, "Ava!"

Ava relaxes visibly and turns toward the woman. "Spirits, I'm glad you found me."

The woman rushes forward and stands between me and Ava. "Drop your weapon," she says to me.

My hand drops immediately to my side, and I let go of the knife. I would have complied even if the woman hadn't used the priestess voice of command, because her face is so terrifying, with her teeth bared and her wide eyes staring down at me. She's at least half a head taller than I am, square-jawed, shoulders broad as a man's. Wisps of the fair hair framing her face seem to glow in the dark, along with the streaks of unusually pale skin visible beneath the mud on her cheeks. Physically, she appears in every way to be Ava's complete opposite, apart from the mud and the ferocity.

Ava seems confused by the woman's command until she looks back and sees the knife I've dropped on the ground beside me. Her eyes widen, and she grabs the woman's arm. I notice for the first time that the woman is gripping something beneath the folds of her cloak. "No!" Ava exclaims. "Mama, wait. It's not what it looks like. Please listen. I—"

The woman seems unmoved by Ava's protests, but she also seems satisfied that I present no further threat now that I've dropped the knife. She lets go of whatever she's gripping under her cloak and raises her hand to interrupt Ava. In a low, urgent voice, she says, "Later, Ava. You've been gone far longer than we planned. We can still make it, but we must go now."

"But I—" Ava begins, then starts shivering so hard she can't say another word. A moment later, I'm shivering, too.

I would normally defer to a girl to speak first, but Ava seems unable to proceed, and given the circumstances I suppose it's all right to interrupt her. I don't recognize this woman, and I've never heard of a sister named Mama before, so I decide to use the respectful form of address for a priestess of unknown rank.

"Mama Mohira," I say. This must be the wrong form of address, because Mama and Ava both give me a strange look, but I push on given the urgency of the situation. I don't understand who this sister is or why she needs to take Ava anywhere in such a hurry, but I'm sure she'll help us once we explain. "Ava needs a healer. We both do. We've had some accident with pharmaka."

Mama looks from me to Ava, then takes Ava's shivering shoulders in her hands and says, "Tell me what happened. Quickly."

"I had to … hide in a barrel of … water while I was in the storerooms." Ava's words are halting, and she winces with each breath. "I had … the amanitai … I still have it … but some … spilled into the water … I think I … swallowed some … but mostly … it stuck on … my skin … I was … confused … in the forest … trying to get … back to you … Dom … found me … and now it's … happening … to him too."

Mama looks up at me, at my shaking bare chest and arms. She jerks back her hands from Ava's shoulders and brushes her palms thoroughly on the outside of her cloak.

"Think, Ava," says Mama, her voice hard. "How much amanitai fell into the water?"

"Maybe … maybe a … third of a bushel?" says Ava. Mama curses under her breath, and Ava hurries to say, "But there's … plenty left … for the boat … I made sure."

"Were you barefoot?" says Mama.

"What?" Ava looks as perplexed by this question as I am.

"While you were walking through the woods. Were you barefoot?"

"Yes … Yes … Of course."

"You said you were confused. While you were confused, did you hear the Voice?"

Ava stares up at Mama, her expression fearful.

"Focus, Ava!"

"Yes," Ava gasps quickly.

Mama takes half a step back from Ava. Her broad shoulders slump as she says quietly, "There won't be a boat. Not for you. Not tonight."

"But you said … there's still time … if we hurry," says Ava, argumentative despite her shivering. "Can't you … give me … counter pharmaka … Once we're … on the boat?"

Mama shakes her head and says, "You've had an overdose of amanitai, Ava. It's the main ingredient in the binding pharmaka. There's only one thing to counterbalance it: unbinding pharmaka."

Finally I'm hearing something that makes a little bit of sense. I know the unbinding pharmaka, of course. The younger girls and boys drink unbinding pharmaka every night for the first few years after they arrive here. The Mohirai say it gives sweet dreams from the Voice, though in my experience it mostly gives very deep sleep, and you tend to remember no dreams at all when you wake up afterwards.

I've never heard of binding pharmaka before, though.

"But …" Ava winces, as her pain appears to worsen. "Maybe … I could … take just a … little bit of … unbinding pharmaka … Just enough to … stop this … this pain … this dizziness."

Mama says, "Even if I had unbinding pharmaka to give you, the amount you'd need is too much for someone so young. You need initiate training, and centuries of memories, to be able to tolerate high doses of unbinding pharmaka."

"Then … what will … we do?"

Seeing the contortions of pain on Ava's face, I feel an echoing pain in my own chest, under my heart, needling at first, then a stab. I suck in a breath through clenched teeth. Ava hears me and looks at me in concern, and my pain grows worse, and then her pain seems to grow worse, and then both of us are hunched over, clutching ourselves.

Mama looks from one of us to the other, then curses again.

"Go to him," says Mama, in a tone of disgust, gesturing toward me while keeping well back from Ava. "Take his hand."

"But why?" says Ava.

"Now, Ava."

Mama's tone of command is so harsh I cringe. Ava stumbles toward me and grabs my hand. I heave a sigh of relief at her touch. My pain gradually eases, and Ava's seems to as well. Cautiously, we both straighten up.

"What is happening?" Ava says to Mama, gripping my hand tightly.

Mama shakes her head, massaging her mud-streaked forehead with a broad hand, studying Ava like she's trying to identify a strange mushroom. She says, "In small doses, binding pharmaka amplifies the connection between two awarenesses. The longer the contact and the larger the dose, the stronger the connection. Too much connection with another awareness can cause great pain, even deadly pain, for one untrained in the arts."

"But—" Ava drops my hand quickly. She winces, and pain prickles in my chest. To my relief, she takes my hand again before it worsens. "But then shouldn't I be trying to get *away* from Dom, to stop the pain?"

Mama's pale eyes flick briefly my way. Frowning, she says, "An awareness like his shouldn't be enough to cause pain." I have no idea whether this is an insult, though her tone is certainly dismissive.

"But he's the only person I've touched since I left the storeroom," says Ava.

"He's the only human you've touched," says a voice, but it's not Mama's.

△▽△

"He's the only human you've touched." The clear, resonant voice of the High Priestess Serapen flows out of the forest behind me. I clench Dom's left hand in my right as my mind reels. How on Dulai could she have managed to get this close without my mother hearing her? She continues, "But he's not the only awareness you've touched."

My mother inhales sharply, and I can see she's realized something, but I don't know what it is, and she makes no sign to me. Slowly I turn around, searching for Serapen. I see nothing but trees. Damn, I wish I had my blade right now.

"Muse Serapen," Dom calls loudly, sounding relieved and taking a step in the direction of Serapen's voice, pulling me after him. "Please, we need your help."

I yank Dom backwards and curse his foolishness. He looks at me like I've kicked him. I suppose I already have kicked him several times already, but seeing his expression, I feel a twinge of contrition for my harsh language. It's not his fault he doesn't know who Serapen really is, or that we need to get away from her, and it's too late to explain now.

The tall, slim figure of Serapen glides out of the darkness a few paces ahead of us, hands clasped before her heart in that peculiar rigid posture. She walks unhurriedly and silently toward me and Dom. The rustling of the forest seems to fade, until the only thing I hear is my own racing heartbeat.

Serapen stops halfway between us and my mother. She pushes back her hood, and tendrils of long snow-white hair spill out around her shoulders. Her dark complexion and the forest shadows make it difficult to see much of her face except for her gleaming eyes, twin pools that reflect every color of the nighttime woods from black and violet to deepest blue. There's something unsettling in the contrast between the fluid movement of Serapen's body and the birdlike flight of her gaze, which flicks precisely from place to place, transitions nearly imperceptible.

Serapen's strange eyes lock on my mother, and there's a crack in the underbrush as my mother steps back. I glance at her, and the tumultuous display of emotions on her usually stoic face confuses me. Is that fear? Grief? Rage?

"Lilith," says Serapen, drawing out my mother's name so it lingers in the stillness. "For seven years I have wondered what work the Voice was doing through you."

"Damn the Voice," my mother says. "The free people serve no Voice."

Calmly, Serapen says, "None of us walk free of the Voice, Lilith, though some choose not to listen."

Two hooded women appear in the shadows behind Serapen, flanking her. I glance sidelong at my mother, expecting her signal. Her eyes never stray from Serapen's, but behind her back, one of her hands signs to me, over and over, *Throw me your pack. Throw me your pack.*

My pack is still looped over my shoulders by both straps. I'll have to let go of Dom's hand to get it off and throw it to her. There's no way to do it without drawing attention. I wonder why she wants it right now. She must want me to be carrying as little weight as possible for whatever comes next. The contrast between her strength and my weakness has never seemed as stark, or as consequential, as it is right now.

"You fools who blindly worship the Voice are doomed to fail, Serapen," my mother says. "There is no purpose to a human life without freedom."

"You speak out of great ignorance, Lilith. What freedom exists may be found only in the Voice."

I mentally rehearse each movement I need to make. We may have only one chance to get it right. I'll drop Dom's hand, shrug the straps off my shoulders, swing the pack toward her. My mother will have to sign to me whatever I'm supposed to do next, but based on what I see, I'm guessing the plan is to run for it. Maybe she's going to make a distraction of some kind. I have no idea how far I can run away from Dom before the pain takes me down, but there's no way to find out except to try. I'll have to go as far as I can on my own, but my mother is strong enough to carry me on her back once I fall.

"Your world is destined for destruction," says my mother, keeping Serapen's eyes on her to buy me time. "You will see."

Serapen makes a long, low, wordless sound, something between a hum and a sigh. She says, "Indeed. I have been called to witness much. So I have. So I shall."

I spring into action, pulling away from Dom, slipping off the pack, tossing it to my mother. It flies in a perfect arc, and she catches it easily by one strap. In an instant, the pack is secure on her back, and she's flying toward the forest edge at full speed on her long, strong legs. She's made no sign to me, though, and I'm so surprised by this that I freeze uncertainly, a moment too long, before I spring after her. Each step brings pain, pain, more pain. I clutch my side.

Behind me, Serapen says calmly but firmly, "Stop her, Dom."

I don't make it ten strides before Dom catches me. I kick and scream and curse at him, but he wraps me in his long arms, pinning my hands to my sides, lifting me right off my feet. I can't get a hold on anything, so I kick his shins as hard as I can with my bare heels. He grunts in pain, but he keeps his hold on me. Each time I land a kick on him, I feel an echoing pain on my own shins. It's awful.

"Mama! Mama! Mama!" I shout.

The forest swallows up my voice. My mother does not return.

RESISTANCE IS FUTILE

WRESTLING AVA TO THE GROUND wasn't easy the first time, and she seems to have recovered more of her strength since then. It takes me plus the two healers to hold her down this time. I pin her hands above her head, and a healer holds down each of her legs. My shins ache in a dozen places where Ava kicked me as I hauled her back here. She more than returned the damage I did to her wrists in our first scuffle. She shouts so loud that I imagine she'll wake everyone in the house of boys, and maybe the girls inside the wall, too.

"Mama! Mama! Mama!"

The woman who ran off—who Ava seems to think is named Mama but Serapen seems to think is named Lilith—is clearly not returning, and Serapen hasn't commanded anyone to follow her. I don't understand who that woman is or why Ava is so distraught, but she's clearly furious at me more than anyone else, because she alternates shouts of Mama with cursing my name.

When Ava stops shouting to catch her breath, I say hurriedly, "Muse Serapen, there's something wrong, something happened to Ava in a storeroom—"

The High Priestess makes a small gesture with her hand to stop me. She says, "I know, little brother. I heard what Ava said."

"Oh …" I say. I don't understand how Serapen heard, but I press on. "Can you help her?"

Ava resumes shouting. Serapen looks like she's in pain,

though she's probably just reacting to Ava, who's gradually growing hoarse but is still excruciatingly loud.

Serapen kneels beside me. She uses two long brown forefingers to probe the exposed undersides of Ava's wrists under my hands, pressing there for a few heartbeats. I've seen Hedi do this before. There's a nerve somewhere in the wrist that the healers manipulate to calm children. Ava stops shouting to look at Serapen's hands, then thrashes with redoubled energy. I guess whatever Serapen is trying to do doesn't work on Ava.

Serapen's hand moves to Ava's forehead. She closes her eyes, pressing her palm against Ava's furrowed brow as she intones, "Listen. Listen. Listen."

Ava moans quietly. "No, no, no. I want my mother. I want my mother."

Serapen opens her eyes again. Her voice is soft as she says, "I know, child. I miss her, too. But she's gone."

Ava stops moaning. Her dark eyes search Serapen's. She says, "Please, Serapen. Please let me go to her. We'll never trouble you again. We'll never return here. Why would you hold me here?"

Serapen sighs. "I am but a servant, Ava. Only the Voice can hold you here."

Ava resumes struggling. Serapen stands and makes a resigned gesture to me and the two healers as she says, "Let her go."

The healers comply immediately, but I look up at the High Priestess uncertainly. I keep my voice deferential but still dare to question her command. "Are you sure, Muse Serapen?"

Serapen nods and extends her hand to me. I look down at Ava, who glares up at me with such fury I flinch. I hope Serapen doesn't change her mind, because I really don't want to catch Ava again. My shins are throbbing.

Cautiously, I release Ava and step back from her. Serapen's fingers close around my wrist. Ava springs to her feet and runs after Mama. This time, to my enormous relief, I feel no pain in my chest as Ava departs. Even the pain in my shins subsides. That tingling resumes on my wrist under Serapen's hand, though.

We listen to the swift rustle of Ava's passage through the underbrush. The sound fades, restoring peace to the forest. I'm relieved, as though I've woken from a nightmare to find myself safe in my bed.

I glance up at Serapen. She listens for something, eyes closed. When she opens her eyes again, she says to me and the other two healers, "Come."

Keeping a gentle hold on my hand, Serapen leads, and the healers and I follow her through the trees. We walk a short distance in the direction Ava ran, until we reach the ferns at the forest edge. Ahead of us, in the meadow, Ava lies curled on her side. She holds her knees to her chest, gasping for breath.

Without further instruction from Serapen, the two healers kneel beside Ava. One draws out a little flask from within her cloak and lowers it to Ava's mouth. Ava presses her lips tight together, refusing to drink it, so the healer lets it drip onto her muddy forehead, hands, and feet instead. The second healer uses a blue cloth to massage the liquid into Ava's skin.

Ava's clenched hands slowly relax, and her labored breathing eases. She stares up at the night sky, limp and unresisting. Moonlight glistens on the tears sliding silently down her cheeks. Seeing her pain subsiding gives me some relief, but I feel yet another kind of pain at the sight of her grief.

"What's happened to her, Muse Serapen?" I ask, looking up at the High Priestess.

Serapen gazes at Ava and says, "She is on a more difficult path than most."

That doesn't sound good. I look back at Ava. "But … why?"

"Hmm." This soft sound of the ineffable resonates somewhere between Serapen's throat and her heart. "Why. That is a very great mystery indeed. A question worthy of the initiate's path."

I lower my head, suddenly aware of my impertinence in questioning the High Priestess. The initiate path is not for boys, so this mystery will remain a mystery to me.

Serapen turns to me, and her voice is kind as she says, "Do not be downcast, little brother. All will be well in its proper time. You will see."

I see myself reflected in Serapen's strange eyes. For a brief moment, I have the sensation—at once exhilarating and frightening—that I'm looking down at the world from a very great height, through her.

She lets go of my hand, and the strange sensation fades. I blink, disoriented and uncertain whether Serapen has dismissed me. Over Serapen's shoulder, I see two windows remain lit on the ground floor of the house of boys: my bedroom and Hedi's. I'm exhausted, and the thought of my soft bed calls to me. Even the prospect of listening to Balashi and Kuri's inane conversation is appealing, after so much shouting and struggling. I could also use a hot bath.

The sea breeze blows over my bare skin. I forgot to grab my tunic before Serapen led us out of the woods. I shiver, then wince at the prickle of pain that returns to my chest now that Serapen has let go of my hand. I roll my shoulders forward slightly to ease the pain. It's uncomfortable, but not yet as sharp as before.

"Should I return to my room, Muse Serapen?" I ask.

"I think not," says Serapen, her observant gaze flicking from my chest to my eyes. "It will be some time before the binding is eased enough between you and Ava to separate you. I cannot keep you with me tonight, and you cannot go inside the city with her. So she must go with you."

I frown. "With me where?"

"Back to your house," says Serapen, as if this is obvious.

"But won't Hedi—"

"Don't worry. I've already sent word to Hedi."

I don't know how the High Priestess could have sent word already, but I nod.

"Stay with Ava," Serapen continues, speaking slowly and clearly to me, waiting for my acknowledgment after each instruction. "Take her to your house when she's recovered enough strength to walk. Attend Hedi's instructions, and make sure Ava does, too. Try to get some sleep."

I nod again, though that last instruction worries me. My mind races ahead. I ask, "What will we do tomorrow, for Calling Day?"

Serapen looks at Ava, limp on the grass between the healers, and says, "Tomorrow will be a long day for you both, I imagine."

"And after that? Will she be all right?"

Serapen turns to me with a softer expression than before. I hesitate to meet her strange gaze again, but when I do I see only the somewhat tired and quite ordinary brown eyes of a woman looking back at me with compassion. She says, "It will take some time to counterbalance the more extreme effects of the dose she's had. A moon at least to get through the worst, I expect. But it will take years of training for her to learn to manage the residual effects. Perhaps centuries. The good news for you is that, since you cannot bind to the Voice in the same way a woman can, you only need to manage the effects of the binding with Ava. Not a small task, either, but you're a strong boy. You'll manage. And you'll both be more comfortable if you stay together for now. Do you understand?"

I don't understand at all. I have so many more questions.

But Serapen raises her hand over me in the sign of blessing and says, "Safe passage tomorrow, little brother. Good night." She departs with the other two healers, slips into the forest, and leaves me in the meadow.

Reluctantly, I approach Ava once more.

△▽△

She left me. My mother left me. Why did she leave me?

I stare up at the stars in shock as the healers' hands move over me. I can't move my arms or legs to struggle—

everything hurts too much—but I won't let them pour their damned pharmaka down my throat as long as I can keep my mouth closed.

But a part of me knows my resistance is futile. Serapen made her point. That final sprint took every last bit of energy I possessed, and the pain that followed was unendurable. As I emerged from the forest, I glimpsed my mother briefly in the moonlight, the shadow of her cloak flying far ahead of me across the meadow. She never slowed, never even looked back, before she disappeared. I think I lost consciousness for a moment, because the next thing I knew I was curled up in the grass shivering, in so much pain I couldn't open my eyes.

The pain eases a little, and I'm vaguely aware of Serapen's voice. The healers rise and go to her. Dom has been standing with Serapen, and now he approaches me. Serapen and her healers slip away into the woods.

Dom sits in the grass at my side. The healers left my hands folded over my heart, and he tentatively takes one of them in his own. He winces at the sight of my wrist, runs his thumb lightly over the place where I'm starting to feel the throbbing bruises he left there. He looks ashamed. Good. I hope his shins are throbbing, too. I hope he feels a knife digging under his ribs just like I do.

But as he sits there, my hand in his, the hunched tension of his bare shoulders eases. The throbbing in my wrists eases. The pain near my heart eases most of all, which is a huge relief. But something else starts seething in its place.

"Ava—" Dom's eyes meet mine, and I see his concern for me in that innocent, open expression. That's what pushes me over the edge. I feel a surge of fury at him: this hand, that voice, those eyes, every part of him a trap. I was supposed to be flying across the sea by now, and instead I'm caught in a snare.

"Go away," I say. I would pull back my hand if I could, but I'm utterly spent.

He sighs. "I can't. Serapen says—"

"Don't," I say. "I don't want to hear what Serapen says. If you won't go away, then be quiet."

There's enough venom in my voice to put down a horse. Dom cautiously releases my hand. He stays quiet, but he doesn't leave. I try to hold my face expressionless as the pain starts up again in my chest. It's not as bad as it was before—whatever the healers did helped a little—but it grows steadily worse and worse, breath by breath. His back and shoulders tighten again, and his jaw clenches, and I know it's hurting him too. I refuse to ask him to take my hand again, but I'm relieved when at last he does.

"I'm sorry, Ava," he says. "I was only trying to help. I don't understand what's happening."

That strange tingling resumes between our palms, and I feel the unfamiliar sensation of … is that humility? I'm not sure I've ever felt that before. But this feeling combined with his words unlock other feelings and thoughts I've been evading. None of this is his fault, not really. I've trapped him as much as the Voice has trapped me. I'm the one who exposed him to pharmaka. I'm the one who screwed up the job.

He looks at me curiously and asks, "What does that mean? The job?"

My mind is clearer now than it was in the forest when

this happened before. I'm sure this time that I didn't say anything aloud about the job. The pain in my chest has subsided enough that I can push myself halfway up to sitting. I try to ignore the fact that Dom helps me up the rest of the way. I study his face, my curiosity momentarily stronger than all my other uncomfortable feelings. "I didn't say anything about the job," I say. "How do you know about that?"

He runs his free hand over his face and rubs his eyes before he meets my gaze. He looks almost as exhausted as I feel when he says, "I just … hear you. Somehow. I guess it's the binding pharmaka, isn't it?"

I guess he's right. Spirits, I wish my mother had taught me more. If I had known, if I'd understood what could happen, maybe I would have done things differently back in the storeroom. None of this needed to happen. Why didn't she tell me what could happen? Why did she leave me here? Anguish at the memory of her running away rips through me, followed by confusion, followed by anger.

Dom winces, stopping my spiraling emotions in their tracks.

"You're not only hearing me," I say, my understanding growing. I remember the jarring sensation of kicking him in the shins and hurting myself. A dozen places on my own shins are still aching. "You're feeling what I'm feeling, too, aren't you?"

Dom nods. "You're … mostly angry. At that woman."

"At my mother," I say slowly.

"What does that mean?" he asks. "Your mother?"

The question is so ridiculous, but it cuts straight to the heart of the matter. I feel sorry for him, but also sorry for myself. Maybe it would have been better for me if I'd never known the answer to this question, either.

The thought of my mother's betrayal brings on a feeling of crushing weariness. I sigh and say, "I'll tell you, Dom, if you really want to know. But not tonight. It's too much. I think ... I really just need to sleep right now."

"All right," says Dom, looking relieved.

We glance down awkwardly at our joined hands, as the particulars of this come into focus. Should I—should we?—sleep in the woods?

Dom, overhearing my thoughts again, shakes his head. With confidence that sounds forced, he says, "No. Hedi will sort us out. Come on, little sister." He offers his arm and helps me to my feet. We walk slowly together toward the house of boys, his arm around my shoulders, mine around his waist.

"You can't call me that, you know," I say, after we've figured out a way to manage his long stride beside my short one.

"Call you what?" he says.

"Little sister," I say. "We're the same age. I'm even a little older than you are. I was already here the day you came out of the woods with Serapen."

He inclines his head, a perfect imitation of deferring to a Mohira. Perfect, except for the mischief in his eyes as he looks pointedly down at me. Something about that look makes me laugh.

△▽△

When Ava laughs, so many memories light up inside my

mind that for a moment I'm stunned.

Her laughter fades. "What's wrong?" she says.

I open my mouth to answer but find no words. Ava reaches for my cheek and tilts my face down toward her, studying me with concern. Soft moonlight illuminates her features, and her dark eyes reflect the stars. I remember so many times I've looked into these eyes and held this hand. But most of all I remember that laugh. Even after she stops laughing, sparkling echoes of the familiar sound seem to drift out from the woods, where we spent so many long afternoons playing together as children.

My gaze turns toward the old cedar, a looming silhouette against the starry sky. I blink, and the shadows of night seem to dissolve into daylight as a memory returns to me.

I'm eight summers again, and I'm sitting beside Ava on the high branch of the old cedar. Ava looks out to sea, but my eyes keep returning to the high stone wall enclosing the temple city. I say, "What's it like, inside the wall?"

Ava turns to me with a delighted expression, eager to share a secret. "Come on!" she says. "I'll show you."

She stands, gripping the branch beneath us with her bare toes as she returns to the opening at the top of the cedar's hollow trunk. She climbs down through the tree, and I shimmy after her. We emerge from the shrubs at the base of the cedar.

I follow Ava along an animal track that leads deeper into the forest. We stop at a sandy hollow beside a clear stream. I've never been here before, but clearly Ava has. Her small footprints cover the sand.

She walks up to an oak snag beside the stream. Its

ravaged trunk is full of holes bored by woodpeckers and other creatures. Ava pulls out treasure after treasure from these holes: smooth river stones, acorns and pinecones, curling strips of bright white birch bark. She arranges her collection in little piles before her, then points out the place where I should stand in the middle of the sand.

I watch closely as Ava places river stones in a curve around my feet.

"Imagine this is the wall," she says.

I recognize the shape immediately. For the first time, with Ava's help, I stand inside the wall.

A golden chip of bark shed by a nearby yellow birch catches my eye, reminding me of the bronze gate in the wall. I pick it up and poke it into the sand so it stands upright where Ava left a gap between two stones. The shape and color of the chip are just right. Ava laughs and says, "Yes, exactly! There's the gate."

Now that I understand the game, I gather new bits and pieces for Ava's collection: iridescent shells dropped here and there by seagulls, bright flowers blooming in patches of sunlight, elegant fronds of ferns, glossy bird feathers, anything I think she might find beautiful. Ava so enthusiastically admires everything I find that my chest swells a little.

She narrates as she places the pieces one by one into their places. "The biggest building behind the wall is the Musaion," she says, arranging a large circle of pinecones some distance behind the wall.

"That's the one with the big dome?" I say.

"That's right," she says. "The sisters give our instruction

in reading, writing, historia, and poetika in the library halls of the Musaion."

She carefully arranges curls of birch bark in a ring around the pinecone Musaion as she says, "And these are the workshops where we practice the arts of tekhnologia." She taps one of the birch bark workshops and says, in an aggrieved tone, "Here's where I was the last few days—the house of weavers. The sisters wouldn't let any of us outside the wall to play until we'd spun all the wool from the spring shearing. Spirits, I hate spinning."

I'd love to learn to spin, but I don't tell that to Ava. She always looks sad when I talk about the things I'm not allowed to do.

Ava considers our collection and selects one of the big fern fronds I gathered for her. She breaks it apart into littler fronds and pokes the pieces into the sand, forming two neat lines of green running east to west inside the wall of the miniature temple city. "These are the kitchen gardens where we learn the arts of pharmaka," she says, running her fingertip along the top of one ferny line. "They're so beautiful, Dom! Walled gardens, and open orchard terraces, and glass houses like enormous jewels. When it's cold and grey outside, the glass houses stay warm and green inside, and they always smell like summer."

I struggle to imagine entire houses made of glass. Perhaps they looks like enormous bottles of pharmaka.

I point to the second ferny line and say, "Are these gardens, too?"

Ava says, "Yes, but the girls never work in those. Those gardens are for pharmaka ingredients that only the initiates are allowed to tend."

Ava lays a grid of pebbles on the east side of the city. She says, "The girls' dormitory is a big stone house through the gate here. Here's where I sleep." She taps a spot near one corner.

From our collection, I select a tawny kuku feather to represent Ava. I poke it into the sand beside her fingertip, so it stands at attention before her. She smiles down at the feather, pleased. My chest swells a little more, until a critical expression flickers over Ava's features.

"But there should be two more, for Hanu and Eumelia," she says, pronouncing Eumelia's name with mild distaste.

This seems easy enough to fix. I examine our collection and select two flowers: one pink for rosy-cheeked, sharp-tongued Eumelia; one violet for solemn, soothing Hanu. I set these beside Ava's feather. Ava claps her hands in approval, then says gleefully, "My turn!"

She steps over the wall and lays a foundation for the house of boys. She searches through our collection and selects two new objects.

First she places a plain dark pebble inside the house of boys. "For Kuri," she says with a giggle, "because he's about as clever as a rock."

She could be right. Kuri never says much, though, so it's hard for me to know for sure.

Next, she places a delicate, perfectly spiraling snail shell beside the pebble. "For Balashi," she says with a more thoughtful expression, "because he's very beautiful."

She's certainly right this time, but I'm deflated, hearing her speak of Balashi this way.

Ava pores over the rest of our treasures, searching intently. I await her judgment on me. At last, her eye falls on an acorn riddled with holes and etchings—the signs of beetles' work. This ruined acorn looks like nothing special compared to the flawless shell she chose for Balashi. But Ava beams at me and holds the acorn up between us, turning it slowly in her fingers.

When the angle is just right, I see what Ava sees: two dark eyes staring out from a round brown acorn shell face, beneath a thick mop of acorn cap hair. She places the acorn between the pebble and the shell. "And that's for you," she says, "because I see you. Always looking."

Ava glances at me with a teasing smile and catches me at it again. I quickly drop my gaze to my lap, trying to hide the hot embarrassment rising in my cheeks. Maybe I do look at her too much. But how can I stop? Does she want me to stop?

"Dom." She says my name playfully. When I don't look up, she takes my hand. Reluctantly, I meet her eyes again. She says, "I like the way you look. It makes me want to show you everything."

My embarrassment ebbs. Our peace is restored.

I say, "Are we friends, then?"

She laughs, and I smile. "Best friends," she says.

△▽△

"What's wrong?" I say again, examining Dom's eyes closely. He's looking at me with a dazed expression, and I brace myself for another unpleasant round of pharmaka side effects.

He opens his mouth, closes it, swallows. At last he says, "I just … I remember your laugh."

I relax. Maybe that is some sort of pharmaka side effect, but at least he's coherent this time. I wrap my arm back around his waist, he wraps his arm around my shoulders, and we keep walking. Wistfully, I say, "What does it feel like, remembering something you've lost?"

"It's a relief," he says. "I'm grateful to have it back."

His gratitude is as sweet as it is heartbreaking. What the Mohirai have done to him—to all of us—should make his blood boil. But I bite back my impulse to shout in frustration at the night sky. I'm too spent for another fight tonight.

We don't say anything else as we make our way up the rest of the path to the front door of the house of boys. There's a light moving behind a ground floor window, and the heavy arched door swings open as we reach the front steps.

I remember Hedi Mohira, the stout, red-cheeked sister who must have raised tens of thousands of boys in this house over the centuries since the time of destruction. I often saw Hedi bustling about around the house when I'd come here to play with Dom. I remember her in the blue healer's dress with the sleeves rolled up above her muscular forearms, herding boys all about her, often with the aid of the long wooden clapper she used to ring the meal bell.

Now she stands before us holding a large candle, wearing a white sleeping tunic and loose leggings under her unbelted sky blue healer's robe, her frizzy curls peeking out under a white sleeping kerchief. She blinks at me in astonishment, but I can see she recognizes me. The Mohirai who raise children remember us all.

"Ava," she says, shaking her head, softly clucking her tongue. Her expression is hard and wary. "Spirits, I could hardly believe Serapen, but here you are. Really, you should be taken back into the city. But all the temple healers are so busy with preparations for tomorrow. I …"

She raises her candle to look at us more closely, and she sees the state I'm in, the state both of us are in. Her expression softens when she looks at Dom. I understand—that face of his would melt a heart of stone.

Whatever Hedi's feelings may be toward me, seeing that we're in trouble elicits the no-nonsense manner I remember, the pragmatism of an initiate healer. She says, "I suppose there's a first time for everything. Come along."

△▽△

By the light of the oil lamps in the entrance hall, Hedi inventories our injuries. We're both muddy and bruised. I'm half-clothed and have a few scratches on my neck from Ava's knife. The cut on Ava's lip has reopened and is bleeding, and her wrists are covered in bruises from me, but the worst of the damage seems to be to her bare feet, which are filthy, covered in scratches, and leave crimson smudges on the grey stone floor wherever she walks. Hedi wakes another of the house sisters for assistance, then leads us to the bathing rooms.

Bathing proves more complicated than the healers anticipate. At first they try to help us bathe in separate tubs, but we both shiver and wince after only a short time apart. Ava and I are starting to understand our predicament better, though, so we quickly sort out that we have to take the bathing in turns. I sit wrapped in a blanket beside Ava's tub, holding her hand when she needs it. It takes two full tubs of hot water to rinse all the sticky residue from Ava's skin, with both healers using long-handled scrub brushes to keep the amanitai off themselves.

Then I have my turn. Ava sits beside my tub holding my hand as Hedi scrubs me down. I have no idea how we're going to keep this up tomorrow, but I'm too delirious to think much further ahead than a bed right now. Hedi puts us in winter sleeping tunics of fleecy wool after watching all our shivering, although I feel warm again after the hot bath. She keeps us in the bathing room to attend to our cuts and bruises with healing pharmaka. My injuries are superficial, but Ava's feet require some time to bandage properly.

Hedi leads us down the corridor toward one of the spare bedrooms where visitors usually stay. She drags the two single beds together and lights two candles for us. From the washbasin stand in the corner of the room, she retrieves two small wooden cups. These she sets on the bedside table.

Withdrawing a silver flask from her robe, Hedi pours a small measure of golden liquid into each wooden cup. I know this routine well; I drank a cup of unbinding pharmaka like this every night at bedtime for my first three years in the house of boys.

Hedi taps the bedside table beside the cups, then looks from Ava to me. "Listen, little sister, little brother," she says. "Any other night, seeing the shape you two are in, I'd say you should drink the full dose and sleep through the whole day tomorrow. But given the circumstances, I suggest you avoid it unless absolutely necessary for the pain. If you must, take the smallest dose you can. Otherwise, you'll be asleep on your feet through the ceremony. Do you understand?"

"I have listened and I have heard, sister," I say automatically. But Ava only stares at Hedi, making no sign of acknowledgment. I wonder whether she's forgotten the correct response.

To Ava, Hedi says, "Listen, little sister. I know you haven't received the proper instruction for Calling Day. But the most important thing to remember is to keep the silence until the High Priestess calls you, and to follow her instructions carefully. You and Dom will walk behind all the others at the end of the lines so you can stay together. You'll see the ceremony repeated several times before you're called forward, so listen carefully and I'm sure you'll learn the correct responses. They're all very short."

Hedi gestures to a shelf holding two folded piles of glossy white clothes, then points to two dark cloaks hanging from pegs by the door. She says, "You'll wear these for the ceremony."

"I can't," says Ava, her voice quavering. "I can't be called." Her expression as she looks at Hedi reminds me of a cornered animal.

Hedi's demeanor toward Ava softens, seeing her fear. She pats Ava's cheek and says, "Don't be afraid, child. The Voice has returned you to us now so you may be called with your sisters and brothers at the proper time. Resisting the Voice will do you as much good as resisting the approach of spring. There's no escaping it, whatever that foolish woman may have told you. All will be well. You will see."

That's more comfort than I've ever seen Hedi offer to anyone, even to the youngest boys. Briskly, Hedi concludes, "The ceremony starts at dawn, despite the night you've had. There's no delaying the equinox. Try to get some sleep."

Ava's hand clenches in mine. Anger seems to pour into me. In the same way snippets of her thoughts flashed in my mind before, her emotion rushes to my head, hot and tumultuous and overwhelming. I'm afraid she's regained enough energy to start another scene with Hedi, so I say quickly, "Thank you, Hedi Mohira. We'll try to sleep. Good night."

Hedi withdraws and closes the door. I turn to Ava and say, "Please, Ava. Please don't fight this. It's a long ceremony tomorrow, and I can't make it through without you. I need you there."

"You don't have any idea what's going to happen after you're called, do you?" she says.

Ava's tone with me is as harsh as Mama's was with her. But it's the note of derision in her voice, not her anger, that sparks my own anger. My voice is louder than I mean it to be when I say, "Just because you're a girl doesn't mean you know everything, Ava. Tomorrow is the one and only time I will ever hear the Voice for myself. You don't know what it will say. I don't know what it will say. No one can know until it happens. But …" I falter, not recognizing this cutting tone in my own voice and alarmed by what I see boiling behind Ava's eyes as she hears it. I've never spoken to a girl this way, or to anyone else for that matter. My anger cools a little, but what follows close behind it is a sickening mix of fear, frustration, and longing that's been accumulating in me for years. I manage to lower my voice somewhat as I finish my thought and say, "It's the closest I'll ever get to knowing what it might have been like to be a Mohira. You can't take this from me."

The small point of Ava's chin rises as she tries to glare down at me, though she has no choice but to look up at me from her little height. Her nostrils flare. She bites back something she's about to say, drops my hand, and turns from me. She blows out one of the candles, climbs into one of the beds, and buries herself in the blankets.

Now that she's let go of my hand, I can't tell what she's thinking or feeling any more. It's a relief to be alone with my own thoughts, which are far less tempestuous than hers. I want to go down the hall to my own bed, listen to Kuri's familiar snore and Balashi's steady deep breathing, and forget this day ever happened. Maybe I could manage it, despite the pain.

But Serapen specifically told me to stay with Ava. As kind as Serapen has always seemed to me, I don't want to find out what she's like when she's disobeyed. And as frustrating as Ava is, I really don't want to cause her any more pain, after all I've seen her go through tonight.

I sigh, climb into the other bed, and blow out my candle. Ava and I lie side by side, not touching, as the pain builds up inside us. I can't bring myself to reach out to her to make it stop, because I dread that burning anger of hers coursing through me again. Sleeping this way is going to be impossible. I close my eyes, trying to relax as the pain grows steadily worse.

But this time, to my surprise, she's the one who ends it. She turns over and reaches tentatively toward me under the blankets. Her fingertips slide down my sleeve until she finds my hand. Her fingers lace through mine, and she squeezes her palm to my palm. The pain trickles out slowly between us.

She whispers something, in a voice so small I can't hear it. I turn my face toward her and whisper back, more sharply than I mean to, "What?"

"I'm sorry," she says a little louder, quite slowly, like she's never said these words before. "You're right. I don't know what will happen. All I know is what I've been taught by my mother, and ..." Her eyes shine with tears, but she blinks them back and simply says again, "I don't know."

I'm stunned by her apology. I don't think a girl has ever apologized to me for anything. My irritation toward her fades. I still feel upset, but most of what I'm upset about has nothing to do with her, really. Ava's anger just unlocked my own.

"All right," I say at last.

The pain ebbs until it's almost gone. She curls up into a ball facing me, her head deep in her pillow. She's asleep almost instantly, and her fingers twitch against my palm. Despite her thick woolen sleeping tunic, Ava's hand feels cold in mine, and occasionally she shivers.

In sleep, the tension around Ava's eyes and lips disappears. I study her face in the moonlight for a while, waiting for my exhaustion to turn into sleep. She looks much younger now than she did before. Long-forgotten childhood memories of Ava drift through my mind, out of sequence and out of context. My eyelids grow heavy, but each time I'm about to drift off I'm reawakened by Ava's shivering or a glimpse of her dreams. Her dreams frequently include jolting flashes of Mama's stern face and ice blue eyes, which sets my heart pounding. I consider taking a sip of the unbinding pharmaka Hedi left for us to help me sleep, but I don't want to wake up Ava by letting go of her hand. Everything is so much more peaceful while she's sleeping. So I watch her sleep, hoping this will help me fall asleep.

Ava's hand grows colder and colder, until at last I pull her toward me, wrapping our two blankets around us, hoping this will stop her shivering. She relaxes against my chest, and for the first time since I picked her up in the woods, her skin feels warm to my touch.

It's nearing sunrise when my exhaustion finally overcomes all the other strangeness, and I slip straight into dreams. But whether they're Ava's dreams or mine, I cannot tell.

THE MORNING AFTER

I STARTLE AWAKE at the sound of footsteps approaching. Heavy arms wrap around me. A warm chest rises and falls against my back. Soft breath courses down my neck.

Overwhelmed by the sense that I'm caught in a trap, I spring away, heart racing. I fall out of a strange bed, tangled in blankets, onto a hard stone floor. My knees and hands and entire body throb, and I moan softly in pain. Where am I?

Dom sits up in the bed, the window silhouetting his mussed halo of curls. Even in the dim pre-dawn light I can see the dark circles under his eyes. He looks down at me with the same expression of concern I remember from last night. It all comes back to me at once. I moan softly again, this time in defeat.

The soft footsteps that woke me stop outside the door. Three loud knocks, and the door swings inward. Hedi stands at the threshold wearing a dark ceremonial cloak over her blue robe. Her deep voice resonates in the room as she says, "Awake, awake, awake. The day of your calling has arrived."

Dom jumps out of bed like it's a reflex, which I suppose it might be, considering all the pharmaka the sisters use to train these boys to the routines of their life. Hedi looks sharply at me sitting on the floor. Wordlessly, she gestures for me to stand up and hurry.

Hedi withdraws, and Dom stumbles groggily toward me. He looks even more exhausted than he did last night, and I feel sorry for him. I open my mouth to speak, but he shakes his head quickly and raises a finger to his lips, reminding me of the ceremonial silence. I wince a little at the prickling pain returning to my chest, and he sees the wince and takes my hands until the pain subsides. Then he pulls me up to stand.

I know this is real, but it feels like a bad dream. My mother spent the last seven years trying to prevent this from ever happening to me. She taught me that Calling Day is the beginning of a woman's unending service to the Voice. It's the end of freedom, the end of choice. It's worse for men in most ways, of course. They have no choice about their calling either, and they have to live almost entirely without the arts and mysteries. Dom should fear this day even more than I do. At least a woman has a life full of comfort and learning, even if she has no control over her path. But both paths are paths of servitude. This is not what I wanted for myself, and not what my mother wanted for me.

But my mother isn't here. She left me. With the clarity of a partial night's sleep, I'm starting to think it makes sense—in a cold, calculating way—that my mother chose to keep her freedom. She's taught me to think that way, too. She must have known from her priestess training what I learned by brute force when I attempted to run after her last night. I couldn't have endured the pain of separation from Dom for long, even if she'd carried me all the way to the boat and we'd managed to sail away.

The boat, my mother, the entire life I thought I was beginning yesterday—all of them are gone. My mother understood, as I'm beginning to understand, that there's no way out for me, at least not until I find out how to counter this overdose of amanitai. My mother couldn't help me, and spirits know what Serapen would have done to my mother had she stayed with me. Whatever it is must be pretty bad for my fearless mother to have looked as frightened as she did. Although … she never actually told me what would happen if Serapen caught her. My mother only told me what would happen if Serapen caught me. Which is what's happening now.

I try to let go of thoughts of my mother. I need to figure out what I'm going to do about what's happening to me now. I take a breath, centering myself in the present. I'll have to get through this like I'd get through anything else, like it's just another job. Of course I don't have a plan yet, but at least I can consider my options.

I look up at Dom, who's still holding my hands. All my options at this point include him. He can't go anywhere without me, and I can't go anywhere without him. The only thing that feels entirely under my control right now is how much pain he experiences and how much pain I experience. I try not to think about the fact that this works both ways, so he has as much control as I do.

Yesterday, I was willing to cause Dom—and myself—any amount of pain in my attempt to follow my mother. But I failed, and we've both paid a heavy price for it. I'm weakened from my ordeal last night, and although Dom is clearly far stronger than I am, he's in much worse shape than he was when he found me. I need to figure out a smarter way to manage the pain for both of us. Any escape will be easier with both of us at full strength.

But Dom made it clear last night that escape is the last thing on his mind. He wants to go to his Calling Day ceremony. He's foolish to want it, perhaps. But how can I blame him? He's been raised to know nothing else, just as I would have been if I'd stayed here. I suppose I could try to stop him, but if he truly wants to be called, he'll find a way. The autumn equinox is considered the most auspicious day to hear the Voice, but the Mohirai could help Dom hear the Voice on another day. I can't think of anything I gain from ruining today's ceremony for him, and I don't want to drive a wedge between us now when I know I'm going to need Dom's help later.

I don't know what I'll do at the ceremony myself, though. Maybe Dom can receive his calling and I can pitch a fit to avoid receiving mine. I'm not sure. I'll have to improvise once we get there.

My hands tingle, and Dom speaks to me, though his lips don't move. *Ava?* His voice sounds tentative, searching, somewhere in my mind. It's an odd sensation, hearing him while the room remains silent. This must be how I sounded to him yesterday.

I don't know exactly how to answer, so I simply think, *I hear you.*

Dom looks relieved. I glimpse a flash of his memory, of Hedi giving him and his trio brothers instructions for today. Dom thinks, *We need to wear the ceremonial clothes with hoods up. Hair stays unbound—no braids or ties of any kind. There's a long walk at the start of the ceremony, and we can't wear shoes. We can't eat until the evening meal, but we can drink water if we need it. And ...*

His voice seems to fade away in my mind, so I adjust my hold on his hands and think, *We can drink water. And ...*

what?

Apprehensively, he thinks, *Well … There's more pharmaka in this ceremony.*

I sigh. Of course there is. I think, *Spirits, I'm not sure I can handle any more pharmaka.*

Dom's worried expression is enough to tell me he's not sure he can either. Hedi's soft footsteps move on to an adjacent corridor, and he thinks, *She's waking the rest of the sixteenth summers. We'll have to leave soon. Do you mind if I …* He gestures at the door to the privy closet.

I wave my hand for him to go. After everything that's happened already, and whatever is bound to happen next, there's no point in being shy.

△▽△

Step by step, Ava and I figure out how to make ready for the day ahead. Taking turns at the wash basin, her hand on my back, then mine on hers, to give each other two free hands. Stepping back to give each other privacy, stepping forward quickly to touch the other's hand before the pain becomes too bad.

Undressing and dressing is the most intricate of these dances. Ava dresses first, and in such close proximity, I can't help watching her. I place my hand on her waist as she pulls her fleecy wool sleeping tunic up over her head. The brightening twilight reveals the warm hazelnut tone of her skin as she slips into the white ceremonial silks embroidered with golden threads. I touch the soft skin above her collarbone as she wraps herself in the white robe. The long

89

black curls loose around her shoulders tickle the back of my hand. All these clothes are far too big on her, though I imagine they're the smallest Hedi could find on short notice. Each movement of Ava's hands and feet seems to linger in the air as excess fabric floats behind her, golden threads gleaming at her wrists and ankles.

Ava's hand moves lightly from my shoulder to my back to my neck as I change into new leggings, new tunic, new robe. The silk against my skin feels cold, almost liquid, until it warms up. I've never worn anything this fine, so smooth and weightless, and I don't expect I ever will again. Usually only the initiate Mohirai wear dyed clothes and delicate fabrics. It's been eight years of undyed wool and leather for me as a boy, and most of the men I've seen wear much the same.

Ava and I argue briefly in the silence when she glances toward her leather belt on the bedside table. She refused to be parted from it last night when Hedi took our other muddy clothes away. I see her visualizing possible ways to hide it under her robe. She reaches for it, but I touch her wrist and think, *We're not allowed to take anything with us to the ceremony apart from the clothes we've been given.*

She thinks, *It's the only thing I have left.* Her emotions, which have been fairly calm until now, grow agitated.

Please, Ava, I think. *I'm sure the Mohirai will give us everything we need after the ceremony.*

She bites her lower lip, wincing when her teeth dig into the deep cut already there. She takes a last look at her belt, looks up at me, and sighs in resignation.

Thank you, I think, relieved she's not putting up a fight this morning.

The footsteps of the sixteenth summer boys shuffle down the adjacent corridor toward the front door. I hurry to put on the cloak of undyed black wool, but I can't figure out the intricate laces, which are different from the children's cloaks. Ava takes over, somehow knowing how these work. Her fingers fly over my heart, tying the little series of knots on my cloak before she laces her own. The footsteps are gone by the time she's done. We're running behind.

I look at Ava and gesture toward the door. She nods and takes my hand. Her lips tremble. Even if I couldn't feel that she's frightened, I would have known it from the look in her eyes as they meet mine.

I squeeze her hand and think, *It'll be fine. You'll be fine. We'll be fine.* Although I have no idea whether this is true. Her lips curve into a wry smirk. Oh spirits, she overheard me thinking that. This isn't going to be easy.

Nope, she agrees.

I try to stop thinking, and we step out the door.

Dawn brightens behind us as Ava and I hurry hand in hand down the path through the gardens, catching up to the cloaked and hooded line of boys following Hedi. My bare feet sting, but I realize quickly that it's not my pain. I glance down at Ava's bandaged feet, just visible beneath the hem of her white robe, and I feel the rough gravel of the path digging into all her cuts and bruises. I wonder how she'll manage the long walk ahead.

Don't worry about me, she thinks. *Compared to all that pain yesterday, this is nothing.*

No one is supposed to look back once the ceremonial walk begins, but Kuri and Balashi decide it's worth risking the wrath of Hedi. As soon as we approach the end of the line, their heads swing back toward us.

Under their hoods, Balashi and Kuri's eyes widen at the sight of Ava holding my hand. Kuri looks confused. Balashi looks impressed. Their faces hold an expression somewhere between, *Who is that?* and *How did you get away with that?* But neither dares to speak, and eventually they have to face forward again so they don't trip over themselves.

They haven't changed much, Ava thinks. I feel her amusement like a warm ripple through my chest, and I have to suppress a laugh.

I realize as we step out onto the meadow that, in our rush to catch up to the others, Ava and I forgot to raise our hoods. I quickly pull the fleece-lined hood up over my head. Ava sees me and raises hers as well.

The hood envelops me in an aroma of pharmaka so intense that for a moment I'm light-headed.

Spirits, here we go, Ava thinks.

It'll be fine. You'll be fine. We'll be fine, I think again, but now it's more for my benefit than hers.

She squeezes my hand and thinks, *Whatever happens, it can't be worse than yesterday.*

I hope she's right.

NOT TOO LATE

HAND IN HAND, DOM AND I FOLLOW the line of cloaked boys walking across the meadow toward the temple city gate. Dawn light gleams on the great bronze dome that peeks over the top of the city wall. I remember standing under that dome many times, looking up at the beautiful ceiling mosaics. The vaulted space beneath the dome connects many different halls of the Children's Temple Musaion, including the library halls. Those endless shelves of parchment scrolls and clay tablets were my favorite place to roam on days the girls weren't allowed outside the city. I remember that when we were little, Dom used to ask me so many questions about the Musaion, and about everything else behind the wall. I spent a lot of time describing the temple city to him as we played together in the woods. I wonder whether he remembers any of that.

More bits and pieces started coming back to me last night, Dom thinks, startling me. He's so quiet when he's listening that I almost forget he's there. But when I focus, I can feel him: a little stillness amidst the churn of my own thoughts.

Across the meadow, the city gate opens inward. Serapen glides out, leading a silent line of eight cloaked girls toward us. The line of boys converges with the line of girls at a footpath that turns upslope into the woods. I scan the shadows beneath the girls' dark hoods, wondering whether I might see either of my old trio sisters. I can't pick out Hanu, but I think I see Eumelia's round, freckled cheeks and smirking half-smile beneath one of the hoods. She and I used to quarrel endlessly, and I feel a flicker of annoyance at the memory, even though I haven't seen her in seven years.

Hedi and Serapen lead the boys' line and the girls' line onto the footpath toward the forest, so we're walking in parallel lines. I realize only as I take my place at the end of the line beside Dom that I complete the trio of trios. Nine girls to match the nine boys.

When we reach the forest edge, Serapen turns to face us. Hedi turns away and walks alone back toward the house of boys. I'm startled by an impulse to cry as I watch Hedi depart. But it's not my impulse—it's Dom's. I catch glimpses of his memories: Hedi introducing him to Kuri and Balashi on his first day here, Hedi leading the blessing in the meal hall, Hedi tending to scraped knees, Hedi kissing his forehead before bedtime. He's realizing he may never see her again.

I feel a pang of sympathy for him, followed by a rush of memories of my mother that rekindle my grief and anger from yesterday. Dom's hand tenses around mine, and I try to calm myself so he won't need to share these painful feelings again. Inadvertently, I take a deep breath of the potent pharmaka in my hood. Dom's memories and mine drift away from me, blurring with distance. His hand relaxes. Although I worry about what this pharmaka might be doing to me, its calming, numbing effect does make me feel better in this moment.

Sorry about Hedi, I think, through the slight fuzziness in my mind. *It's hard to lose someone like her.*

Hedi wasn't warm toward me, probably because she cares

about Dom and doesn't like seeing him tangled up in this situation with me. But despite that, she was efficient, pragmatic, even kind. I understand why Dom would miss her, how he could love her, especially since he doesn't know what she's done to him.

I even notice some similarities between Hedi and my mother. I love my mother not because she's ever been particularly warm toward me, but because I admire her knowledge, strength, and self-reliance. I've wanted to be like her since the day she led me out of the Children's Temple and explained what had happened to me. She taught me everything I need to be self-reliant like her, and to trust myself over anyone else. All that will be useful now that she's gone, since all I have left is myself.

And me, thinks Dom.

Spirits, it's so weird having him overhearing all this. It's hard to tell when he's listening and when he's not.

Sorry, he thinks. *Do you want me to let go of your hand?*

Even the thought of the stabbing pain returning makes me feel tired. *No,* I think. *You feel even more exhausted than I do. Let's not make it worse.*

Thanks, he thinks. His gratitude soaks into me like warm sunlight, so disproportionately strong in response to my very small kindness that I'm ashamed of everything I put him through yesterday.

Let's also try not to think about yesterday, Dom thinks.

Good point. No need to re-live any of that right now. Better focus on what's ahead.

The eighteen of us stand facing Serapen. The first light of dawn peeks beneath Serapen's hood, revealing the sharp lines of her jaw beneath the shadows of her hood. In a ringing voice that fills the meadow, she says, "The sun rises on the day of your calling. Listen well, for I tell you a mystery.

"There is a Voice that speaks within all. Within each stone, within each tree, within each breath of the wind. The Voice speaks clearest in stillness. Give yourself to stillness, and listen for the Voice that calls within you."

Serapen turns and walks into the cedar forest. We follow her, walking in silence along a wide footpath through the trees. I know this forest well, having found food and shelter and safe passage beneath its canopy in every season over many years of travel. But I've never seen the forest look as beautiful as it does this morning.

The sun rises, transforming the dark violets and blues of morning twilight into the bright greens and blues of full morning. As we walk deeper into the woods, my toes sink into soft beds of star moss. I look down at the velvety mosses, tenacious lichens, and mysterious fungi springing up around my bare feet. I'm a giant passing over this tiny world, even as I'm the tiniest field mouse scampering beneath towering trees.

I breathe in the resinous sweetness of the cedars. For a moment, I forget to step forward. I stare up at their ancient forms in simple awe. Each one of their vast trunks holds a shape unique from all the rest. This one twists like the muscled torso of a farmer straining against a plow. That one bends like a Mohira over her lyre. Their branches spread overhead in a dance with the dazzling sun, weaving a canopy so dense that only a rare sunbeam penetrates to the forest floor. Drifting shafts of light illuminate tiny motes of dust and winged insects spiraling overhead. The late summer birds call out to one another from perches all around us, gossiping about what we're doing here, occasionally revealing themselves with a flutter of wings or a darting flight from one treetop to the next.

Every familiar tree, herb, mushroom, insect, and bird call seems so mesmerizing to me this morning that I wonder whether the pharmaka in my hood is affecting my senses. I certainly felt some strange distortions in my vision and hearing last night. I glance at Dom, wondering whether this is happening to him, too. He gazes upward with that look of intense focus, the look he turned up at the stars last night, the look I caught him giving me as we were getting dressed this morning. That look is now focused on the canopy. Is this how Dom sees the forest? Does he see like this all the time?

Dom glances back at me.

Don't you? he wonders.

No, I think, astonished. *Not even close.*

Serapen turns off the wider footpath onto a narrower trail. The girls' line and the boys' line press closer together, our long cloaks brushing against each other and catching sometimes on the tips of the branches on either side of the path.

The trees grow ever larger, older, grander. I step carefully over the gnarled roots that surface more frequently through the soft soil here. Herbs reach out with tender green fingers into the opening of the trail, tickling my bare feet and ankles.

Bright sunlight streams through the thinning trees ahead, and we follow Serapen into a grassy clearing. At the center of the clearing lies a large spring, its surface reflecting the blue sky. On a flat rock beside the pool stand a large silver chalice and a tall silver ewer, gleaming in the sunlight.

Serapen turns to face us and pushes back her hood. Her eyes reflect the blue and green of the clearing. In the morning sun, her long snow-white hair shines brighter even than the chalice behind her. She unlaces her dark cloak and lets it fall around her bare feet, revealing her dazzling white robes, her ornate sleeves and collar worked in golden thread. Looking at her is like staring at the sun.

Serapen says, "Keep your silence until the Voice calls for you. Remember your instructions as you approach. Do not look down into the waters as you step into the sacred pool. It is dangerous to look upon the waters unprepared. Look only to me, listen only to me, as I receive the Voice's words for you."

Serapen approaches the pool. We stand waiting. She lifts the silver ewer from the flat rock and bends to dip it into the pool. The glassy surface of the water, now disturbed, shimmers in the sunlight. I struggle with an impulse to look down at the surface, but I remember Serapen's warning and keep my eyes locked on her.

Serapen pours a stream of clear water from the ewer into the chalice. From within the folds of her white robe, she withdraws a small cloth pouch and empties it into the chalice. She lifts the chalice in both hands, swirls it slowly, drinks deep, and lifts it up toward the sun.

She carries the chalice back toward us. She nods, and all the boys and girls around me push back their hoods, so I follow their lead.

Serapen walks along the line of boys, holding the chalice

to each boy's lips in turn. Each boy drinks until she withdraws the silver cup. My apprehension of whatever is in that cup builds. I'm afraid of what might happen to Dom, and to me, if we drink. What if we get sick? I saw that happen many times during ceremonies in my year at the Children's Temple. Would we both feel each other's sickness? What if we start seeing things or hearing things or become confused? Will we both feel that way? Will we amplify those feelings between us? My stomach churns.

Calm down, Dom thinks. *Serapen's the most experienced healer in all of Dulai. She wouldn't give us anything that would hurt us.*

Poor Dom. He still doesn't know the first thing about Serapen.

What do you mean? he thinks. *What do you know about Serapen?*

I know that she takes away memories and people and choices that should belong to us. My mother showed me how the men in the villages live, how the initiates in the temple live, how the priestesses called to bear children live. I've heard what some of the men say in secret about the injustice of the sisters, about all that was stolen from them when the Mohirai took control of Dulai after the time of destruction.

The withered faces and voices of the old men I've seen die, the sounds of women in childbirth, the look in the eyes of the mothers and children as they are unbound—all flash before my eyes, the things my mother showed me so I could understand what she'd learned through centuries serving the Voice as an initiate priestess.

I feel Dom's confusion as he glimpses my memories

without context or explanation. But I also feel his desire to understand.

I'm sorry, Dom, I think, growing frantic. *There's not nearly enough time to explain it all at once. But ...* Serapen is approaching Dom fast, working her way down the line of boys with the chalice in her hands. A desperate plan forms in my mind, spilling out from me to him.

No, Ava, he thinks. *Don't. Don't run now. Please.*

Do you really want to spend your entire life as a slave to the Voice? I think.

I don't know what that means, he thinks.

A slave ... I try to remember the words my mother often used. *A slave is someone whose body and mind and life belong to someone else. A slave is someone who must obey commands. A slave is someone who makes no choices of their own.*

But everyone has to obey the Voice, even the Mohirai, he thinks.

No, I think. *That's just what the priestesses want you to believe.*

Dom's jaw clenches, and I feel his resistance to this thought rising between us like the wall around the temple. Serapen reaches Kuri, two boys ahead of Dom. Kuri drinks from the chalice. We're almost out of time. I pour every last drop of my conviction into my next thought, willing Dom to believe me.

Please listen to me, Dom. It's not too late. We can escape from here, if we run together. I know these woods like the back of my hand. But I can't go without you. You saw what happened to me last night.

Dom turns to me, and despite the tired circles under his

eyes, his acorn brown complexion looks rosy, glowing with the effects of whatever pharmaka we're breathing in from these hoods. His eyes are bright but unfocused. He looks at me with that awed expression again. I wonder whether he's heard me, or whether the pharmaka has him in its grip, making him compliant, unresisting, unthinking.

Inside my head, I scream in frustration. Dom overhears me and winces. His eyes refocus as he searches my face.

You're wrong, Ava, he thinks. *The Mohirai would never do anything to hurt us. The Mohirai don't lie. I don't understand what you saw, but you must be mistaken.*

The lamb. The fool. The damned fool lamb. The vitriol surges inside me until Dom drops my hand like I've burned him. Serapen stands before him, and he looks up at her.

The pain in my chest prickles as the High Priestess raises the chalice to his lips.

ANSWERING THE CALL

AVA'S WORDS ECHO in my mind even after I drop her hand: *Do you really want to spend your entire life as a slave to the Voice?*

Each thought that spills from Ava into me feels like another push toward some dangerous precipice. And I don't want to follow her there. She thinks she's telling me the truth, but somehow I know she's wrong. I've received nothing but kindness from the sisters my entire life. As much as I've wished for another fate than my own, I trust the Mohirai. I believe the Voice has a plan for me just like it does for every other creature in its care. I want to give myself over to the Voice. I want to know my purpose.

And I definitely don't want to run away with Ava. Most of what I've experienced with her since yesterday has been pain, pain, and more pain. The life of an uninitiated man may not be the richest or fullest life, but it can't be nearly as painful as a single day bound to Ava this way.

Ahead of me in line, Balashi finishes drinking from the chalice, and Serapen moves on from him to me. Even though I've let go of Ava's hand, somehow I still feel her agitation. I try to shut out my thoughts of her, which is easier when I look up into Serapen's eyes. The High Priestess raises the silver chalice before me. I look down into a swirling brew of dark blood red.

I breathe in a faint bitterness, but when the cool liquid meets my lips, the taste is mostly sweet. I swallow and swallow until Serapen pulls away the cup. A buzzing sensation spreads over my tongue, down my throat, into my belly.

Serapen turns from me and walks back to the front of the line of girls. She passes her hand once more over the chalice and raises it to the first girl's lips.

The needling pain has been rebuilding in my chest since I let go of Ava, but now she tentatively takes my hand again. My pain eases at her touch.

I'm sorry, Ava, I think, *but this is what I want. You can't take this from me.* A feeling like grey fog sweeps through me, and I recognize Ava's grief. But this time, her grief is for me, not for her mother.

I never wanted to take anything from you, she thinks.

I look down at her, and she looks up at me. The morning light reveals flecks of yellow, amber, and green in her dark brown eyes, which gleam with unshed tears.

She thinks, *I wanted to share everything with you. Don't you remember?*

I search Ava's face, trying to remember. In her eyes, I see my reflection—impossibly young—as a memory returns to me.

Ava and I are small children again, and I smile shyly at her as we sit side by side in the high branch of the old cedar on a warm, clear afternoon. Ava smiles back at me, then looks out toward the sea. She tips her head to the side and says, "I wonder if we can see all the way to the ocean from here."

"What's the ocean?" I say.

Ava gasps with delight at having a new secret to share

with me. She sweeps her hand across the watery horizon to the south and says, "The sisters say the ocean is an even greater sea beyond the sea. And," she looks at me for emphasis as she shares the best part, "beyond the ocean, they say there are whole other worlds beyond Dulai!"

Awed, I say, "What's in the other worlds?"

Ava frowns and says, "I don't know. The sisters won't tell me. But," her voice rises with new conviction, "I'll be a Mohira one day. And when I find out—" she leans toward me, dropping her voice to a conspiratorial whisper, "I'll let you know."

The whisper fades back into my memory as Ava thinks, *Please, Dom. Come with me. Where I'm going, you won't need to serve the Voice. I'll hide nothing from you. We'll share everything as equals. I promise.*

I struggle to hold my focus on Ava's words. *I'll hide nothing … We'll share everything … I promise.* I want to ask what she means. But the pharmaka is hitting me hard. It's difficult to think of anything except how beautiful this clearing is, how this is the only place in the world I want to be.

Ava's hand relaxes in mine. Distantly, I wonder whether she's experiencing some effect of the pharmaka through me, even though she's taken none of it herself.

Serapen reaches the end of the line of girls and looks down at Ava. A profound stillness falls over the clearing. Even the dust motes swirling in the sunlight seem to cease their motion. The High Priestess raises the chalice to Ava's lips. I hold absolutely still, listening intently to Ava's thoughts, expecting an explosion of some sort from her. What will she do? Throw the chalice back at Serapen? Break away from me again to run?

Ava's awareness coils like a snake preparing to strike. My whole body tenses in anticipation of whatever is coming. But I hear nothing in her mind but a rippling reflection of my own memory, the sound of her child's voice overflowing with confidence: *I'll be a Mohira one day.*

I can't believe my eyes when Ava accepts the raised chalice in Serapen's hands without a single protest. And yet there she stands: swallowing, swallowing, swallowing. I feel her tasting the bittersweetness of the dark brew, the tension melting from her awareness.

At last Serapen lowers the chalice from Ava's lips.

What am I doing? Ava thinks.

Serapen returns to the pool, pours out the last of the pharmaka onto the soil, and returns the chalice to its place beside the ewer on the flat rock. She turns to face us and closes her eyes.

"Listen," she says.

"Listen," she says again.

"Listen," she says a third time.

We listen. A breeze stirs in the clearing. A prickle runs down my neck.

Serapen steps into the pool, wading in until she stands submerged to the waist. She turns back toward us and calls Ubar, the first boy in the line ahead of me.

Ubar unlaces his cloak, and the dark folds drop around his ankles. He makes his way toward the High Priestess. His gaze doesn't stray to the forbidden surface of the pool as he steps in and takes her outstretched hands. His white silk robe rises around him, floating on the surface like a lotus blossom.

Serapen looks down at him. "Listen, Ubar, for the Voice that calls to you," she intones. "Listen."

"I listen," he replies in a low, soft voice.

Holding hands, they close their eyes and wait. The breeze stirs. Serapen says, "Listen, Ubar, for you are called as farmer. Will you answer the call?"

"Yes," he says, in a voice more confident than before. "I will answer."

They open their eyes. Serapen smiles at Ubar, embraces him lightly, and kisses his cheek. He allows her to lower him gently into the water, so he floats face up toward the sky. He closes his eyes and mouth tightly just before Serapen presses him briefly down beneath the surface.

He re-emerges with a gasp, wet hair hanging over his eyes. Serapen helps him find his footing and leads him by the hand out of the pool. His soaked ceremonial garments gleam in the sunlight.

I'm startled when a man steps out from behind a large tree at the edge of the wood behind the pool. He calls in a deep voice, "Welcome, Ubar, to the order of farmers."

Ubar turns toward the man, who holds out a new cloak dyed a rich chestnut brown. The man wraps the dry cloak around the wet boy and leads him off into the woods.

And then Ubar is gone.

Serapen calls the next boy, and the next, and the five that follow. One by one, they're called to join the farmers and fishermen, hunters and gatherers, masons and smiths. Kuri disappears under a dark green gatherer's cloak. My last sight of Balashi is of his handsome face disappearing beneath an inky black smith's cloak with silver threads.

My head swirls. My heart races. At last, I'm going to hear my calling. As if from a great distance, Serapen calls, "Dom."

I let go of Ava's hand. My fingers fumble on the cloak laces Ava tied for me this morning. Vaguely, I wonder when the prickling pain will return to my chest, but all I feel is the tingle of pharmaka in my belly, radiating out along my arms, steadying my hands. The heavy cloak falls from my shoulders.

I step out into the bright sunlight of the clearing, walking forward until my bare feet reach the rocky edge of the pool. When I step in, the water closes cool around my toes, and Serapen's fingers close warm around my hands.

The water ripples at the bottom edge of my vision, enticing, but Serapen's words of warning were very clear. I hold my gaze steadily on hers, never looking down into the pool.

Serapen looks back at me through eyes that reflect all colors of the rainbow. I feel so connected to this woman, and through her to the stones beneath our feet, to the water rising up around my body, to the trees holding up the sky above us.

"Listen, Dom, for the Voice that calls to you," she says, in a voice that holds more richness, more certainty, more promise than any single voice can hold.

The breeze encircles us. Nothing moves, and yet I lose all sense of my body's orientation above the ground, of the ground's orientation beneath my feet. I find myself standing alone in the wood. Even Serapen is gone. Panic flares in me for a moment, but her unseen hands grasp mine tight.

She says, "Listen."

The reply rises within me. "I listen."

I don't know how long I stand in this place where the wind blows between layers of the unseen.

The Voice calls up from the depths of the pool, from the height of the sky, from the tips of every branch, but I can't make out the words.

I strain to listen. The sun and moon and stars swirl in the bowl of sky, dissolving time and space. Their passage fills me with wonder. I know for the first time that the Voice calls not only within this world, but within all the worlds.

The sky's swirling stops. I gaze up at an infinite darkness pierced by innumerable stars, and I listen.

I listen.

I listen.

And then I hear.

You have asked it. We may give it. But there is a price. Do you accept it?

As the Voice says this, I feel Ava's hand in mine. She's with me here, and at the same time she's elsewhere. I'm not sure whether I've asked for Ava or Ava is the price of what I've asked. In this moment there are no such distinctions. All I comprehend is that the choice—to have all I've asked—lies before me.

So I choose. I think, *Yes. Yes. Yes, I do accept the price.*

The Voice says, *Listen, Dom, for you are called as Artifex. Will you answer our call?*

Artifex. I've never heard this word before. But it resonates within me, and I've never been more certain than I am when I say, "Yes. I will answer."

The stars wink out above me. I look no longer into the

infinite darkness, but into the twin reflecting pools of Serapen's eyes. She doesn't smile at me like she smiled at the other boys. Instead, she looks at me with knowing. Her face draws near to mine, and she kisses my cheek.

"May you find peace on your long journey, Dom Artifex," she whispers in my ear.

She holds me gently in her arms and lowers me into the pool. I see the blue sky above for just a moment before I close my eyes and sink beneath the surface.

When I step out of the spring, no man steps out of the forest to claim me. Confusion clouds the certainty I felt just a moment ago when I heard the Voice. Serapen takes me by the hand and leads me back to the place I was standing before, beside Ava. Serapen picks up the dark cloak from the place I left it. I had expected it to be replaced with one of some other color, after seeing what happened to all the boys before me. But Serapen simply wraps this cloak back around my damp shoulders, re-tying the laces with practiced fingers.

I reach for Ava's hand, and her cold fingers grip mine.

△▽△

Dom stands beside me, dripping beneath his cloak, his warm hand wrapped around mine. I overhear him thinking, *Why am I still here? What's an Artifex?*

I have no idea what's going on, but I remember overhearing the word Artifex. This is what the two healers in the storerooms were discussing last night while I searched for a hiding place. What does it mean? Why hasn't Dom been sent off with the other men?

It's hard for me to focus on these questions, though. I'm still reeling from the fact that I drank Serapen's pharmaka. All I could think about as the awful chalice rose to my lips was how desperately I want to be a Mohira, even though I know that's not what I want. I haven't wanted that for seven years. I want to get out of here. But somehow Serapen's gaze pinned me in place as easily as Dom's strong arms did yesterday.

I also can't make sense of what happened when Dom walked away from me into the pool. Why was there no pain in my chest? Has Serapen given us some kind of antidote to the binding pharmaka? Could it be safe for me to run away now?

There are so many unknowns, so many risks, and the buzz of pharmaka seems to be slowing down my thoughts, making reasoning difficult. Still, as I've watched all the other boys follow different men off into the woods, a plan had been forming in my mind. It seemed so simple, really. I'd follow Dom, go to whatever village he was destined to labor in for the rest of his life, and work out my next steps far from Serapen's watchful eyes. It didn't seem likely that Serapen would try to stop me—I'd be senseless with pain if Dom left without me, anyway.

But now Dom's here, and he doesn't seem to be going anywhere. So I'm stuck here, too. Spirits blast it all, what game is the Voice playing with me now?

Calm down, Dom thinks. *It's wonderful. You'll see. You'll see.*

His conviction floods through me, and I feel my resistance disappearing like the tide pools beneath the waves.

Narua is the first of the girls called to join the Mohirai. She's followed by her trio sisters Bel and Tashlu. Kor, Piroza, and Kishar follow in their turn. Hanu is called. Eumelia is called. Mohira after Mohira after Mohira.

And then Serapen calls, "Ava."

I try to resist one last time. But Serapen's eyes watch me steadily across the clearing, and I find my fingers trembling as they untie the laces at my throat. My dark cloak falls around my bandaged feet. I walk unsteadily toward the pool, step into the water, and look up into the uncanny eyes of the High Priestess.

"Listen, Ava, for the Voice that calls to you," she says.

The reply rises unbidden to my lips. "I listen."

The strange breeze that accompanies all of the callings stirs again around me. But here in the sunny clearing I don't hear the Voice, even though I heard it easily last night in the woods. There is no call for me, at least none that I can hear.

The long silence stretches. I feel a tentative sense of relief. Perhaps the Voice doesn't want me. Perhaps the Voice is going to let me go. Perhaps I don't have to be a Mohira after all. Serapen says she's a servant of the Voice, so if the Voice doesn't want me, who is Serapen to force me to do anything?

I'm about to laugh in triumph, to pull away from the High Priestess, to step back out of the pool with my freedom, when a cloud passes briefly over the sun. The sun re-emerges, momentarily dazzling me, and its light flashes bright on the surface of the pool, drawing my eye irresistibly downward. I gaze into the reflection.

I find myself in a bed in a room I've never seen before, looking out a window toward a sparkling bay. Beyond the bay, across a bridge, behind a pinkish haze, rises the city of glass towers.

A man sits in a chair at my bedside. Though he's changed from the boy I know, I would recognize the concerned expression in those deep-set eyes anywhere. The worried crease between his eyebrows is chiseled deep. The look he gives me breaks my heart.

I look more closely at the face of this Dom, who is at once familiar and unfamiliar. Yes, they're the same eyes in some ways, but they're shadowed by … is it grief? Is it anger? Is it hunger? It's a feeling far too complicated for me to identify. Instinctively, I want to reach out and touch him, so I can feel what he's feeling and understand it. But somehow I know this Dom before me is far, far away—in every way that far can be measured.

I open my mouth to speak to him, but the room vanishes, and I'm trapped in Serapen's long, sinewy arms. She whispers in my ear, "Don't look, Ava. It's too much, too soon."

I look across the clearing at Dom, who gazes at me with an open, hopeful expression. I struggle a bit in Serapen's grasp, unsure what's happening.

In a louder voice, Serapen says, "Listen, Ava, for you are called as Mohira. Will you answer the call?"

I stare up at her in shock. I didn't hear the Voice say that. She must be lying. But the response again rises unbidden to my lips, "Yes. I will answer."

Before I can even close my eyes, Serapen presses me down beneath the surface of the pool. For a heart-stopping moment, I'm sinking an unfathomable depth, water piling over me, pulling me under.

The strange sensation vanishes, and I gasp for breath as Serapen helps me back onto my feet. I sway dizzily, leaning on the High Priestess as she leads me out of the pool, across the clearing, back to Dom's side. The girls' eyes follow me as I pass, though none of them dares turn her head.

At the end of the line, Dom smiles at me. My heart aches as I look into the eyes of this eager, hopeful boy while the gaze of that intense, grim man I saw in the pool lingers in my mind. What's happening? What have I done?

△▽△

Ava and Serapen stand in the pool across the clearing from me. Just like all the other girls before her, Ava says, "I listen."

The silence stretches so long after Ava speaks that I grow uneasy. Serapen takes Ava into her arms and whispers into her ear. Nothing like this happened to the other girls.

But then Serapen says the words, "Listen, Ava, for you are called as Mohira. Will you answer the call?"

And Ava says, "Yes. I will answer."

I can't see Ava's face, but I imagine that if she heard the Voice like I did, she must feel elated. I'm happy for her and eager to have her by my side again so I can find out what the Voice sounded like to her.

As I watch Serapen lower Ava into the water, I'm jolted by the bizarre impression that Ava has slipped like a stone through Serapen's hands into the depths of the pool. This must be some trick of the light or of the pharmaka, though, because as soon as I blink, I see Ava on her feet again, soaked and leaning on Serapen's arm. She looks pale and stricken, and my residual awe at having heard the Voice gives way to worry.

Serapen takes Ava's hand. The pair step out of the water and return across the clearing to where I stand with the rest of the girls. Serapen's white hair flows over the shoulders of her long robes, white and gold threads reflecting the sunlight. Ava's wet clothes cling to her like moonlight, her long dark hair trailing gleaming droplets like falling stars behind her.

Ava returns to her place beside me. Serapen draws Ava's dry cloak up over her small shoulders, tucking the warm folds around her shivering body. I take Ava's hand, and I overhear her thinking, *What is happening? What have I done?*

Serapen returns to the center of the clearing, the sun directly above her at its zenith on the autumn equinox. She faces us and says, "Today you have listened, and you have heard the words of the Voice in all. Remember this day. Remember the Voice. Remember the Voice speaks loudest in the stillness.

"I wish you every blessing on your journey. Be patient with yourselves. Be helpful to one another. Be open to the mysteries you will encounter.

"The Voice has called you all to paths rich in mystery. Not every step will be clear. You will find yourself lost at times. Remember to listen, when you are lost, for the Voice is in all.

"But for now, your path is wide and clear. Today, your training begins. Today, you depart for Velkanos."

THE CARAVAN

Serapen leads me and the nine girls out from the clearing by the same narrow trail that led us in. Ava's hand remains ice cold in mine despite the dry heat of midday. I wonder whether it would be all right for me to give my cloak to her now that the ceremony is over.

Overhearing my thought, Ava thinks, *You don't have to take care of me.*

I'm just trying to help, I think.

No one can help me now, she thinks.

A numb sensation spreads from her to me, so different from the afterglow of excitement I feel. I wonder, *Didn't you hear it? The Voice?*

Not today, she thinks. *But I saw something.*

An image forms in her mind. It's a bedroom, though the furnishings are unlike any I've ever seen. A man sits beside the bed, and through the window I recognize the city of glass towers I saw in Ava's thoughts last night.

Where is that? I wonder.

No idea, she thinks, *but I think that's you, sitting beside me.*

I take a closer look at the man in her memory. I don't recognize him, and he looks far too old to be me. But I suppose she could be right. I've only glimpsed my own face occasionally in a watery reflection, and never from this perspective.

What do you think it means? I wonder.

No idea, she thinks again.

She and I walk in silence. Well, everyone has been walking in silence, but Ava and I also manage to silence our thoughts for a while, too.

I look sidelong at her, walking unhooded beside me, her wet hair dripping down the back of her cloak. I hazard another thought. *Thank you.*

For what? she thinks, meeting my eyes.

For staying here with me, I think. *For letting me hear the Voice.*

Ava's curiosity feels like tentative fingers in my mind. *How was it for you?* she thinks.

I remember what I saw, standing alone in the woods beneath the vast night sky, hearing the stars speak. The Voice's words return to me. *It has been asked. It may be given. But there is a price. Do you accept it?* And my answer returns. *Yes. Yes. Yes, I do accept the price.*

Ava frowns, puzzled. *What do you think it means?*

No idea, I think.

I don't like it, she thinks.

What's an Artifex? I wonder.

No idea, she thinks.

We reach an intersection between the footpath and a wider dirt road with deep cartwheel ruts. Twelve horses munch the grass beside the road, while two Mohirai I've never seen before stand by chatting. A few of the horses and both Mohirai turn curious eyes toward us as we approach.

Serapen embraces her sister priestesses in greeting, then turns to introduce us to them.

"Today the Voice has called nine new sisters to the house

of novices," says Serapen, gesturing to each girl in turn. She names Narua, Bel, and Tashlu; Kor, Piroza, and Kishar; Hanu and Eumelia. The two Mohirai greet each girl with friendly nods. Serapen concludes with Ava. Several girls ahead of us in line glance back at the sound of her name, but no one dares to fully turn around.

Next, Serapen introduces the two Mohirai from Velkanos.

First is Thalia, Muse of the house of poetika. She wears a robe of summer green. Her sash, richly embroidered with gleaming copper threads, coils artfully around her figure, displaying her ample bosom to advantage. Her laughing eyes twinkle brighter still when she catches me looking. She tosses her long auburn braid behind her shoulder, her painted rosy lips curving into a smile that reveals perfect rows of bright white teeth.

Second is Arkhi, Muse of the house of tekhnologia. I've never seen a complexion like hers: the color of the night sky between the stars, deepest blue-black. She wears a robe of inky black, and around her shoulders hangs a fine black stole with a delicate pattern worked in silver threads. She doesn't smile like Thalia, but her expression is kinder.

Arkhi raises her hand toward us in greeting, revealing a pale palm painted in swirling patterns of dark blue dye that spread all the way out to her fingertips. Her eyes fall on me. "And who is this?" she asks Serapen.

Serapen settles a hand lightly on my shoulder and says, "The Voice has called a novice Artifex to the path of mysteries today. This is Dom."

My heart rises to my throat at Serapen's words. I must

have misunderstood. Did she say that I've been called to the path of mysteries?

That's what she said, Ava thinks.

But ... how is that possible? I wonder.

Arkhi and Thalia examine me with interest. The girls seem to take this as permission at last to turn around and satisfy their own curiosity. I squirm under their collective gaze. I've known these girls for as long as I can remember, but in this moment they remind me of nothing so much as a pride of hunting lionesses—beautiful but terrifying.

△▽△

Thalia observes the group of girls staring at Dom like they've never seen a boy before. "What a stir we'll cause in the house of novices," she says slyly, winking at Dom. A hot wave of his embarrassment floods through me as Thalia's tinkling laugh fills the air. I want to smack the smile off her painted mouth, but I don't quite dare to strike a Muse. Not yet, anyway.

These girls are another matter, though. "Leave him alone," I say, glaring at each of them in turn. "Can't you see you're bothering him?"

Kor returns my glare with a distant, disinterested nod. Her younger trio sisters Piroza and Kishar look at me and, to my immense irritation, burst out laughing. Narua ignores me completely and takes her time studying Dom. Her younger trio sisters Bel and Tashlu avoid my eyes, sneaking glances at Dom when they think I'm not looking. Hanu searches my face for a long time with a confused, foggy expression. I wonder whether she'll remember me like Dom did last night, but she doesn't seem to. None of these girls seem to recognize me. That's a relief. Hopefully we can all remain strangers and avoid difficult questions.

Hanu's gaze travels down to my hand gripping Dom's. She and Dom look at each other, and an image flashes in my mind of Hanu's gorgeous naked figure lying on the beach at sunset. I'm confused for a moment before I realize what's happening. I stifle a giggle when Dom realizes, too. He looks away from Hanu quickly, and I feel his desperation to distract himself before he accidentally shares any more intimate memories of Hanu.

In a tone of perfect kindness, Hanu says to me, "Never fear. Dom will come to no harm at our hands, little sister."

"Don't call me that," I say sharply.

My rudeness startles her, but Hanu recovers quickly, inclines her head peaceably, and says, "Of course. My mistake. Sister."

Watching this exchange with undisguised delight, Thalia says, "Truly there is no joy greater than sisterhood." Each syllable shimmers with her amusement.

My anger fades into embarrassment. I realize I've made a spectacle of myself in front of all the other girls and the Mohirai, and I hate Thalia for enjoying it.

I open my mouth to return some choice words of my own to the Muse of poetika, but before I say anything, Arkhi cuts in, saying, "Peace, Thalia." All eyes turn to the Muse of tekhnologia, who speaks with a quiet composure that commands attention. "We have a moon of riding ahead, long enough already without your teasing."

Thalia tips her head in deference to Arkhi, though her

eyes still sparkle with mirth. I step back beside Dom, feeling foolish for standing up to defend him against what I realize now are just a bunch of silly girls. Though I'm wary of all Mohirai, Arkhi's deft diffusion of the tension earns her my respect. Arkhi appears to be the complete opposite of Thalia, who has about as much substance as a butterfly.

Arkhi continues, "None of you have ridden before, I assume?"

The girls and Dom all shake their heads. Determined to avoid any more unnecessary attention, I suppress a sigh of resignation and say nothing. I guess Arkhi's right—this is going to be a painfully long journey. I've been riding since my ninth summer, but for some reason girls and boys at the Children's Temple aren't allowed to ride.

Arkhi introduces each of the horses by name and demonstrates the proper way to approach them, how to mount the saddle, how to use the reins. She's very thorough in her instruction and answers questions patiently. It's all quite tedious, except for the feeling of Dom's excited anticipation spilling into me through our joined hands. I smile to myself. Riding is one of my great pleasures. Perhaps it will be one of his, as well.

As Arkhi's lesson wears on, I study the horses. Three of them appear to belong to the Mohirai, judging by the saddle blankets that match the patterns of the Muses' sashes and stoles. Serapen's horse is the speckled grey mare called Amisos. Arkhi's is the pure black mare Khaos. Thalia's is the white mare Rurata. So I probably won't be riding any of those. I eye one of the smaller horses, a spirited-looking palomino called Nisaba. She and I would be pretty well matched. I wonder whether I'll be allowed to choose my horse.

A few of the other girls look as eager to ride as Dom, but most seem apprehensive. The girls' nervous energy around these obviously gentle creatures is ridiculous, but I suppose none of them have handled horses before. Dom should know his way around a horse, though, since the boys keep the stables outside the Children's Temple.

"Looks like you forgot a horse," says a bored voice behind me. "Or does Dom have to walk all the way to Velkanos?"

I look back over my shoulder. For the first time since early this morning, I see Eumelia. Where has she been standing all this time? Her hood is pushed back, so I can see her face clearly now. Her round freckled cheeks have slimmed down since we were little, but she still has that mocking half-smile and the pert nose I remember taking more than one swing at. She's quicker than she looks, though; I never landed a punch. In our eighth summer, I was the only girl smaller than she was, and she loved finding ways to demonstrate her incremental superiority over me at every opportunity. I'm glad she can't remember me.

I feel Dom's disappointment at the realization that Eumelia must be right, that he's not going to ride. I'm about to feel sorry for him. But then I have a sinking realization: I can't ride without Dom. Maybe we're both going to have to walk for the next moon.

Arkhi looks at me like she's read my thoughts. Spirits, can she read my thoughts? I hope not. I don't think I can bear having yet another person in my mind, and having a Mohira in my mind would make planning an escape impossible.

In a calming voice, Arkhi says to me and Dom, "Nothing has been forgotten, though we do have an unusual situation to manage with you two." Despite my distrust of the Mohirai, I can't help appreciating how Arkhi addresses Dom, without overlooking him or dismissing him like sisters often do while talking around brothers. She continues, "So you'll be riding together on Eridu for this journey."

Arkhi gestures toward a tall chestnut gelding, the largest of the horses by far, who stands behind her mare Khaos. Eridu has a star on his forehead, four white socks, and a calm intelligence in his big brown eyes. He's a larger horse than I would have chosen for myself, but I've ridden horses his size without difficulty. I'd be quite happy with Eridu on my own, but the prospect of riding him with Dom is not appealing, especially not for such a long journey. Dom doesn't even know how to ride.

Sorry, he thinks. I curse inwardly. Yet again, I've forgotten he's listening. His humility is so complete and sincere that I'm appalled by his servility, but not nearly as appalled as I am at myself. I'm as bad as any Mohira, ignoring and forgetting him when it's convenient for me.

It's all right, Dom, I think. *We'll … figure it out, I guess.*

Maybe it'll be fun? he thinks. *You can just hold on to my back.* He looks from Eridu to me, and I glimpse that teasing expression I remember from last night.

Vastly preferring his teasing to his humility, I smile and think, *Not a chance. I'm holding the reins.*

He inclines his head deferentially. I roll my eyes and think, *You don't have to treat me like them. I'm not a Mohira.*

Not yet, he thinks.

Not ever, I think.

Arkhi matches each of the remaining girls with a horse. I'm impressed by the speed with which she pairs the more skittish girls with the steadiest mounts, accounts for size variations between the girls and the horses, and redistributes the saddlebag weight more evenly once she's completed the pairings. She's clearly done this many times before. I agree with all her pairings, except that she gives Eumelia the spirited palomino I wanted.

Some of the girls pet their mounts, tentatively getting to know them. Others flinch every time a hoof stamps or a tail swishes or an ear flicks. None of these novices look like they're going to be great riders any time soon, but hopefully the horses and the Mohirai know what they're doing.

In a voice that carries surprisingly well considering her lightweight laughter, Thalia calls out, "Your riding clothes and boots are here, novices." She demonstrates where to look on her own horse's saddlebags. "Go ahead and change out of your wet things. Then, onward to the Mountain of Muses!"

△▽△

Changing into riding clothes requires me and Ava to repeat our undressing routine from this morning in front of all the other girls. Despite the unwanted audience—or perhaps because of it—we're more efficient the second time. Most of the girls shoot only occasional curious glances our way, but Hanu and Eumelia stare at us openly. Eumelia studies Ava with intense interest. Hanu's gaze drifts often to my hands on Ava's body.

I swallow, trying to keep my focus on Ava so I won't think of Hanu again.

Ava glances at me. Embarrassed heat rises to my ears as I realize she's overheard this. I lower my gaze to my feet and try to clear my mind completely. Ava taps my hand. Reluctantly, I look at her again. She thinks, *Don't be embarrassed. I wish I could give you more privacy, but I really don't mind if you think of Hanu. She's always been the best of these girls, anyway.*

Ava's sincerity helps me relax, but her own irritation grows as Eumelia's eyes linger on her. At last she wheels around, still half-dressed, and snaps, "What?"

Hanu immediately looks away from us both. But Eumelia doesn't flinch, back down, or even acknowledge Ava's tone. She continues studying Ava's face as she says, "Where did you come from? And what on Dulai are you doing to Dom?"

Before Ava can answer, Serapen steps up behind us and says calmly, "The Voice has returned Ava to us after a long time away. She and Dom had an accident with binding pharmaka last night. It will take some time for them both to recover, and until then they need to remain close to each other. But all will be well again in time."

From Eumelia's expression, it's clear that this answer only multiplies her questions. But Serapen's tone of finality invites no further questions.

△▽△

Arkhi, Thalia, and Serapen untie the lines of horses so each novice has plenty of space to mount for the first time. The

Mohirai walk among the girls giving pointers and adjusting saddle straps.

Dom and I stand at Eridu's side. After considering our unique situation, Arkhi adjusts the stirrups to Dom's height, but I've insisted on keeping the reins. I've lost control over pretty much everything else in my life since yesterday, so I'm not giving this up without a fight. There's also no way I'm looking at Dom's back for this entire journey. Fortunately, neither Dom nor Arkhi pushes back on this.

Do you need help getting up? Dom wonders, looking from me to the high saddle. In answer, I drop his hand, grab the saddle pommel, and swing myself up easily. I pat Eridu's glossy chestnut shoulder and take the reins, then move as far forward as I can in the saddle to make room for Dom.

Dom mounts with surprising grace for someone who hasn't ridden before. He and I adjust our bodies against each other in the saddle while Arkhi makes a second check of the stirrup length for Dom. Eridu's saddle accommodates two, but it's close quarters. Dom's warm chest against my back reminds me of waking up in his arms this morning. The feeling of entrapment and the memory of my clumsy tumble out of bed follow close behind. Hopefully I can avoid any more falls like that while we're riding together.

Even pressed this close to Dom, the pain in my chest returns because we've lost skin contact. I gather the reins in my right hand and set my left hand on Dom's knee where he can reach it. His palm presses the back of my hand.

How do you want me to hold you while we're riding? he wonders.

Let me think … The last time I shared a saddle, I was a

small girl holding on to my mother's back, but I remember the basic mechanics of how it felt to ride that way. I imagine how Dom's body and mine will collide as Eridu walks, trots, canters, and gallops. I imagine the difficulties he'll have without the reins, and the difficulties I'll have without the stirrups. I consider the added complication of maintaining skin contact throughout the ride. I visualize what I think might minimize our saddle soreness tomorrow, sharing the idea with Dom.

I untuck the front of my shirt, and he slips his right arm inside and across my waist, his right hand resting over my left hip. I noticed while we were grappling with my knife last night that Dom's left-handed, and I think he'll want that hand free. He pulls me gently back into him with his forearm, anchoring me to the saddle. He rests his left hand on my thigh, so he can reach forward for the saddle pommel if he needs it.

How does that feel? I think.

Against my ribs, the pulse in his wrist speeds up. He remembers the way my body looked to him this morning as we dressed. He jerks his hand quickly out from under my shirt, but not before I feel another wave of his embarrassment.

"Sorry," he says quietly.

I dig one of my elbows playfully into his ribs and say, so only he can hear, "Relax. It's just another body. But if you have to think about one, better stick with Hanu's. She's more fun to look at, anyway."

Dom doesn't answer, and I glance up at him. He meets my eyes briefly with an expression I can't quite decipher. I wonder why he feels so embarrassed. Seeing my body from his perspective is a little strange, but it's nothing I haven't seen before, and it's certainly not embarrassing to me.

Dom keeps his hands to himself long enough that the prickling pain resumes in my chest. I want to give him as much privacy as I can, because I know it's tiring to have someone else always observing what you're thinking. But eventually my shoulders twitch involuntarily in pain. As soon as Dom feels that, he wraps his arm around me again. My hip tingles under his palm.

Thanks, I think, as the pain eases. *It's not quite as bad as yesterday, but it still hurts.*

I know, he thinks. *Sorry I made it worse.*

Stop saying sorry, I think. *None of this is your fault, remember?*

Fortunately, there's not much time to dwell on these pointless apologies. Arkhi mounts Khaos, glances back at us, and says, "That looks like it should work. Ready to go?"

Are you? I think to Dom.

His eagerness to ride floods through me in answer, and I can't suppress a smile as I call out to Arkhi, "Ready!" I won't deny myself—or Dom—the pleasure of a ride after the wretchedness of the last day. I'll just have to keep my eyes open as I start working out my next plan.

SHELTER FROM THE STORM

ARKHI LEADS THE CARAVAN north on the cart path. Ava and I follow behind her on Eridu, and the rest of our company spreads out in a long line behind us. I'm unfamiliar with the motion of a horse beneath me, so at first I sway in the saddle, pulling Ava off her balance. She patiently shows me how to make small adjustments in my posture to complement Eridu's movement. This helps a lot, and the ride becomes more comfortable for both of us. Her body fits against mine perfectly in the saddle, though I try to avoid thinking about her body. Fortunately, I can see everything easily over Ava's shoulder, so there's plenty for me to look at to keep my mind off of her.

The girls behind us call out to each other occasionally, but most of us ride in silence after the long, tiring day.

Ava's awareness feels lighter and happier as she rides. When the cart path widens, she thinks, *Want to try something fun?*

Curious, I think, *Maybe? Yes?*

Without waiting for me to change my mind, she tugs Eridu's reins, and he steps out of the plodding line of the caravan.

Hold on tight, she thinks, leaning forward and tapping her heels against Eridu's sides.

Eridu springs forward. Instinctively, I grab for the saddle pommel in front of Ava with my left hand and hold her tight in my right arm so she and Eridu don't both fly away from me.

The combination of Ava's breathless laughter and the delight spilling from her into me is intoxicating. Eridu's gallop transforms the forest around the path into a blurred tunnel that shimmers with every shade of summer green. I've never moved so fast before.

Arkhi calls out behind us, almost too faint to hear. Ava urges Eridu onward, but he slows to a trot, then to a walk. Ignoring Ava's indignant tugs on his reins, Eridu turns and walks slowly back toward the caravan.

Although she's a little disappointed by the abrupt conclusion of our ride, Ava mostly radiates exhilaration. "Thanks," she says to Eridu, scratching between his shoulders. "I needed that." She twists slightly against my tight grip on her waist and reaches up to touch my cheek, laughing as she says, "And you need a shave."

I realize only now that the rough stubble on my chin has been digging into her neck since Eridu started galloping. "Sorry," I say quickly, before remembering she hates apologies. I loosen my hold on her and make space between us. "I'll ask one of the Mohirai for a blade when we make camp."

She glances up over her shoulder at me, a mischievous look in her eyes, and says, "Or I could lend you mine."

"What?" I say, astonished. "Where did you get another blade?"

"Never lost the first one," she says.

I try to remember what happened to her knife after I dropped it in the woods last night. I can't imagine how she's kept it with her all this time without me noticing. "You're full of surprises," I say.

She shrugs. "Isn't everyone?"

Eridu comes to a stop when we near Arkhi at the front of the caravan. Some of the girls riding behind the Muse watch us with interest, probably wondering whether we'll be reprimanded, but Arkhi only adjusts the silver-threaded stole around her shoulders and makes a clicking noise with her tongue. All along the caravan, horses' ears flick forward at the sound. Eridu turns and falls into step alongside Arkhi's horse Khaos.

"You've trained them well," Ava says to Arkhi, clearly impressed. But there's a bite in her tone as she adds, "Is that to keep us from running away?"

Arkhi says impassively, "It's to keep the caravan together. There's a vast wilderness between here and the temple lands of Velkanos, far too vast for novices untrained in the arts of navigation to travel alone. But you're welcome to ride Eridu as you please, as long as you don't lose sight of the caravan or wear him out. Remember he needs to carry you both for an entire moon, not just today."

Ava inclines her head slightly in a gesture of obedience, chastened by the reminder of Eridu's welfare. She guides Eridu back in line behind Arkhi, and we ride on for a while in silence.

A landscape of rolling grassy hills dotted with trees opens before us as the narrow cart path emerges from the dense cedar forest and joins a wider road. The road is intermittently paved, so the steady thud of hooves on dirt alternates with the ringing clop of hooves on stone. There are few other sounds besides our horses and the occasional call of a kuku bird. The rainclouds Arkhi predicted earlier gather on the southern horizon, and now even I can feel the approaching storm in the air. Arkhi leads the caravan a short distance east before she calls us to a halt at a small clearing beside the road.

We all dismount, and Arkhi gives instructions to each novice to help make camp. Kor, Piroza, Kishar, Tashlu, and Eumelia unload the horses under Arkhi's supervision, settling them for the night under the shelter of some trees on a grassy stream bank. Narua, Bel, and Hanu gather wood to build a fire and help Serapen prepare the evening meal. Ava and I are useless for many tasks in our present condition, but we can carry gear while walking hand in hand, so we attend Thalia as she lays out the camp. The wind picks up as the rain approaches, so she chooses a spot on the leeward side of a stand of trees, and we help her stake out four canvas tents.

The rapidly darkening sky looks ominous, but Arkhi says we have enough time to eat outside before the rain begins. So the nine girls and I sit in a circle around the fire. Most of the girls chat in little groups. Ava and I sit apart from the others in a comfortable silence. Her hand rests lightly on mine. She watches Serapen with close attention as the High Priestess draws ingredients out of a leather satchel and carefully pours and mixes them into whatever she's brewing over the fire.

I'm not as hungry as I'd expect after the daylong fast, but I'm completely exhausted now that it's been almost two days since I've had any real sleep.

Ava overhears me and thinks, *You do look exhausted. Do you want us to just go to bed? I'm not really hungry.*

Serapen looks over at us and says, "The evening meal will help restore you, and afterwards I'll give you instruction to help you ease your binding. Just stay put a bit longer, all right?"

"All right," Ava says cautiously, thinking, *Do you think she can hear us?*

Not sure, I think. *I don't notice anyone else in my head besides you, though.*

I don't like it, she thinks.

I glance at her, amused.

What? she thinks.

There's a lot you don't like, Ava.

She gives me a playful shove, and I laugh.

Hanu and Eumelia have been speaking with Thalia on the far side of the fire from us. They stand up and cross over to our side.

Ugh, Ava thinks, looking at Eumelia. *Not again.*

Hanu sits facing me, her back to the fire. I try to focus on Eumelia, who takes a seat facing Ava, just out of her arm's reach.

"What do you want?" Ava says to them, not quite civil, but not as rudely as before, either.

Hanu glances at me, then looks at Ava and says, "Thalia says the tents usually hold three. And the other trios want to stay together. So that leaves us four to share the last tent."

"Should be fine," Eumelia says to Ava with a shrug. "You take up hardly any space at all."

Ava manages to hold her tongue, but I feel her distaste for smirking Eumelia like a knot in my throat.

Take it easy, I think. *None of us will get any sleep in that little tent if we're fighting.*

"But also, you would complete our trio," Hanu adds

gently, seeing Ava scowling at Eumelia. "Will you be part of ours, Ava? We've always been missing our third sister."

Not always, Ava thinks.

In the awkward silence that follows, Hanu looks hopefully from Ava to me and back again. I hope Ava says something soon, because I'm struggling to fend off more thoughts of Hanu. She's leaning a bit forward toward Ava, awaiting an answer. Hanu's riding shirt, slightly damp with sweat, is translucent over her breasts now that she's backlit by the fire.

Are you going to say something? I think.

Ava glances at me, then at Hanu. Her scowl fades. Her lips twitch in a mischievous smile. I would be apprehensive if I weren't so exhausted.

All right. Fine. Maybe it'll be fun, she thinks, tossing my earlier words back at me.

"Sounds good," Ava says, with an indifferent shrug that's almost a perfect imitation of Eumelia's. Hanu beams at Ava, then at me. Eumelia continues to watch Ava through slightly narrowed eyes. I'm relieved when Serapen announces to the group that food is ready. Hopefully this will give all the girls something else to focus on for a little while. And maybe Hanu will turn around to face the fire so I can safely look up again.

Serapen ladles out a fragrant stew. Bowls pass hand to hand around the circle. The three Mohirai stand around the fire and turn their palms up toward the darkening sky. We all join them in speaking the familiar words of the meal blessing.

We give our thanks for gifts of sun

Of water, soil, and seed
For gifts of many seasons
Gathered here to meet our need
To build our strength so that our hands
May in their time return
The gifts received from mother land
Improved with gifts our own

The ritual is comforting, even spoken in this unfamiliar setting beneath the open sky. When I say the words, I'm transported to my old table in the meal hall packed with boys, where I recited this blessing a thousand times before.

Do you miss them? Ava thinks, pressing my hand in sympathy.

I think, *Everything today happened so fast. I haven't had time to think about them until now. But I'll miss them, in some ways, yes. Things are ...* I feel Hanu's eyes on me, Ava's hand touching mine, Eumelia's quirking half-smile that Ava keeps avoiding. I keep my eyes on Ava's hand as I think, *Things are simpler when it's just boys.*

Ava's amusement at my predicament with Hanu drowns out most of her other emotions at the moment, but she's trying to be encouraging when she thinks, *Still, you always wanted to be a Mohira, right? Seems like the Voice gave you exactly what you wanted. Or as close as you could get as a boy, anyway.*

It's the first time I've thought of it that way, that the Voice gave me what I wanted. I've always thought of the Voice as something wise and powerful but completely indifferent to what I want. Ava's words make me realize I should be feeling deeply grateful. And I do feel grateful, in a way. But I also feel regret, which confuses me. Maybe that's Ava's regret I'm feeling, though.

What about you? I think. *This was what you wanted once, wasn't it?*

Ava sighs. *It doesn't matter,* she thinks. *This is what I have to work with now.*

But what did you really want? I think.

An image of the sea flashes before me. A deep blue vastness beneath a brighter blue bowl of sky. A green headland rising in the west. Wind through my hair. Freedom.

I'm sorry, I think. *I wish you could have that.*

Don't apologize, she thinks, bumping my shoulder with hers. *I'm happy for you, anyway. From the looks of it, you're going to be much better off as an Artifex than you would have been in the men's villages. Although ...* she glances at Hanu, and at some of the other girls looking at me. *I still think you should have made a run for it with me. These girls look like they're going to eat you alive.*

She and I both laugh at this, and we catch some puzzled glances from the others.

My stomach growls, reminding me of the untouched bowl of stew I'm holding in one hand. Ava and I decide through a quick exchange of ideas that the best way to manage eating at the same time is by making use of our feet. We each pull off a boot, and Ava rests her bare foot alongside mine.

"You're so weird," Eumelia says, more bewildered than malicious, as she watches Ava's toes wiggling absent-mindedly beside mine in the grass.

Ava ignores her, and the four of us eat in silence for a while. Ava hardly touches her food, but the rest of us dig in with good appetites.

"I always wondered why we were missing a girl in our trio," Eumelia says thoughtfully, her eyes still fixed on Ava. "What did Serapen mean, when she said you were lost? Where were you?"

△▽△

"What did Serapen mean, when she said you were lost? Where were you?" says Eumelia.

She, Dom, and Hanu all look at me. Spirits, the last thing I need right now are shrewd questions from Eumelia drawing more attention to me. The less anyone knows about where I've been and where I'm going, the better.

I struggle to think of an answer that would put an end to further questions. Fortunately, I don't have to say anything, because the High Priestess stands up from where she's been sitting with the other Muses and approaches us.

"Have you had enough to eat?" she asks me and Dom. We both nod. I'm grateful for the well-timed interruption, even coming from Serapen, whom I'd otherwise be trying to avoid. There's a hint of concern in Serapen's expression as she looks at my nearly untouched bowl beside Dom's empty one, but she makes no comment about it. Instead, she gestures for us to follow her and says, "Very well. Come walk with me."

We quickly pull on our boots and hand our bowls to the girls helping Thalia and Arkhi wash up after the meal. The first few raindrops fall as we follow Serapen across the clearing, toward the grassy stream bank where the horses are sheltered beneath the trees.

I've been expecting something like this to happen. Now that Dom has to stay with the girls, and I have to stay with Dom, I figure the Mohirai have to silence me in some way. Serapen can't possibly want the other novices to find out what happened to me or learn what I know about the Mohirai. So what does she plan to do with me? Negotiate for my silence? Manipulate me with one of her arts? Dispose of me somewhere in the wilderness?

I've allowed the pleasure of riding this afternoon to keep my mind off these darker thoughts, mostly for Dom's sake. I'm worried about the trouble I've already caused him, and how much worse it could get the longer we're together and the more he learns of my plan. He seems determined to stay among the Mohirai, so the sooner I can escape from here, and from him, the better everything will be for both of us.

But where would you go? Dom wonders, looking at me with that worried expression again.

It's good I have no escape plan right now, since Dom seems able to overhear so much of what I'm thinking. But this overhearing is going to be a real problem.

Serapen leads us to a large beech tree by the stream and turns to face me. From inside her robes, she withdraws a silver flask. The surface of the flask reflects her sky blue sleeves with their delicate embroidery of golden threads.

Holding out the flask to me, she says, "I suppose you know what this is."

Warily, I say, "Unbinding pharmaka."

She nods and says, "Keep this with you at all times. If you

experience acute pain from your binding, you can take the unbinding pharmaka to weaken the bond, which should reduce the pain."

I know very little about the arts of pharmaka, but most of what my mother taught me is about the effects of unbinding pharmaka. I would have been willing to take unbinding pharmaka from my mother's hand, but not from a priestess, and definitely not from the High Priestess Serapen, whom my mother fears more than any other Mohira. I say, "I don't want it."

Patient but unyielding, Serapen says, "It's wise to be cautious. The use of unbinding pharmaka comes at a cost to memory, and it is challenging even for a skilled initiate to control what memory is lost. These arts require time to master, but the only way to attain the skill is through practice."

"I'm not going to take it," I say. "I want to remember."

Serapen says, "You do not need to fear the arts of pharmaka, little sister. Pharmaka is a gift to us all from the Voice. Accept the gift. No child under my care will be left helpless, as you were in the forest last night."

I detect reproach in these words, but the reproach doesn't seem directed at me. It occurs to me suddenly that Serapen must be speaking of my mother, and of what my mother has taught me—or not taught me—about pharmaka. Why did my mother leave me so helpless? I chew my lip, worrying this is a trick of some kind. Perhaps Serapen's trying to confuse my thoughts. Still, I can't see the harm in accepting the flask as long as I don't drink from it, and I can see Serapen won't take no for an answer. So I take the flask, securing it to my belt with a leather strap.

Serapen continues, "Your amanitai overdose is unlike any case I've seen before, Ava. There's always an experimental component to pharmaka, but usually experimentation is done by an experienced initiate with small incremental changes in dose. Your overdose was extreme, and you had no prior tolerance to moderate the effect. Even among my most experienced healer initiates, no one has ever taken such a large dose all at once.

"The overdose alone would have made the healing work significant, but it's complicated by the fact that you formed not just one bond, but two."

"Two?" I say. I've been so focused on managing my bond with Dom that the thought of a second bond is truly awful. How on Dulai could I have formed a second bond? As soon as I wonder this, a memory from last night resurfaces. Apprehensively, I say, "I told my mother that Dom was the only person I'd touched, after my accident. But then you said …" I struggle to remember exactly what Serapen said, given all the confusion that followed.

"He's the only human you touched," says Serapen. "But he's not the only awareness you touched."

I frown. "I don't understand."

Serapen says, "Surely Lilith taught you where the Voice in all dwells."

"Well … It's in everything, isn't it?" I say.

"It is," says Serapen. "But in some places the Voice's awareness is much stronger. It's more concentrated in rich soils, like a forest floor. That's why forests are sacred to the Mohirai. Even without binding pharmaka, walking barefoot through a forest creates a weak connection with the Voice. But walking barefoot through a forest under the influence of binding pharmaka, as you did last night, would create a connection far stronger."

So this is why my mother asked if I was walking barefoot. Why didn't she warn me this could happen?

Serapen continues, "Connecting awareness with binding pharmaka safely takes years of training, even with low doses of binding pharmaka, even for initiates of the mysteries. Too much connection creates overwhelming sensation. Imagine the pain if you tried to swallow the ocean all at once. In a way, that's what happens when an unprepared human awareness connects too fast with a non-human awareness like the Voice in all."

The warmth drains out of my face and hands as I remember the excruciating pain I felt when I tried to run after my mother for the last time. I don't think I could have endured it a moment longer than I did. Shutting my eyes, I struggle to suppress the memory so I can think clearly again.

Dom squeezes my cold fingers in his warm hand as he thinks, *You're all right. It's over now.*

Is it? I wonder. I'm afraid to ask my next question, but I summon my courage. This may be the only question that really matters. I take a deep breath and look up at Serapen. "Are you saying I'm bound to the Voice in all?"

My heart pounds louder and louder as I wait for Serapen's answer. I sway dizzily on my feet. Dom wraps his arm around my shoulder to steady me, and Serapen reaches out and grips my wrist. Briefly, I feel her awareness probing mine—light, swift, and precise as a hummingbird—but she withdraws her hand even before I react. I look at her suspiciously, wondering what she did to me with that healer's touch. Despite my worry, I'm relieved when my dizziness passes.

"All are bound to the Voice, little sister," Serapen says. "But you ..." Her gaze drifts upward as she searches for words. I notice her long fingers moving absent-mindedly through the air between us, like she's untangling invisible threads. "The depth of connection you formed with the Voice should have been fatal. In truth, I don't understand how you survived. But perhaps it has something to do with your double binding."

I have no idea what to make of this. I say, "If one bond should be fatal, wouldn't two be worse?" Can anything be worse than fatal?

Thoughtfully, Serapen says, "Two are more complex to manage than one, certainly. But complexity creates possibility. Every bond presents unique possibilities, for good and ill, and one might offer counterpoint to another.

"For example, humans are far more similar to each other in their awareness, and far less complex than the Voice in all. A human mind has fewer sensory perceptions, less attention, less memory to manage.

"So your binding to Dom, even though it formed without preparation, is far less painful than your binding to the Voice in all. Dom's awareness is concentrated in a single human body with only sixteen summers of memory, not spread out over a vast area of ancient perceptive awareness like a forest, certainly not as vast as the entire perceptive awareness of the Voice that dwells in all. And Dom cannot hear the Voice as you can, so it cannot overwhelm him the same way it overwhelmed you. For you, Dom's awareness might therefore be like … the calm at the eye of a storm. As long as you're within the eye, you're safe from the storm."

"Muse Serapen," says Dom. He's been listening so quietly that I'd almost forgotten he was here, even while his arm is wrapped around me, supporting me. I'm not sure whether he has an uncanny ability to fade into the background or I have a deplorable tendency to forget him.

"Yes, Dom?" says Serapen.

He says, "The Mohirai teach that men can't hear the Voice in all, apart from our Calling Day. And you said it again now, that I can't hear the Voice like Ava does. Why not?"

It's a good question. There are few advantages to being a boy, but I suppose this might be one. If I'd been a boy, maybe I couldn't have formed an accidental bond with the Voice in the woods last night. If I'd been a boy, maybe I would have succeeded in my escape.

Serapen says, again in the tone of instruction, "Listen, novice Artifex. You, and all the men of Dulai, pay the debt of the men who came before you. Ever since the time of destruction, men have been cut off from direct experience of the Voice. The Artifexi alone among men may live and work among the Mohirai, but even an Artifex may experience the Voice only through his Muse.

"You will learn more of this mystery in the proper time, from the Muses as well as from your brothers among the Artifexi."

This answer only multiplies my questions, but I suppose I

should let Dom ask these questions. They do pertain to him more than me. So I'm surprised when he asks nothing else, reciting only the ritual response to instruction. "I have listened, and I have heard, sister."

I'm disappointed in Serapen's answer, and even more disappointed in Dom's failure to question. How typical for a Mohira, to cloak something so important in mystery. And how typical for a boy, to accept what is given and ask for no more. Ah, well. I suppose that's none of my concern. Dom can muddle through the mysteries however he likes, but I want answers.

To Serapen, I say, "So ... If Dom is like the eye of the storm, and the Voice is the storm, what can I do to get out of the storm?"

"I'm not sure," says Serapen. "There's little we can do to escape a storm around us, other than take shelter. But I think the work ahead of you might be the inverse of most novices' work. The usual goal of novice training is to ensure the connection to the Voice deepens slowly and steadily over time without becoming overwhelming. Usually it is only when the mind and body have been suitably prepared by pharmaka that a novice seeks deeper connection to the Voice through initiation.

"But the Voice has set you on a different path. You have begun your novice training with a connection that's far too deep. Dangerously so. Your work will be to change this connection into one you can manage safely on your own.

"The other Muses and I will do our best to instruct you in this work. But even we will not always know how to help you. Only you will be able to judge when you've found the right balance for yourself between connection to and freedom from the Voice in all."

Everything about Serapen's voice and presence conveys knowledge so deep that my instinct is to trust her. Yet I can't trust her words. She speaks of connection and freedom as if they complement each other and can coexist peacefully. But my mother taught me that connection to the Voice is the trap that holds an initiate back from true freedom, that the Voice's will eventually subsumes the initiate's own. Once that happens, there is no way for an initiate to judge for herself the path she should take. She can only follow the Voice's call.

My mother also warned me about the subtle ways the Mohirai maintain the Voice's control over initiates. I've stumbled upon the least subtle way by overdosing on binding pharmaka. But the Mohirai practice many arts drawn from their mysteries, and they have many tricks up their richly embroidered sleeves. Maybe Serapen's apparent trustworthiness is one of these tricks. Maybe trusting her will ensure my own enslavement to the Voice.

But, as impossible as I find it to trust the High Priestess, I know I need her help. I have to ease this painful bond with the Voice. I can't remain tied up with Dom forever. Cautiously, I say, "What exactly is this work?"

The rain falls a little faster, but the old beech above us offers adequate cover, so we remain dry. Serapen sits at the base of the tree, in a crook formed between its gnarled roots. She gestures for us to sit like her. Dom and I find similar spots at the base of the tree and sit, then peer around the trunk to watch Serapen. She pulls off her riding boots and tucks her legs beneath her. The tops of her bare feet and her ankles press into the soft, dark soil. She presses her back against the trunk and extends her hands, palms up, on either side of her, inviting me and Dom to join her. He and I pull off our boots again, lean back against the trunk, and take her hands. Serapen's fingers are strong, warm, and dry like Dom's, but much softer and smoother than his, like fine oiled leather. We form a ring around the tree, facing outward.

"Listen, novice Mohira," Serapen says to me, raising her voice over the patter of the rain. She speaks in the tone of instruction, though from her it sounds far gentler than it ever did from my mother. "Close your eyes, if you like. The work of unbinding is not so different from the work of binding. Both are works of transformation. One is the complement of the other. Unbinding inverts binding. Binding inverts unbinding. In either case, whether you work to bind with or unbind from another awareness, you must first focus on the connection you wish to change. In your case, the connection you need to change is between your awareness and the awareness of the Voice in all.

"When we speak of awareness, it is helpful to imagine it as whole with many parts, like a year has many moons, or a lyre has many strings. But most often, the Mohirai speak of awareness like a soil with many layers.

"Each layer of an awareness creates the possibility for some aspect of experience. The more layers an awareness possesses, the richer those experiences may be, just like the richest soils may support the most life.

"We give names to the more familiar layers of our human awareness. There are passive layers of bodily sensation and emotional reaction, like sight and hearing, touch and scent, fear and desire, anger and joy. There's the sense of self—those many inner voices speaking words we think are our thoughts, telling us stories we believe are our identities. There's imagination—that most active part of awareness, always generating ideas, meaning, and purpose with the help of the other layers. And there are some layers that remain cloaked in mystery, like intuition and the sense of knowing.

"Every creature possesses some layers of awareness, though not all creatures share all the same layers. The Voice in all differs from other creatures because its awareness includes all layers—many beyond our human ability to experience.

"Each layer of an awareness has the potential to connect with a layer of another's awareness. Awareness in fact hungers to connect in this way, so it may receive more, give more, experience more.

"Awareness grows in power through expanding connection. But in that power lies the danger. It is easy for us to damage another awareness, and for another awareness to damage our own, especially when that awareness is deeply connected to ours through binding pharmaka. Binding pharmaka strips us of the protection that comes from separation and unawareness. Without separation, one awareness may flood into another in unexpected ways.

"You have experienced a bit of the consequence of this, Ava. You experience pain because your awareness is unprepared to receive the awareness of the Voice. But pain is not the only possible consequence of a poorly formed connection between two awarenesses. Without the protection of separation, it becomes easier to manipulate another awareness, or to be manipulated. It becomes easier to force an idea or a desire upon another awareness, or to have one forced upon our own.

"It is possible to injure and even to destroy layers of awareness through such ill use. Just as rich soil may turn to desert, or an eye might be blinded, or skin might be burned away."

I cringe at these vivid images. The High Priestess continues, "We sit now in a place where the Voice's awareness is more concentrated than most, at a living intersection between water, soil, air, and sun. The Voice's awareness travels beneath us, above us, and all around us. Your pharmaka-amplified connection to the Voice would be too strong for you to endure here alone, Ava. You would be aware of everything connected to this tree across all of Dulai, and you would have none of the protection from that awareness that comes from initiate training. You would experience pain from all this unfamiliar sensation, and that pain would quickly become deadly, for an unprepared mind cannot hold so much awareness.

"Here and now, however, you have shelter from your awareness of the Voice. All initiate Mohirai learn to bond lightly to a new awareness on contact, and we learn to manage connection to the Voice without allowing it to overwhelm us. So while you hold my hand, my awareness offers yours shelter, as would the awareness of any other initiate Mohira. Dom's awareness offers shelter to yours as well, while his awareness resides in you and yours resides in him.

"Your work of unbinding will require you to find places

like this one, where you can practice the art of connection to the Voice with enough shelter to protect yourself from ill effects. Most of the work is simply observation, allowing yourself to encounter the awareness of the Voice. The best way to encounter another awareness is without resistance and without using force, letting each layer of your awareness find balance with its counterpart within the other awareness. You will know when you have found balance—it will feel like pain easing, like awareness expanding.

"Finding the balance takes practice and self-discipline, like any art. You may find that some layers of awareness reach balance with another's easily. But sometimes you will struggle, and many times in the beginning you will fail. When the struggle seems too great, or when you find you're no longer making progress, that is when the unbinding pharmaka is useful. You can use the pharmaka to weaken your bond to another awareness while you're in contact, and this will reduce the intensity of painful connection, like wrapping yourself in a cloak to protect yourself from the elements.

"But you should not rely on unbinding pharmaka alone to protect you in this practice. Memory should never be given up lightly, and the amount of unbinding pharmaka you would need to counterbalance your overdose all at once would have catastrophic effects on your memory, since you are so young and have so few memories. The Voice has given you a gift in Dom. Let him help you in your practice. In time, you should be able to manage your connection with the Voice without great loss of memory."

I consider Serapen's instruction carefully, comparing it to

what my mother said in the woods. If I had any hope before that this unbinding work could be done without Dom, that I might be able to take care of this predicament on my own, it's now gone. Whether or not I trust Serapen, her guidance and my mother's seem to agree on this point: I can't risk using unbinding pharmaka alone to counteract my overdose. I'll need Dom's help if I want to remember who I am when this is all over.

I say, "If I do need to take the unbinding pharmaka, will it weaken my connection with Dom as well as my connection with the Voice?"

The gentle rain transitions into a downpour, and a translucent grey curtain falls over our view of the camp. All the other girls and Mohirai withdraw to their tents. The beech boughs above still manage to keep us dry, though.

Over the rushing sound of the rain, Serapen says, "The unbinding pharmaka will work most strongly on the connection with which you have the most physical contact. If you take unbinding pharmaka while you're in a place like this, with a high concentration of the Voice's awareness, the bond with the Voice should weaken more than if you were to take it in a desert, for example. However, since Dom's awareness is so concentrated in his body, you may also affect your bond with Dom, especially if you need his contact soon after you've taken the unbinding pharmaka. This is why it's important to do the work in small steps. You must keep your connection with Dom strong enough to offer shelter as you work to balance your bond with the Voice, to minimize the need for unbinding pharmaka."

I say, "And then, when this work is done, will I be like I

was before? Able to walk on my own, free of this pain?"

The High Priestess takes so long to answer that I grow alarmed. At last she says, "There is no returning to the condition you were before, Ava. A thing once known can never be fully unknown. An awareness once experienced can never be entirely forgotten. But the bonds between awarenesses can be strengthened and weakened, relative to one another, once they are connected. The art lies in balancing the strength of your bond and your freedom from the bond."

Serapen stops and looks at me expectantly, and I realize she's waiting for the proper response to her words of instruction, which means this is all that I'm to learn tonight. This would all be fascinating, if it weren't so hopelessly complicated. Dispirited, I say, "I have listened, and I have heard, sister."

"Good," says Serapen. "Then it is time to act."

"I'm still not sure I know what to do, though," I say.

She says, "Sometimes the only way to know is to do."

Well, at this point doing seems preferable to knowing. My mind can't possibly hold much more than the knowledge Serapen's already poured into me. So, tentatively, I let go of Serapen's hand. I hold on to Dom's hand a moment longer, anticipating the unwelcome return of the pain, but then I let him go too. I lean back against the trunk of the tree and close my eyes.

I'm aware of nothing at first but the sound of the rain in the leaves above me. Next I feel the tingling where my ankles press into the soil, the same feeling that comes when Dom and I share thoughts in a particularly vivid way. My insides clench as I remember how this feeling came over me for the first time last night when I touched the forest floor outside the cave, just before I heard the Voice in all. Fortunately, the memory prepares me somewhat better this time for the disorienting sensation of my awareness slipping away from me and sinking down into the ground. I have an impulse to panic, but Serapen's words return to me. *Observe ... without resistance ... without force.*

So I try to relax, despite my disorientation. My body drifts away from me, and I let it drift. Freed from my body, my awareness spreads outward through the ground. I feel my awareness drawn into the tree. I stretch deep down along old roots through the soil, toward rock. I rise up along strong branches through the air, toward the sun. My young leaves tremble in the wind. My tender rootlets soak in the rain.

The Voice, when it returns this time, is louder than before. The weight of it slams into me from all directions. The pain comes on fast, much faster than before, so fast I only fleetingly perceive it as pain before I'm lost inside of it. A tiny voice inside me screams as I shrink to a grain of sand, a point of nothingness, swallowed up in an infinite vastness. There is no I. There is only ...

We are the bridge joining light to darkness. We are the wheel turning season to season. We are the threads binding realm to realm. We are—

The Voice fades. There's a hand. My hand, pulled out of nothingness by another's hand. Dom's hand. The rest of myself returns in pieces, slowly reassembling. I am an I again.

Are you all right? Dom thinks.

Am I? I wonder, dazed.

Serapen takes my other hand and says, "Breathe, Ava. Breathe." I gulp air, and each breath seems to draw blades deeper into my back. My pulse is erratic. Dom's and Serapen's hands on my skin feel so hot they might burn me, but it must just be my fingers that are so cold. I lean weakly back against the trunk of the tree and look up into its branches. For a strange moment, I think, *up into my branches.* The wind stirs the leaves, and I'm nauseated by their motion.

Serapen and Dom wait silently at my side as I attempt to recover my composure. The rain pours down harder, at last breaking through the protective cover of the beech boughs. Warm raindrops patter on my upturned face, sliding down my cheeks.

Eventually my breathing steadies. The stabbing pain ebbs. My pulse returns to something like normal. Serapen squeezes my hand and says, "It will get easier with practice, little sister. Head back to the tents, when you're ready. Try to get some sleep tonight. You both look like you need it."

Serapen stands, pulls her dark hood low over her forehead, and runs through the rain back toward the camp.

I remain sitting, uncertain whether I'm strong enough to stand yet. Dom reaches toward me and lifts up my hood to cover my head from the rain. I hadn't noticed how much water was running down my neck until he makes it stop.

"Thanks," I whisper.

Dom studies me with worried eyes. He says, "Do you want me to carry you back?"

I say, "Do I look that bad?"

"You look … not good."

"Still better than you, though," I say, forcing a weak smile.

He chuckles. "Can I give you a hand up at least?"

I nod. Dom pulls me up. I stand without too much difficulty, but when I try to step forward, my legs move like a newborn colt's, as though I've never walked before. I wobble, grip Dom's hand hard, and throw out my free hand to catch myself against the beech trunk. I grit my teeth and breathe sharply through my nose, trying to focus. I feel almost as weak as I did last night when I collapsed in the meadow, and my sense of helplessness infuriates me. Propped up here between Dom and the tree, I hunger for their strength.

Both my palms tingle, and warmth floods through me. To my surprise, I feel steadier on my feet. Tentatively, I withdraw my palm from the tree and look up at Dom.

"Did you feel that?" I ask.

"I felt your hand get warmer," he says. "Is that what you mean?"

I nod and say, "Do you feel all right?"

"Me? Same as before, I guess. Just tired."

Whatever happened, it's a relief, and the exhilaration of my renewed strength rushes straight to my head. I look out at the curtain of heavy rain separating us from camp.

"Shall we run for it?" I say.

"Maybe we should take it slow," he says, his brow furrowing.

I disagree. I pull him after me into the downpour.

THE TROUBLE WITH TRIOS

HAND IN HAND, AVA AND I RUN back toward camp. Her bright laughter as the rain pours over us reminds me of galloping with her on Eridu this afternoon. Hearing her, I can't help myself from laughing too.

But despite her apparent recovery from whatever just happened to her, I haven't recovered from my alarm. When Serapen and I let go of her hands beneath the beech tree, Ava had closed her eyes and briefly relaxed. I watched her, waiting for the prickling pain to return in my chest like it usually does when we're separated, but at first I felt nothing amiss, so I thought Ava must be fine. Then all at once she'd gone so pale. I'd felt a crushing sensation, an unbearable pressure all around me, so I'd grabbed her hand. Her fingers were ice cold, and although her body sat beside me, I could tell some part of her was gone. For a terrifying moment, I thought she might not return. Even after her eyes opened again, she looked translucent, as if some part of her had dissolved into the air.

It's like none of that ever happened, though, as we burst through the door flap into the fourth tent, breathless and soaked.

"Ugh!" Eumelia shrieks as a light spray of rainwater from my riding cloak splashes her in the face. Hanu catches a bit of it as well, but she only laughs in surprise.

"Sorry, sorry," I say to Eumelia, wiping water out of my eyes. Eumelia grumbles but accepts my apology.

Ava attempts to use the hem of her damp riding shirt to dry her drenched hair. I shift my hand to her bare hip to free up both her hands. Hanu's eyes follow my every move.

Eumelia asks, "Where did you two go with Serapen?"

I wait for Ava to speak, but she seems preoccupied, so I say, "Over to the stream."

Dom, Ava thinks. *Let me handle this. We need to be careful about what we say to them. I don't want anyone else tangled up in this, all right?*

Sorry, I think automatically.

You don't need to be sorry, she thinks. *I'm the one who got you into this mess.*

Eumelia raises an eyebrow, then says, "What did she want to talk to you about?"

Ava's thoughts churn with possible answers to this question, evaluating the risks and advantages of each possibility so fast I can't keep up. I wait. At last she says, "She's teaching me and Dom how to ease the binding between us."

"Oh, I'm glad there's something she can do to help you," says Hanu. "Did she say how long it will take?"

How long do you think Hanu can tolerate? Ava thinks. A hint of a smile plays at the corner of her mouth as she glances at me.

Please stop, I think.

"She didn't say," says Ava. "I don't think she really knows. I hope it won't take too long."

Hanu nods sympathetically and says, "It must be difficult for you both to manage."

"It is," says Ava. "I wish I could trade places with you." Her tone is all innocence, but her mischief feels like a squirrel on the loose inside me.

Hanu says, "Tell me if there's anything I can do to help. Really. If you need extra hands, or anything like that."

Ava surveys the tent. Hanu and Eumelia have already laid out their bedrolls on one side, leaving the other side open for me and Ava. All I want right now is to spread out my bedroll at the far edge of the tent and collapse into it.

But Ava says, "You know, there is one thing that would be helpful."

I see what Ava's thinking before she says it. I grip her hand. *Please don't,* I think urgently. *Please, Ava.*

Oh come on, she thinks. *I'm doing you a favor.*

Ignoring my silent protests, Ava says, "One of the side effects of the binding pharmaka is that I get cold very easily, and Dom does too. Could we sleep between you and Eumelia for warmth?"

"Of course!" says Hanu. She looks at Eumelia. "Is that all right with you, Mel?"

Eumelia shrugs. "Fine with me as long as you sleep on Dom's side. No offense, Dom, but you smell like boy sweat. That's more Hanu's taste than mine."

Ava and Hanu laugh. I want to say that I'll be fine sleeping on the outside edge of the tent, that actually I'd prefer it. But there is some merit to the idea that we two should sleep in the middle for warmth, at least until we've both recovered more of our strength. And Ava knows, because she can hear what I'm thinking, that I don't want to hurt Hanu's feelings by saying I don't want her next to me. I'm irritated that Ava's put me in the middle of this situation, but her amusement pours into me, drowning out my annoyance.

You're terrible, I think.

You're welcome, Ava thinks.

Hanu folds up her bedroll and moves to the other edge of the tent beside me.

Ava and I help each other get ready for bed. In these tight quarters, with Ava and Hanu undressing on either side of me, there's not much that's safe to look at. I keep my eyes on Eumelia's side of the tent. There's no risk of any uncomfortably intimate memories popping up involving her. Eumelia and I have always been friendly enough, but nothing more than that.

Eumelia's face is less mocking, less guarded, and more thoughtful when she thinks no one is watching. Her gaze follows my hands on Ava's back with undisguised enjoyment as Ava pulls a dry sleeping tunic over her head. Eumelia catches me looking at her, and I'm so surprised that I don't think to look away. Eumelia winks at me. I suppress a laugh.

Ava glances up at me and thinks, *What?*

I do my best not to think about Eumelia's expression. *Just appreciating how clever you are,* I think. Ava narrows her eyes suspiciously, but I manage to keep a straight face.

Ava and I spread out our bedrolls, and Hanu lends a hand when we need help. The rain and wind pick up outside the tent. Darkness falls. There's nothing left to do for the night but try to sleep as best we can. So the four of us crawl under our blankets.

Ava curls into a ball, pulls her blanket up over her nose, and reaches for my hand. The damp chill from the rain creeps inside the tent, emanating up from the ground through my thin bedroll. The warmth drains slowly from Ava's fingers, and eventually she's shivering even harder than she was last night.

I'm delirious with exhaustion, but I feel her growing discomfort like it's my own. I overhear Ava's thoughts as she chastises herself for weakness and tries to fall asleep despite the cold.

Come here, I think. *I'll warm you up.*

I'll be fine, she thinks. *I'll ask Thalia for an extra blanket tomorrow.*

Come on. I reach for her sleepily. *I can't sleep if you can't. You'll be doing me a favor.*

Her gratitude overcomes her resistance. She lets me draw her against me, her back to my front. She grows warm again and relaxes. I fall almost instantly into a deep and dreamless sleep.

△▽△

Before sunrise, I wake to the familiar sound of the first morning birds outside the tent. I recognize the weight of Dom's arms around me and the steady cadence of his breathing against my back. Yesterday returns to me through all the scents still clinging to him: pharmaka, sweat and leather, grass and campfire. His hand rests on the bare skin of my hip. Being held this way still feels like a trap, but this morning I have no impulse to spring away from him. For a moment I simply enjoy his warmth and the feeling of a good night's sleep. I guess even a trap can become comfortable, once it's familiar.

But I can't let myself get comfortable. I can't let myself forget that Dom, innocent though he may be, is just another tool the Mohirai can use to hold me here against my will. When I asked him to come with me yesterday, to run from the Voice's calling, I was driven by an impulse to save him as much as to save myself. How foolish I was. Of course he trusts the Mohirai more than he trusts me. Of course he wants to stay here; he knows nothing but what they've taught him. I need to focus on saving myself, before the Mohirai have me lulled into complacency the way they've lulled him and all the rest of these girls.

I open my eyes to find Eumelia watching me, her nose a handspan from mine. I'm so surprised that for a moment I simply stare back at her. I never before noticed the ring of blue encircling her hazel irises, or how pretty her mouth is when she's not smirking at me.

Her expression has changed dramatically since yesterday. Yesterday, Eumelia and Hanu both studied me with the same foggy look Dom gave me the first time he saw me in the woods. Neither of my former trio sisters could remember me. But the fog is gone from Eumelia's eyes this morning.

The soft, smooth hand on my hip slides away, and I realize that what I thought was Dom's hand is actually hers. She finds my hand beneath my blanket, and my fingers tingle against her palm.

I remember, she thinks. A memory of my younger face flashes before me. Eumelia's memory.

My eyes widen. *How do you remember?* I think.

I don't know, she thinks, shaking her head slightly against her pillow. *I was dreaming that I was flying over a beautiful city made of glass. When I woke up, I could still see it so clearly in my mind. Then I realized I was touching you, and I pulled back my hand, and the city disappeared. Then I touched you again, and I saw the city again. So I knew that image was coming somehow from you.*

And now when I look at you, I remember all sorts of things. I've seen you before. We know each other, don't we?

It hadn't occurred to me earlier that anyone who touches me, not just Dom, might experience some effect of the binding pharmaka. Serapen didn't warn me about this. Perhaps she didn't know; she did say she's never seen an overdose like mine before. In my head, I curse extravagantly.

Eumelia's lips twitch into her usual smirk as she overhears me, and something about that familiar expression erases the years that have separated us. A memory returns to me.

I'm eight summers old, standing with Dom in a crowd of children outside the sheep paddocks. Eumelia's exasperated voice calls out from behind me, "Ava! Where were you? Why are you never where you're supposed to be?"

I look back over my shoulder at Eumelia, irritated by everything about her, from her plump freckled cheeks to the infuriating way she always talks to me, like I'm hers to command. Eumelia and Hanu stand waiting for me as the crowd of children disperses around us. I gesture sharply for Eumelia to wait, then turn back to Dom and say gently, "I have to go."

Dom looks crestfallen, and I feel guilty for leaving him. It's his first day here, and I can see he's nervous to be left alone among all these unfamiliar boys. I remember my first day, coming out of the woods with Serapen, so I know how confused he must be feeling. But he's not allowed into the temple city with me, so there's not much I can do. He has to go with the other boys back to their house outside the wall.

"Don't worry," I say, doing my best to sound cheerful. "The sisters will let us back out after we finish preserving the temple garden harvest. Should only take a quarter moon or so. I'll look for you at the old cedar when we're done, all right?"

"Ava, come on!" Eumelia marches toward me. She looks at Dom shrewdly and says, "Don't let her get you into trouble. She has a lot of funny ideas in her head."

My hands clench as I resist the urge to push Eumelia to the ground. Why can't she ever just leave me alone? I say, "You couldn't fit an idea in your head if you tried, Eumelia."

Eumelia rolls her eyes at me and says to Dom, "You'll see."

Dom looks uneasily from Eumelia to me. Hanu approaches, stepping between me and Eumelia, joining hands with us. She's much taller than both of us, with large, watchful eyes in her dark, solemn face.

"Come on," Hanu says in a soothing, grown-up voice. "You'll both feel better once you've eaten."

I refuse to look at Eumelia as Hanu draws us back toward the city gate. I cast one last look over my shoulder at Dom, who stands alone beside the paddock, looking completely forlorn as he watches us go.

The memory fades, and I'm back in the tent, lying nose to nose beside Eumelia. *Ugh,* she thinks. *You're such a sucker for that sad puppy face of his.*

I blink, horrified to realize Eumelia's just witnessed that entire memory. I try to pull back my hand from her, but she tightens her grip around my wrist, inadvertently digging into the bruises Dom left there yesterday. I wince, and she loosens her grip slightly but doesn't let me go.

Wait, she thinks. *I want to know what really happened to you.*

It's difficult to stop my thoughts from spilling into her while she's holding on to me. I consider wrenching my arm away, but she's always been stronger than me, and I don't want to cause a scene that wakes up Hanu or requires the intervention of the Mohirai. The last thing I need right now is more hands touching me, more awarenesses tangled up in mine.

Let me go, Eumelia, I think. *Whatever's happening to me with the binding pharmaka is dangerous, and Serapen doesn't really know how to fix it. I don't want to hurt you, all right?* More importantly, I don't want to be worrying about yet another person overhearing my thoughts while I need to be planning my escape.

Eumelia studies my face. *You're not going to hurt me,* she thinks. Her confidence is as infuriating as it is misguided, considering all the ways I managed to hurt Dom yesterday. I briefly consider slipping out of Dom's arms just to give her a taste of the awful pain, to prove I can hurt her. That seems unnecessarily cruel, though. There must be a better way.

I consider the memory of Dom's sad puppy face, which, however pathetic it may seem, is pretty effective at arousing sympathy. Maybe a little bit of his submissiveness would do the trick. Eumelia always seemed to enjoy being superior to me when we were little, after all. *Please let me go,* I think, summoning up the closest thing I can find to humility and hoping it feels authentic. *Please, Eumelia.*

You can tell me, she thinks insistently. *We're trio sisters, Ava. You can trust me.*

I stifle a derisive laugh. How could I trust Eumelia? For the brief time we lived together, she was nothing but a constant source of torment. Just looking at her fills me with irritating memories. She's the most unlikable person I've ever known.

Eumelia's lips tremble slightly. Oh, blast, she overheard that. *Sorry, Eumelia,* I think. *You're just ... Well ...*

Listen, Eumelia thinks, setting her lips in a firm line. *I can't change what I did when we were little. Maybe I was irritating. Maybe I was unlikable. Maybe I still am. But I promise you can trust me. Just give me a chance.*

I chew the inside of my lip, considering. *You want me to trust you?* I think.

She nods.

I think, *Then don't tell anyone about what happens when you touch me, all right? Not Hanu. Not the Mohirai. Not the other girls. I don't need anyone else in my head right now. Dom's too much as it is.*

All right, thinks Eumelia, *I promise. I won't tell anyone else. So tell me what happened.*

Prove you can keep a promise first, I think. *And let me go when I ask you to let me go.*

To my relief, Eumelia finally lets go of my wrist. But just as she withdraws her hand, a series of confusing sensations swirl through my awareness. The curves and colors of my face, lips, and body. The smoothness of her skin against mine and mine against hers. Arousal stirring deep inside of me— or is it inside of her? Understanding dawns on me, followed by awkwardness. Heat rushes to my cheeks. I curse inwardly.

My agitation seems to disturb Dom's sleep, and his waking sensations unfold clearly in my awareness. First he's so cozy that he doesn't want to open his eyes. Then his arms tighten slightly around me, and he's glad I'm still here and still warm. Then his pulse speeds up when he realizes the reason he's so cozy is that Hanu is draped around him, still asleep. He recognizes the feeling of her long legs tucked behind his, her full breasts pressed against his back, her forehead touching his shoulder, her hand resting on his thigh. Then he's alarmed because he realizes I'm awake and overhearing all this.

Good morning, I think, amused enough by Dom's predicament to momentarily forget my own. Eumelia's expression softens, and I realize with dismay that I'm smiling at her as I'm thinking of Dom. She's smiling at me because she thinks my smile is meant for her. And she's happy because this is how she wants me to smile at her. I curse inwardly again.

Now it's Dom's turn to be amused. *Good morning*, he thinks. *Turns out two can play at this game, eh?*

I roll over to face him so I don't accidentally send Eumelia any more mixed messages. Dom only half-opens one eye at me, but it's enough for me to see his teasing expression. I can't begrudge him his amusement. I was the one who thought playing games with our sleeping arrangements would be harmless fun, after all. This was a more serious mistake than I could have imagined. I need to get out of here before this gets any more complicated.

Dom's drowsy expression sharpens into wakefulness, overhearing me. *You can't get out of here without me,* he thinks. *You need to tell me what you're planning to do.*

Spirits, he's almost as irritating as Eumelia. I flop onto my back and stare at the canvas roof so I don't have to see Dom's concerned eyes or Eumelia's eager smile while I try to think.

My abrupt movement wakes Hanu. Through Dom, I feel the warmth of her body stretching alongside his, the gentle touch of her fingers on his side, the light kiss she presses to the back of his neck. All of these sensations seem familiar to him; I guess they've woken up together like this before. Her sleepy hand trails up Dom's thigh, and his concern for me disappears into a panicked surge of arousal.

He sits up, letting me go and extricating himself from Hanu's arms.

"Sorry," he says hoarsely. "I'll be right back."

Dom rushes out of the tent wearing nothing but his sleeping tunic. I sit up, my chest prickling in pain as soon as the tent flap falls closed behind him. Hanu yawns softly and sits up. "What's wrong?" she asks, looking from me to Eumelia.

Eumelia's expression is a perfect imitation of complete mystification.

All of this might have seemed funny to me yesterday, but now all I can see is how reckless I've been, tangling myself even deeper in this web of complications. I hastily pull on my boots, wincing alternately at the stabbing pain in my chest and the stinging pain in my bandaged feet. Eumelia watches me, and when our eyes meet I can see what she's thinking, almost as if she's still touching me. *Your secret is safe with me. I promise.*

I don't like the idea of anyone being the keeper of my secrets, especially not her, but there's no help for it now. I knot my boot laces, hop to my feet, and head out after Dom.

GOOD INTENTIONS

Ava calls out from behind me, "Dom! Wait! Please, wait!"

I'm already halfway across the clearing, heading toward the stream. A few of the grazing horses look up at my approach, and Eridu whinnies a friendly greeting.

I walk faster. As the distance grows between me and Ava, the ache in my chest returns, although I notice my pain doesn't escalate as fast today as it did yesterday. It occurs to me for the first time that I shouldn't think of this pain as mine. It's Ava's. She feels this pain because she's able to have a connection to the Voice. I feel the pain indirectly through her, and the idea that my feelings are only an echo of hers bothers me.

Knowing these are her feelings does nothing to lessen their intensity for me, though. I wince as the pain sharpens, and I know this means her pain is growing worse too. But I can't go back to her yet. I don't want an audience while I sort through my confusion.

Yesterday, when Ava pleaded with me to run away with her, she thought, *I'll hide nothing from you. We'll share everything as equals. I promise.*

Yesterday, I wanted so deeply to hear the Voice that I couldn't imagine doing anything that might interfere with my calling, especially not running away. But when I woke with Ava in my arms this morning, her words were the first thing I remembered. *We'll share everything as equals.* Those words give shape to a desire I've felt for a long time but never really understood until now. I want to know what it feels like to be treated by Ava as an equal.

But how can I trust her words? It's clear from all I've overheard her thinking that she's hiding plenty from me. She has yet to explain where she's been for the last seven years or what happened to her. She does exactly what she pleases with no regard for how it affects me. She seems to forget I'm here one moment, then toys with me for her own amusement the next. I don't know what it's like to be treated as an equal by a girl, but I can't imagine it's like this. With other girls, at least I know where I stand, what to expect, how to behave. With Ava, I'm completely confused.

It's not only confusion I feel, though. I also feel regret, wondering whether I made the wrong choice. What might have happened, if I had agreed to run with her? Maybe the reason Ava doesn't see me as an equal is because I didn't have the courage to go with her. Maybe if I'd agreed to go, she'd treat me differently. Maybe I deserve to be treated this way.

"Dom," Ava says breathlessly, catching up to me as I stop beside the stream.

I sit on the grassy bank. "You didn't need to come out here," I say, not looking at her. "I would have come back before the pain got too bad for you."

"That's not why I came," she says. She sits beside me, but she doesn't take my hand, even though I can feel her pain worsening. "I came to apologize. I'm really sorry, Dom. You asked me to leave things alone with you and Hanu, and I ignored you. I shouldn't have done that. I wish I hadn't. I honestly thought it was just a bit of fun, and that you'd like having her close to you after having to spend so much time with me. But I see now that …" She trails off.

I look at her straight in the eye as I say, "What? What do you see now?"

She shrinks back a bit but holds my gaze. In a small voice, she says, "What's between you and Hanu is private. And I forced you into a situation where I'd see things you didn't want me to see. I wouldn't want you to do that to me, but I did it to you. I'm really sorry. I won't do it again."

Her eyes as she looks at me are wide with contrition. She tries not to look away, but her eyes close briefly in a wince as a searing stab of pain pierces both of us.

"All right," I say, relenting. I take her hand, and when her skin touches mine, her awareness floods into me. I feel her relief as the pain subsides, but mostly she feels guilty about all the pain she keeps causing me, uncertainty about why she decided to play games with me and Hanu in the first place, and anxiety about something that happened between her and Eumelia this morning. Ava's thoughts are as confused as mine, and this, even more than her apology, somehow makes me feel better.

You know, I think, *you've misunderstood, about me and Hanu.*

What do you mean? she thinks.

I hesitate, then think, *You thought I'd rather have Hanu close by, after spending so much time with you. But I …* Ava watches me, waiting for me to finish my thought. Embarrassed heat rises to my ears as I think, *I like being with you. I don't feel like I need to hide anything from you about Hanu. But I thought those sorts of memories might bother you.*

I feel Ava's genuine surprise as she wonders, *Why would*

that bother me? Then her eyes widen as she thinks, *Oh …*

She slips her hand out of mine, so we're both alone with our thoughts when she says, "I like being with you too, Dom. But this is so difficult already, hearing each other's thoughts and seeing each other's memories. I think anything more would be unbearable."

My throat tightens. I run my hands over my face and rub my eyes, trying to decide what to say. Thoughts are so much easier to convey when I'm touching her than when I try to find words to speak aloud. The words I settle on are entirely inadequate to express what I mean when I say, "I know. You're right."

She says, in hopeful tone, "I think once I've practiced more of what Serapen showed me last night, this will get easier."

I look down at my bare toes in the grass, trying and failing to match her tone as I say, "Yeah. I hope so."

Ava shifts uncomfortably beside me, clasping and unclasping her hands in her lap as the pain rebuilds. At last, she says, "May I touch you?"

I hold out my hand uneasily, wondering which of my emotions might spill into her next. She takes my hand and thinks, *I just don't want to hurt you, Dom.*

I can feel that she means it, but I'm beginning to realize that no matter what she does, it's going to hurt me.

△▽△

My heart sinks as Dom thinks, *No matter what she does, it's going to hurt me.* I worry he's right. The sooner he's cut loose from me, the better for him. Unfortunately, my silly prank and its aftermath have used up what little free time we might have had this morning to practice what Serapen taught me. Now the Mohirai are stirring back at the camp, rousing the girls from their tents, instructing us to make ready to leave.

A number of girls, Hanu among them, hurry toward the stream where Dom and I sit. They strip off their clothes and wash away yesterday's dirt and dust as best they can, chatting amiably with one another. Hanu glances occasionally at me and Dom, but we both avoid her gaze.

I long to bathe, and I can feel that Dom does too. But I'm uncomfortable at the thought of joining Hanu and the other girls now that I understand Dom's feelings about her and me a bit better.

Please can we think about something else right now, he thinks, keeping his eyes fixed on his toes.

Right, I think. *Quick—give me something else to think about.*

How about Eumelia? he thinks.

I laugh, then he laughs, and that makes everything easier.

"Come on," I say, hauling Dom up by the hand. I lead him to a spot a little farther downstream from the other girls, behind a screen of trees, so he doesn't have to look at any of them while he's also in contact with me.

"Is this all right?" I ask.

He nods. "Thanks."

I'm self-conscious undressing in front of him now, even though I've done it several times already without a second thought. But I can't do much to minimize the awkwardness of this apart from turning a bit away from him and averting my eyes. Once we've shed our sleeping tunics and I've gingerly removed my boots and bandages, I take his hand and lead him into the water. I rest a hand on his shoulder as Dom scrubs his hair and body with sand and lets the current rinse him clean. He does the same for me as I wash up and make a quick check of all my little injuries. The cuts on my feet are healing cleanly, thanks to the salves Hedi used, though it'll probably take half a moon before it's entirely comfortable to walk barefoot again. My lower lip is swollen under the scab where I bit myself, but that will heal even faster than my feet. Delicately, I wash my arms, examining the purplish shadows around my wrists and the darker purple spots where Dom's fingertips dug in hardest. They're going to take a while to fade, but they don't hurt much today.

I feel Dom's shame as he sees me looking at my bruises. I look up over my shoulder at him. "Don't feel bad," I say. "You didn't mean to hurt me."

"I still did, though," he says.

I run my fingertips lightly along his shins, which look far worse than my wrists. "I actually did mean to hurt you when I did this," I say, wincing as the ache of the tender marks on his legs echoes in my own shins. "Sorry."

"We need to be more careful with each other," he says.

I nod. "I'll try to do better. I promise."

"Me too," he says.

We hurry to follow the other girls back to camp, change into our riding clothes, and help Thalia break down and pack up the tents. Arkhi and Serapen set out a cold meal. My stomach felt strange all day yesterday after drinking the Calling Day pharmaka, but I'm ravenous this morning.

After we say the meal blessing, I sit in the grass with Dom. I tuck my bare foot under his bare ankle and start to eat. He chuckles, watching me.

What? I think, chewing an enormous mouthful of delicious dark bread spread with soft goat cheese. It's pretty useful to converse this way right now, since I don't have to pause eating for talking.

That bread tastes as good to you as harvest cakes do to me, Dom thinks. *It's like you've been fasting for half a moon.*

I shrug and think, *It's been a while since I've had bread. Or cheese.* My mind flicks back over the few small foraged meals I ate with my mother in the forest on our last few days on the road to the Children's Temple. I'm used to going days at a time without eating much.

Really? Dom thinks, and his amusement fades.

I roll my eyes at him and think, *Don't feel sorry for me. I've always had enough to eat. Maybe not as much as you have, but I don't need much. And there's always something to eat in the forest, if you know where to look.*

Dom looks up, and through his eyes I see Arkhi approaching behind me and glimpse a bit of his perspective. In her inky black silks, she weaves through the bright morning light like a ribbon of midnight.

Like a ribbon of midnight? I think, delighted by Dom's impression of Arkhi. I glance over my shoulder at her, and I hardly even notice her clothes. What I do notice is how she's looking at me, with that uncomfortably perceptive expression. I turn back to Dom and smile. *Everything is more beautiful through your eyes, Dom,* I think. He shrugs, looking a bit embarrassed, but I can feel he's pleased.

"Good morning," says Arkhi, taking a seat across from the two of us on the grass. "Did you manage to sleep, all four of you in that little tent?"

"We did," I say.

No thanks to you, Dom thinks. I can't suppress a giggle, which turns into a choke as I inhale a bit of the bread I'm chewing. Dom thumps me on the back.

Arkhi waits until I've recovered, then says, "The two of you are sharing thoughts quite frequently."

Dom and I glance at each other. I wonder how Arkhi knows this. She hasn't really asked a question, but she seems to be waiting for an answer. I can't think of anything I'll gain by lying to her about this, so I say cautiously, "Yes. I guess we are."

"Listen, novices," says Arkhi. She speaks in the tone of instruction, but in her voice it's more inviting than it ever sounds from my mother, or from Serapen—like we're friends, not just her wayward little sister and little brother. "I know it may seem easier to share thoughts directly with each other. And sometimes sharing this way will be unavoidable, especially while you both must remain in such close contact.

"But every shared perception, emotion, and thought strengthens your bond, just like using the binding pharmaka itself. Strengthening the bond between you two may not seem dangerous, compared to the far greater danger posed by Ava's bond with the Voice. But a binding between two human awarenesses should not be taken lightly. Awareness is unruly by nature, and most novices find it challenging enough to manage their own awareness without the added trouble of another's. This is why initiate Mohirai approach binding with great caution and allow the bond to form slowly over time. You and Dom have already formed a far deeper bond than any initiate would create by choice, and the more you use the bond between you, the stronger it will become."

I don't like the sound of this at all. My chest prickles painfully, and I realize I've unconsciously withdrawn my bare foot from Dom while Arkhi's been speaking.

Arkhi must see my apprehension, because she continues in a slightly more encouraging tone. "Even the most unruly awareness can be shaped by the arts of mindfulness—especially the art of intention. Intention will serve you well in the house of novices, but it will make the journey ahead more comfortable for you both, too. You'll receive deeper training in this art from the Muses at Velkanos, but there's no need to wait. To begin building an intention, simply choose an intention, focus on it, and remember it.

"I'd suggest you choose an intention to use your bond with each other in a disciplined way. As you focus on that intention, you might practice distilling your thoughts into speech rather than allowing unfiltered thoughts to spill into each other. Or you might choose carefully which experiences you allow yourself to have, knowing both of you must share them. Or you might try to anticipate which of your actions could create which sensations for the other."

I can't help remembering what happened in the tent this morning, and I feel guilty about it all over again. "I didn't mean to hurt Dom, by sharing thoughts this way," I say.

"The absence of good intention can be as dangerous as the presence of bad intention," says Arkhi. She says this kindly, but her expression is deadly serious. "You can still hurt each other, even if neither of you intended to."

I glance down at my bruised wrists and nod slowly. "All right," I say. "I'll be more careful."

"We both will," says Dom.

Arkhi nods and rises from her seat beside us. She calls out to the rest of the group, "Grab your saddlebags, novices. It's time we're on our way."

△▽△

Only after Arkhi's warning do I realize how much of Ava's awareness I'm perceiving, and how much of mine I'm sharing with her. I have no idea how to stop sharing while we're still touching each other. I try to clear my mind entirely of thoughts, but this only seems to make thoughts spill out faster.

Ava, overhearing all this, says wryly, "I'd never shared a thought with anyone two days ago, and now it feels like a hard thing to give up. Speaking is so much harder, isn't it?"

I chuckle ruefully and say, "I was thinking exactly the same thing."

But, even as I say these words, I realize that Arkhi's suggestion—*practice distilling your thoughts into speech*—works. The search for words, and speaking them aloud, temporarily stops the flood of shared thoughts between us.

Ava and I hurry to finish eating, then stand and brush crumbs off ourselves. Following Arkhi's instruction, we head toward the pile of packed camp gear to pick up our saddlebags.

Ahead of us, Kor grabs her saddlebag and turns in the

direction of the horses. She pauses mid-turn, a puzzled expression on her face. Following her gaze, I look back to see a tawny female kuku bird pecking at the breadcrumbs Ava and I left behind in the grass. The dark bars across the kuku's chest tell me it's her first autumn.

Kor lowers her saddlebag and walks slowly toward the bird, kneeling in the grass a few paces away. Girl and bird study each other for a moment. In a sweeter voice than she ever uses with humans, Kor says, "Hello, little sister. What are you doing here so late in the season? Have you lost your way?" She extends her open hand toward the kuku, offering her a few dried bits of fruit from our morning meal. The bird hops toward Kor and eats out of her palm. When all the fruit is gone, Kor points toward the south and whispers to the kuku, like she's sharing a secret, "The sea's that way. Off you go." The kuku takes wing, flying off into the clear blue sky.

Ava watches this exchange with wide eyes. Muffling a giggle, she whispers to me, "Getting stranger by the year, isn't she?"

Kor does have an odd way about her, but there's a gentleness to her that I like. I see no need to make a joke at her expense, so I say nothing and pick up my saddlebag. I reach for Ava's bag automatically, from long habit of carrying things for sisters, but she stops me and picks it up herself. "I've put you through enough already without making you my packhorse, too," she says.

Hand in hand, we walk toward the horses. Eumelia and Hanu fall into step on either side of us carrying their saddlebags.

Eumelia says to Ava, "I saw you teaching Dom how to

handle himself in the saddle yesterday. He was riding beautifully by the end. Would you teach me how to do that?"

"And me, please!" says Hanu. "You and the Mohirai seem to be the only ones walking normally this morning. My whole body aches from riding."

Ava's happy to share something she loves with an eager audience. She says, "I'll show you some things that can help with the saddle soreness once we're out on the road."

Eumelia and Hanu thank her and say they'll rejoin us once the caravan is underway. They hurry off toward their horses.

"Oh," Ava says, looking at me with dismay. "I've done it again."

"Done what?" I say, as she and I quickly part ways to buckle our saddlebags on opposite sides of Eridu.

"I didn't ask what you wanted," says Ava, taking my hand again once her bag is secure. "Is it all right with you if Hanu rides near us? I can make some excuse if you'd rather she doesn't."

I'm so rarely asked what I want that Ava's question takes me by surprise. She waits a long time for me to speak, and her touch conveys her worry that she's hurt me again, right after she promised to do better. I wonder whether this is what it might be like to be treated by Ava as an equal.

At last, I say, "I want you to teach them what you taught me. You're a good teacher."

Ava smiles. "All right. Thanks."

"And—" The next words slip out before I have a chance to consider all they might entail. "I want the four of us to be friends."

An image of Eumelia's most irritating smirk flashes in Ava's mind. Ava sighs dramatically, then says, "Well. I'll try my best."

"Thanks," I say. It would be nice if she'd try to be friendlier to everyone else, too, but I decide not to push my luck. Peace in our tent would be a good start.

She squeezes my hand and says, "Ready to go, then?"

I nod. She mounts Eridu. I give her a moment to settle herself up there while I treat Eridu with some apples I pocketed from the morning meal.

"No fair!" says Ava. "He's going to like you better."

"He already likes me better," I say, swinging myself up into the saddle. She laughs, and the sound makes me smile.

I settle myself in the saddle and start to wrap my arm around Ava's waist. But the memory of what happened when I did this yesterday stops my hand at the hem of her shirt. My self-conscious hesitation stretches into an uncomfortably long pause.

At last Ava says, "It's all right, little brother. You can come out." I hardly recognize her voice as she speaks in this steady, soothing way. Then it hits me that she's mimicking my voice. These are the words I called out to her in the forest the other night. It's a pretty good impression, and I chuckle. She takes my hand and slides it under her shirt, settling my palm lightly at her hip. Her skin feels cool under my hand. Not as cold as she was last night, but not as warm as she should be, either.

"Do you want your cloak?" I say.

"I'm fine, Dom. Don't worry about me." She taps Eridu lightly with her heels, and we follow Arkhi back onto the road.

△▽△

Dom and I haven't been on the road long before Eumelia calls my name. I turn to see her trotting toward us on Nisaba, followed by Hanu on an elegant silver mare called Baba. I wince at the sight of the two girls bouncing along in their saddles, their bodies jarred by every movement of their horses. It's obvious why they're so sore after yesterday's ride.

"What, you don't think I'm as graceful as the Muses?" says Eumelia, seeing my expression. Her mocking half-smile is clearly meant only for herself now, and we share a laugh.

I call out to Arkhi at the head of the caravan, "Is it all right if we ride behind so I can give Eumelia and Hanu some pointers?"

Arkhi raises a hand in assent and says, "Just stay in sight of the caravan."

I pull Eridu out of the line, and Eumelia and Hanu follow me. We stand at the roadside and wait for the rest of the caravan to pass.

Using the open space on the wide road, I give the girls a lesson I received from my mother long ago. I show them four paces on Eridu, passing back and forth before them at a walk, trot, canter, and gallop. It's a bit complicated with Dom behind me in the saddle, but I manage to demonstrate certain postures and leg grips that can jostle a rider at each pace. Then I show them how I can move more smoothly with Eridu, sitting deep in the saddle, opening up my legs and hips. I ask first Eumelia and then Hanu to ride back and forth at a walk and trot, calling out suggestions. The caravan seems unlikely to move much faster than a trot for a while, so I figure the other paces can wait.

Ahead of us, the caravan begins to disappear around a bend in the road. I'm about to tell the girls we need to catch up when Eridu, Nisaba, and Baba all trot ahead without our direction.

"How is Arkhi doing this?" I mutter to myself. The Muse must have summoned the horses to keep us close, but I didn't see or hear her do anything.

Nisaba trots so close beside me that Eumelia overhears. "Don't you know?" she says, looking at me with genuine surprise. "Why were you using binding pharmaka, if you don't know what it's used for?"

I want to protest that I wasn't using binding pharmaka—at least, I hadn't meant to—but that would only raise more questions about what I was doing, so I remain silent.

Hanu, riding on my other side, says kindly, "How could you know, without a Mohira to teach you?"

For once, Hanu's words annoy me even more than Eumelia's, because they remind me that my mother could in fact have taught me, but instead chose not to. I ask Eumelia, "Do you mean Arkhi is controlling the horses with binding pharmaka?"

"The Mohirai would say communicating, not controlling," says Eumelia. "But yes, essentially. The main use of binding pharmaka is communication at a distance. After the destruction, with so few people spread out across such a large region, communicating with binding pharmaka was much more practical than sending messengers.

"The Mohirai use bonds to communicate directly with each other, but they also use them with animals, to send deliveries between temple cities without using riders. Once I even saw Muse Serapen send a dove out from the aviary to forage for her."

I'm fascinated by this. I also wonder why my mother never told me that the Mohirai could communicate with animals. "But how does it work?" I ask Eumelia. "Does Arkhi have a bond with all the horses in the caravan?"

Eumelia shrugs and says, "I'm not sure how it works, exactly. The Mohirai don't teach any advanced pharmaka until we start novice training. But I have a general idea from watching the sisters in the Children's Temple. You've seen Arkhi's stole, haven't you?" I nod, remembering the long silver-threaded black stole the Muse wears over her robes. Eumelia says, "Some of the higher arts involve weaving with pharmaka. I've seen sisters use ribbons, robes, stoles—all sorts of things, really—to communicate with each other. I'd guess some threads in Arkhi's stole let her communicate with the horses the same way. See this?" Eumelia pats her saddle blanket.

For the first time, I notice the subtle gleam of silver threads in all three of our dark wool saddle blankets, much like the silver threads in Arkhi's stole. Then, with a jolt, I recall the golden threads worked into the white ceremonial silks all the novices wore to the Calling Day ceremony, and the ornate golden embroidery of Serapen's robes. During the ceremony, I'd been conscious of the effects of the pharmaka I inhaled from my hood, but I'd assumed that pharmaka had been smeared or soaked into the hood. I hadn't considered that pharmaka might be woven into the fabric itself.

I look down at the riding shirt I'm wearing, which Thalia gave me yesterday. I think of the coppery threads of the long sash she winds so artfully around her green robes, and I search my sleeves and hems for any gleam of copper, silver, or gold. I see nothing but undyed linen, without ornament or embroidery of any kind. I examine the legs of my riding breeches and the tops of my leather riding boots. Are any of these things what they seem?

My mind races through all my memories since my overdose. I consider Arkhi's uncanny perceptiveness, my suspicion that Serapen was somehow reading my thoughts, my unaccountable decision to drink from the chalice at the Calling Day ceremony. Struggling to keep the alarm out of my voice, I say, "Do the Mohirai use binding pharmaka to control us, too, then?"

With ambivalence I find both shocking and impressive, Eumelia shrugs and says, "I doubt the Mohirai would use binding pharmaka on novices. Only initiates are supposed to use it, because of the tricky side effects. You've already broken that rule, of course. But you're not the first." Eumelia flashes a cheeky smile at Hanu. Hanu looks back at her coolly. Puzzled, I look from one girl to the other.

"That mouth of yours is going to get you in trouble one day, Mel," Hanu says with dignity. She urges Baba ahead with a light flick of the reins, leaving the three of us behind.

Eumelia groans. "Oh, come on, Hanu!" she calls. "You can't have thought that was a secret!"

What do you think that's about? I wonder. Dom shifts uneasily behind me, and I sense more of his embarrassment.

Must be something else to do with him and Hanu. Well, let him keep his secrets. I have no desire to revisit the awkwardness from this morning. I have far more pressing concerns.

Hanu's parting words chasten Eumelia somewhat, and her mocking expression fades. She changes the subject. "Thanks for the lesson," she says to me.

It's hard for me to focus on Eumelia as my mind churns with all these new questions about pharmaka. But I did tell Dom I'd try to be friendly, and it's a little easier to be kind to Eumelia after Hanu's put her in her place. "Glad it helped," I say. "You and Nisaba ride well together."

Eumelia brightens at my compliment. She leans forward and pats Nisaba's shoulder, saying, "Well, that's more to her credit than mine. Nisaba's splendid. She looks like she'd be fast, too, doesn't she?"

Eumelia's landed on one of the few subjects I find irresistible. For a moment, I forget my other concerns, looking longingly at Nisaba, imagining how well she and I would ride together, if I weren't stuck with Dom and Eridu. "She sure looks fast," I say.

"Want to find out?" Eumelia says, giving me a sly smile. "I seem to remember you love racing."

Dom's hand tingles at my waist, and I feel his surprise as he thinks, *Eumelia remembers you, too? When did that happen?*

I didn't have a chance to tell you, I think, showing him my memory of what happened between me and Eumelia this morning. *It's my fault. I'll stay at the edge of the tent from now on so there's no more accidental touching.*

Dom's amusement is palpable. *You think that was accidental?*

I ignore him, lower my voice, and say to Eumelia, "You can't tell anyone you remember things like that. It's a secret. You promised."

Eumelia's smile widens. She guides Nisaba so close to Eridu that her knee almost touches mine. I look at her warily. So swiftly that I don't have time to pull away, she reaches out, taps the back of my hand lightly with her fingertips, and thinks, *All right. I don't remember all those times I beat you.*

A jumble of memories, mine and hers, flashes before me. Foot races across the meadow. Swim races at the docks. Climbing races in the woods. Races up the stairs of the city alleyways, through the kitchen gardens and temple orchards, even in the library of the Musaion. In most memories, I'm half a stride or half an arm's length behind Eumelia.

I'm stunned that so much can be shared through such a brief touch. Thoughts and emotions seem to flow between me and Eumelia even more easily than they do between me and Dom. The strangest part of re-experiencing these memories through Eumelia's perspective is that, while they look nearly identical to mine, they feel entirely different. I understand for the first time that I love racing because moving at speed feels like freedom. Winning isn't the point, for me. But Eumelia craves the feeling of triumph as much as I crave freedom. Winning is the entire object for her. There's something intriguing about this difference between us. Something that could be useful.

I study Eumelia with new interest. Slowly, I say, "I'd love to race, but the roads through these hills are too winding for an inexperienced rider. And there's Dom to consider. We're not evenly matched with two riders on Eridu and one on Nisaba."

Eumelia dismisses these concerns with a wave. "Arkhi told me we'll be on open plains for days, until we cross over the Purattu. And Serapen told me you should be able to go brief stretches without Dom soon, if you practice what she showed you properly. So practice! Whenever you're ready, I'll be waiting."

Eumelia winks at me and rides off after Hanu. I stare after her, stunned by the idea Eumelia just planted in my mind. A smile spreads slowly over my face. Of course. The Purattu.

Overhearing me, Dom says, "What's the Purattu?"

"Oh …" I think fast. Talk, Ava. Talking makes the sharing stop. "The Purattu. It's a river. It's the outer boundary of the Velkanos temple lands." I try to think of other innocuous facts about the Purattu, but fortunately Dom has more questions.

"Have you been to Velkanos before?" he says with interest.

Not in the way that Dom's thinking, but that's a bit too complicated to explain right now. I say simply, "No. I've crossed the river before, though."

"Is the river far from here?" he says.

"Maybe half a moon's journey," I say, more to myself than to Dom. Half a moon. Will that be enough time?

CHILDREN OF THE VOICE

DOM AND I RIDE at the end of the caravan. Dom has endless questions about the places I've traveled in Dulai, and I'm grateful for all his questions now, since the longer we keep talking, the longer I can keep my thoughts of escape planning to myself.

So I chatter on to Dom, hoping he doesn't notice my divided attention as I study the road ahead, looking for landmarks to help me estimate more precisely how far we are from the Purattu river crossing. I've tramped through quite a lot of Dulai, and I've had a general idea of our location since Arkhi called us to make camp yesterday afternoon. The lightly forested hills we're approaching are distinctive, so now I know exactly where I am.

There, on the north side of the road, is the hilltop grove of oaks where my mother and I made our last camp together three days ago. It was warm and cloudless that night, so we hadn't raised our tent, and we'd had a good view of the surrounding terrain. I remember lying awake past midnight, looking up at the stars through the branches of those oaks, wondering what it was going to feel like to sleep on a boat among the free men.

We hadn't built a fire at that camp because my mother said we might be spotted by Mohirai on the road. Her concern had seemed strange to me at the time, because we'd so rarely encountered anyone on the roads, in all our years of travel. But she must have known the route of the three

Mohirai I'm following now. She would have been familiar with the usual comings and goings of the sisters around the time of the autumn equinox. She likely made this very journey herself, centuries ago, after her own Calling Day ceremony. It's possible she too led a caravan of novices like this one back to Velkanos when she was a priestess, perhaps many times. Perhaps that's how she came to know the roads of Dulai so well. I never thought to ask her. Maybe, if I manage to pull this off, I'll have another chance to ask.

My eyes linger on the hilltop grove as I remember many routes I've taken with my mother that passed by this place. I think I may have estimated right the first time: at the pace our caravan is moving, it should be about half a moon's ride from here to the Purattu ferry crossing that the Mohirai use on the route to Velkanos. My mother and I always steered clear of that ferry crossing—my mother said the ferryman Urshanabi couldn't be trusted—but there's a men's village upriver from Urshanabi's crossing, at the edge of a wide ford. My mother and I crossed the river there several times. I remember a boatwright in that village, with fair hair and pale eyes like my mother's. He accepted a bribe from her about a year ago to pass a message to a sailor headed downriver. My mother never allowed me to speak to the men who were involved in arranging our westward passage, and she usually prevented me from even seeing them, but I still managed to glimpse a few of their faces. If I could find that boatwright, or any of the other men who helped my mother, maybe they would help me like they'd helped her. Maybe they could send a message to my mother. Maybe I could tell her I'm working to counter the effects of the amanitai. Maybe once this work is done, I can return to her, if I can only find out where she's gone.

"Ava," says Dom. I straighten up in alarm. I realize I fell silent some time ago, and my mind has been wandering. I'm not sure how much of this he's overheard.

"A lot of it," he says. "It's hard to block it out. But I don't understand much. Would you just explain it to me? I won't tell anyone else. I promise."

After Arkhi's warning, I'm worried about how much of each other's thoughts we're overhearing, and how much worse our binding is becoming. My thoughts seem to be private only when we're talking or separated. It's going to be impossible to talk indefinitely for the entire journey to the Purattu. And so far I can only endure separation from Dom for very brief stretches of time. Under the circumstances, it's inevitable that I'm going to let something slip. Eventually, whether I like it or not, Dom's going to know something I'll need him to keep secret.

But can I trust Dom? As a boy, he has the most to lose by staying among the Mohirai, and therefore he seems to be my most likely ally as I plan my escape. He's instinctively obedient to the Mohirai, which presents difficulties for me, but it's obvious that he cares about me, too. More than that, he's genuinely curious about what I know. Perhaps, even though he refused to run with me on Calling Day, he might still be persuaded to help me get away on my own.

My stomach twists indecisively. I wish I could trust him, but all my instincts tell me it's foolish. This entire situation is impossible. I yearn for the days when escaping a job gone sideways was as simple as disappearing into Dulai's endless trackless wilderness. Unconsciously, I rein Eridu to a stop, overcome by the desire to dismount and run back toward the woods from which we've come.

"Please don't," says Dom. "You know you can't go without me."

I sigh. He's right. I'm being ridiculous. And if I had even a shred of hope remaining that I might escape here, it's stripped away when Eridu resumes trotting ahead after the caravan without my direction. Arkhi must have summoned Eridu again through this damned saddle blanket. He's as much a part of my trap as Dom, it seems.

"I never meant to trap you," says Dom. "I want to help you, Ava. But how can I help if you keep me in the dark?"

I'm struck by the familiarity of Dom's frustration as it spills into me. It's the same frustration I always felt when my mother withheld something in an effort to protect me. But despite all my mother's efforts, here I am, trapped in a situation that could have been avoided entirely if she'd just been more open with me about what the amanitai could do. As much as I want to protect Dom from the consequences of what I must do, keeping him in the dark is no guarantee he'll be protected from anything.

So I decide I'm going to trust him. What other option do I have? I glance ahead to confirm we're still out of earshot of the others. I say, "All right. I'll explain."

How did my mother explain this all to me for the first time? I think back to that day she found me alone in the woods outside the temple city, at the start of my ninth summer. I remember that she started with what was possible for a child to understand. Dom's a lot older than I was that day, but he can't really know much more than I did then.

So I guess I'd better start with the basics. "Do you know where children come from, Dom?"

△▽△

Ava glances over her shoulder at me. The emotion that spills from her into me is a peculiar mix of apprehension, amusement, and pity. She says, "Do you know where children come from, Dom?"

Feeling foolish, I say, "I've only ever seen children come out of the woods with Serapen."

"You must have seen hundreds of lambs and kids and calves born, though," she says.

"Sure," I say. "I've had to help plenty of their births along."

"Did you ever think we too must have been born, like every other animal?" she says.

I consider this. There are many similarities between us and our animals. They have most of the same basic needs we have—water, food, shelter, companionship. We separate them by male and female for their separate purposes—meat or milk, work or breeding. It's not so different from how the Mohirai separate boys from girls and how our paths diverge.

And like all boys, I've managed the breeding of animals. The way animals conceive and bear young is no mystery to me. However, even if there are some similarities between the sexual appetites of humans and animals, sex seems to serve a different purpose for us than it does for them. Animals rut by instinct, and the act seems to serve no purpose other than breeding for them. But the Mohirai treat sex like music, painting, or pharmaka—an art to be practiced and perfected, one of many ways to experience the mystery in all. No girl or Mohira has ever given birth after sex, to my knowledge. So the purpose of sex for humans, if I had to guess, seems to be pleasure, not breeding.

At last I say, "I guess, if I ever thought about where we came from, I assumed it's another mystery the Mohirai keep. You know how few of the mysteries are explained to children, especially to boys. But I never heard anyone say we're born like the animals are. I've never seen a child born. And I don't remember being born myself."

"It's true, though," says Ava. "All of us were born. I've seen children born."

"You have?" I say, fascinated. "Where?"

"In the villages," she says.

"What? Among the men?" I say.

She laughs and shakes her head, "No, not in the men's villages. There are other villages, outside a few of the larger temple cities, where Mohirai give birth to children."

"I never heard of those villages. Are they another one of the mysteries?"

"I don't think the existence of the villages is a mystery, not exactly," she says. "But very few of the Mohirai are ever called by the Voice to bear a child. How the Voice calls for a child is among the mysteries kept by the initiates, according to my mother."

There's that word again. "Your mother," I say. "Will you tell me what that means? I've only ever heard of mother land, like we say at the meal blessing."

"Mother," Ava says the word softly. "It's an old word. Maybe the oldest word. But the Mohirai don't use the word mother any longer in the old way. The Mohirai changed the meaning of kinship words—mother, sister, brother—after the time of destruction.

"But before the destruction, a mother meant any creature who gives birth and raises young. So my mother is the one who gave birth to me. Your mother is the one who gave birth to you."

"My mother." I say the phrase slowly. The possessive word sounds strange in this context. How can a mother belong to me, when I've never even known such a person existed? "But I don't remember having a mother."

"You're not supposed to remember her," says Ava. "That's why all the young children receive unbinding pharmaka. The Mohirai use it to weaken the connection between mothers and children, so our memories of them and their memories of us are lost."

We ride in silence for a long time as I consider this, searching my memory for some sign of this supposed mother of mine. My mind roams through eight years in the house of boys. Hundreds of identical repetitions of wake-up calls, meal blessings, chores, and bedtime pharmaka blur together across the seasons. The faces of Balashi, Kuri, Hanu, Eumelia, and all my other brothers and sisters grow younger and younger the further back I go, while the faces of the Mohirai remain always the same.

Somewhere in the early days of my time at the house of boys, I reach a place in my memory that seems cloaked in fog and shadows. Vague forms hover just at the edge of my perception here, and whenever I reach out for one of these memories, it retreats from me, always just beyond my grasp. Focusing on this unsettling fog requires enormous effort, and it's a relief to give up trying to remember.

I say, "But why do the Mohirai do this, unbinding children and mothers?"

Ava doesn't answer me as quickly this time as before. I recognize the feeling spilling from her into me. It's grief—silent tears in the moonlight as she realizes her mother has left her. But now her grief is for me, feeling the loss of my mother on my behalf. I wonder whether I should be feeling this for myself. But I can't grieve the loss of something I can't remember. She squeezes my hand and says, "Did any of the Mohirai ever say to you, when you were sad, something like this? Peace, child …"

I repeat the familiar words of soothing, "Peace, child. The Voice loves you. You belong to the Voice."

Ava nods and says, "The Mohirai teach that all children born since the time of destruction belong to the Voice in all. They teach that our purpose is to serve the Voice. The Mohirai unbind children from mothers to ensure that the strongest bond we'll ever know is the bond with the Voice that's formed on Calling Day."

I don't understand Ava's anger as she says this. Tentatively, I say, "But isn't it better for all of us to have a strong bond with the Voice? Doesn't that make it easier to answer our calling and perform our service to the Voice?"

Ava says, "It's only better if you believe what the sisters teach: that we belong to the Voice. But that's not what my mother taught me. My mother says we belong to ourselves.

We can choose how to live our lives. We don't have to serve the Voice in all."

Of all the strange things Ava's told me, this is the strangest by far. The Mohirai say that the purpose of my life is to serve the Voice in all, and they've never given me reason to doubt their trustworthiness or truthfulness. Ava contradicts the sisters' fundamental teaching with deep conviction, but what she's saying doesn't make sense to me. I say, "If your mother is right, then why are you here?"

"What do you mean?" she says.

"Well, Serapen said the Voice is the only thing that keeps you here. If it's true that you don't have to serve the Voice, why can't you leave?"

MUTUAL FEELINGS

"IF IT'S TRUE that you don't have to serve the Voice, why can't you leave?"

Until Dom asked this question, I thought I was persuading him to help me. I'd hoped that once he knew what I knew, he'd believe what I believe: the Voice must be avoided and the Mohirai can't be trusted. Now I realize I've persuaded him of nothing. Instead, he's turned my own conviction into doubt.

Why can't I leave? The most obvious answer may be the right answer, and I'm afraid of this answer. But my mother always says that understanding comes from facing reality without fear. Reluctantly, I let myself consider that maybe my freedom from the Voice ended with my overdose. Maybe this unwanted bond is irreversible. Maybe I've lost, the Voice has won, and all that's left to me now is the life my mother tried so hard to save me from.

Dom's arm tightens around my waist, and I realize I'm swaying in the saddle, shivering. He takes Eridu's reins from my shaking hands and pulls us to a stop. "What's wrong, Ava?"

I grip the saddle pommel to steady myself. "I don't want to talk about this any more right now," I say, pushing away the hopelessness that's closing in on me from all directions. "Can we just ride?"

Dom keeps the reins and nudges Eridu onward. After a while, he says, "I think I understand a little of what you're feeling. I was feeling the same way, just before I found you."

My curiosity dispels some of my gloom. For the first time, I wonder what happened to Dom that led him to be in the woods the night he found me.

Dom says, "For almost as long as I can remember, I thought I'd spend my life far from the arts and mysteries. I didn't want that life, but I knew I had to go where the Voice called me." As he remembers how this felt, I feel it too: dread, uncertainty, powerlessness.

I say, "But if you felt like that, why didn't you come with me when I asked you to run on Calling Day?"

"The whole idea seemed like madness," he says. "It still does. Even if we weren't bound together this way, how far could we possibly get on our own, without supplies, without horses, without any help from the Mohirai?"

"I would have figured it out," I say. "I've done harder things than that before."

"Have you?" he says. "Well, I haven't. And I wasn't going to risk my one shot at hearing the Voice."

I overhear a bit of his next thought and say, "You think it was the right decision, not to come with me."

"Not exactly," he says. "It's more that I'm glad I heard the Voice. I've never been more certain about anything than I was in the moment I answered my call."

"And I'm happy for you," I say. "But you don't even know what it means, to be an Artifex. How do you know that's what you want?"

Dom shrugs. "I don't know whether it's what I want. Like you said, I have no idea what it means to be an Artifex, apart from the little bit Serapen told me. But … I don't know if this makes sense, but have you ever wondered whether wanting something is useful? I spent so much time wanting to be a Mohira because I thought that was the only way I'd ever be allowed to learn the mysteries. Now it seems like all that wanting—and all the unhappiness I felt because I wanted something impossible—was such a waste. None of it changed what's happened to me, and what's happened is actually better than I'd expected.

"I might have been happier all this time if I hadn't been so focused on what I thought I wanted. Maybe it's better to accept things as they are and trust in the Voice, like the Mohirai teach. Maybe it's better not to worry so much about what I want."

I shake my head in disbelief, disagreeing with so many aspects of what Dom's said that I don't know where to begin.

Dom chuckles and says, "So you think I'd be better off worrying about it?"

"You know I don't think worrying is useful," I say. "For that matter, I wish you'd stop worrying so much about me. But wanting is useful. If you don't want anything, how can you ever know what you need to do next? Until this accident with the amanitai, I knew what to do because I knew what I wanted. I wanted to escape from the Voice and the Mohirai. I wanted to get on that boat."

"But your wanting to get on the boat didn't matter in the end," he says. "You've ended up in exactly the same place you would have been if you'd never heard of that boat."

"That's not true," I say, growing heated. "I'm not in exactly the same place as the rest of you. This—" I sweep my hand in a gesture that encompasses me and him, the caravan, this entire situation. "This isn't permanent. Eventually, I'll find my way out of this. And when I do, it will be because I wanted to find a way out."

He says, "You think that wanting to find a way out will be enough?"

I say, "I didn't mean that wanting is enough. But it's a start. I'll need your help, too."

"Only mine?" he says.

Clearly Dom is trying to get me to see something, but I'm not sure what it is. I consider the vague outline of the plan I'd been contemplating earlier: making my way to the nearest coastal village, negotiating a deal with the boatwright, sending a message to my mother through the sailors on the delivery routes. "Well, no," I say. "I'll need a lot of people's help."

"And you think all of those people will help you, if it's not something the Voice wants, too?" he says.

"What are you trying to say, Dom?" I can't keep the frustration out of my voice. "That I should accept there's nothing I can do about any of this? That I'm helpless?"

"No, no, that's not it at all," he says. "Sorry, it's so much harder when we're trying to talk this way. What I mean is—" His palm tingles against my waist as he thinks, *The Mohirai teach that the Voice works toward its own purposes, in its own time. If the Mohirai are right, shouldn't you try to understand what the Voice wants? Maybe you can work with the Voice, rather than fight against it.*

My fear of the Voice runs so deep that I've never really tried to understand what it might want, beyond its desire to control me. Imagining the Voice as an ally rather than an opponent is an intriguing change in perspective, opening up many possibilities. I'm surprised by Dom's insight.

"Why are you surprised?" he says, in a tone that would sound joking if I couldn't also feel the bitterness behind his words. "You think because I'm a boy, I can't have ideas of my own?"

Gently, I say, "Of course I don't think that, Dom." I know Arkhi warned us against sharing thoughts and feelings, because we could hurt each other. But something has already hurt Dom, and I want to understand what it is. I close my eyes to focus, searching for the source of Dom's bitterness. He lets me find it, and the feeling flows into me: his frustration with being always underestimated, always assumed to be less capable, always treated as less worthy of respect.

I know this feeling. For both of us, the frustration is rooted in the constraints of our bodies—mine so small, his so male. Neither of us fits into our world the way we wish we did.

I wish there was something I could do to change these constraints, for Dom and for myself. But I can't change his physical form any more than I can change my own. I think, *It always seemed wrong to me how the Mohirai treat the boys so differently from the girls. I never really understood why it was wrong, though, until you and I were connected this way. What we have in common is so much more than what separates us.*

Something about my thought sends Dom's own thoughts reeling. I don't understand why until I overhear, *I'll hide nothing from you. We'll share everything as equals. I promise.* I recognize these words as my own. But hearing them from his perspective, feeling his reaction to them, I realize they mean so much more to him than I could have imagined. Despite all Dom's said about how pointless it may be to want anything, I feel how desperately he wants the inclusion every girl can take for granted.

Did you really mean it? he wonders, *Would you have treated me as your equal, if I had gone with you?*

Dom's desire for me to say yes is almost strong enough to pull the words out of me before I'm ready to answer. I resist, alarmed by the sensation of his awareness trying to control mine. For the first time I understand the danger Serapen described, how the bond between us could be used to manipulate each other. Fortunately, this time, what Dom wants to be true is the same as what's actually true.

I did mean it, I think. *And I still want to share everything as equals, even if you don't want to come with me.*

Dom's awareness usually feels much calmer than mine, but my words stir a whirlwind of conflicting desires in him. He wants to trust the Mohirai, and he wants to trust me. He wants to follow his calling, and he wants to follow me. I'm momentarily drawn toward this fascinating tumult in his mind, until I realize I'm losing the ability to differentiate his thoughts from my own. It's an unsettling sensation, far too much like the loss of my self-awareness that happens when I hear the Voice.

I panic at the thought that I've accidentally erased some critical boundary between myself and Dom. Frantically, I try to remember what Arkhi said to us this morning, when she warned us of the risk of sharing thoughts. *Choose an intention, focus on it, and remember it.* I grasp for something that seems like a good intention: for Dom to decide for himself what he wants, whom to trust, whom to follow. I focus my entire awareness on this intention as best I can.

Though my focus wanders again and again, I pull it back to this intention, and the intensity of Dom's thoughts slowly recedes from me. I become more aware of the steady clop of Eridu's hooves, the distant sound of girls' voices from the caravan ahead, the rush of wind through the grassy hills. Gradually, I relax. I can't quite block out my awareness of Dom's agitation, since he's still holding on to me, but the boundary between our innermost thoughts seems to have solidified once more.

I'm still struggling with my unruly focus when Dom says, "I believe you. And I'll help you leave, when you're ready to go. But not as a brother obeying a sister's command, or as a man serving a Mohira. Just as a friend helping a friend."

I hadn't considered that he might want to help me purely for friendship's sake. Over the last seven years, I've learned to see everyone else as either an opponent or an ally. To secure an ally usually requires shared interests, persuasion, sometimes bribery. I've been so focused on turning Dom from an opponent into an ally that I'd failed to see he might be something else entirely.

"So we can be friends again?" I say, surprised by how much I want this. It's been so long since I last had a friend.

"I don't think we ever stopped being friends," says Dom. "It's more like our friendship was lost, and now we've found it again."

Dom speaks with the same unguarded sweetness as the little boy who sat beside me in the forest seven summers ago, playing with river stones. I'm startled by my fierce protectiveness of his innocent openness, because I fear that somehow it must lead to that grim-faced Dom I glimpsed on Calling Day, a man so changed from the boy I know. As much as I want Dom's friendship, I worry that my friendship will do nothing but harm him.

Overhearing my thought, Dom says, in a bright, animated voice utterly unlike his own, "I'm fine, Ava. Don't worry about me."

I look over my shoulder at him and shoot him a mock glare. "Is that supposed to be me?" I say.

He grins. I elbow him in the ribs. "Ow!" he exclaims. "I thought we agreed to be careful with each other."

"I thought you wanted me to treat you like any other girl," I say.

"Is this how you treat other girls?" he says.

"I'm not this gentle with other girls," I say, and he laughs.

△▽△

Ava and I settle into a routine over the next several days on the road. Our mornings begin well before dawn. Ava always wakes first. She tries to keep perfectly still beside me, to let me sleep as long as possible. But as soon as she's awake, her mind begins to race. She's always eager to start the new day, hoping for some breakthrough in her work to ease the binding between us. Her anticipation spills into me, making it impossible for either of us to fall back asleep, so we make our way together out of the tent, as quietly as we can.

Each morning, we see Serapen somewhere at the edge of camp in the predawn twilight. She's nearly invisible in her dark cloak, seated cross-legged on the ground, facing east. Sometimes she raises a hand to us in greeting, but she always remains silent, listening as the early birds herald the sun. I have no idea when, or whether, the High Priestess sleeps.

Each morning, Ava finds a new spot to practice her unbinding. There we sit until sunrise. I stay close beside her, so she can reach my hand if she needs me, and I can reach hers if I need to intervene. The work consumes all of Ava's focus, so we speak very little until she's done. At the end of these morning sessions, when Ava takes my hand, I often notice residual effects of her time alone with the Voice. I feel traces of unfamiliar sensations, overhear peculiar thoughts, and glimpse strange images. Sometimes I ask her what these things mean, but she seems as mystified by them as I am.

After each session, as the sun rises, we return to camp, make ready for the day's travel, and resume the long eastward march.

Each evening, we raise the tents and eat the evening meal. The other novices and the Mohirai often relax around the fire if the weather is clear, but Ava always wants to resume practicing, no matter how tiring the day's journey has been or how bad the weather might be. Our evening sessions are longer, continuing long past sunset, until she's completely spent.

Although the work is exhausting, Ava's progress is rapid. Each day, she's able to sit apart from me for longer before the pain becomes too much to bear. Sometimes we practice walking along the road, back and forth, without holding hands. Each time, we walk farther before Ava's breathing turns into painful gasps.

Almost every day, she tells me how much better and stronger she feels, her eyes bright with hope, even though the rest of her looks pale and weakened. Often, after particularly difficult sessions, I notice that strange translucency about her that I noticed our first night on the road, like some part of her has dissolved into the air. And every night, she needs more and more time to warm up in my arms before she falls asleep. I worry that she's pushing herself too hard, but every time I suggest we take a break this evening, or end a session sooner, she pleads with me to continue. "You said you'd help me, Dom. Please, do this for me." I find it impossible to refuse.

Between these morning and evening sessions, we ride. We use all sorts of tricks to pass the time and practice shielding our thoughts from one another. We join in enthusiastically, if not particularly tunefully, with the rest of the girls whenever Thalia proposes a caravan song. We listen to Narua recite epic poems in a rhythmic voice that carries over the hoofbeats of the caravan—poems that hold Ava's attention long after I've gotten lost in all the unfamiliar names and places. On flat stretches of road, we race ahead on Eridu, often chased by Eumelia on Nisaba, until Arkhi recalls us.

Despite our best efforts, though, it's impossible to maintain perfect mental discipline all the time, and these games and distractions have their limits. At times, I catch glimpses of unguarded thoughts in Ava's mind that show me she's still keeping secrets from me, even though I've promised I won't tell anyone about her escape plan. I wish she would trust me. Things would be easier between us that way. But I know trust is built over time, and it can be destroyed in an instant. Ava's trust has been destroyed so many times in so many ways that I can't blame her for distrusting me.

Increasingly, as the journey wears on, Ava slips into long silences. When she does, it's hard for me to stop myself from following her wandering thoughts and daydreams. Her mind fascinates me. It's so entirely different from my own.

What I notice most about Ava's awareness is how she questions the meaning of everything. When a Mohira says something mysterious, or we pass a ruin at the roadside, or Eumelia and Hanu exchange a look, Ava's mind generates a hundred penetrating questions before I realize there's a question worth asking. She can be deeply perceptive when she focuses her attention.

And yet Ava often fails to see what's directly in front of us. To me, each landscape we pass appears entirely solid and real, full of color and texture and movement. But through Ava's eyes, this solid reality seems to melt away into abstractions. What surrounds Ava is a bright foreground of the possibilities she finds most interesting, against a blurry background of uncertainties, complexities, and interconnections still to be untangled.

Where I see picturesque roads winding through forested hills, Ava notes specific patches of woods thick with beechnuts and blackberries, worth remembering for a return journey if she manages to escape before the winter snows. Where I see washouts that mar the level symmetry of the ancient paving stones over which we ride, Ava focuses on the dried-up streambeds that lead to a river that leads to a village where she once raided the food storerooms. Where I see the interplay of light and shadow on a rocky scree, Ava marks the cave openings where she could take shelter from rain, wind, and cold. Ava sees the world as a collection of opportunities to be seized and risks to be avoided.

I understand now why Ava was so frustrated with me when I suggested that perhaps it's better to simply accept things as they are. She spends so much time imagining how things could be and what she needs to do to make those things happen. She's always planning ahead.

But Ava's thoughts aren't all as practical as planning her escape. When she daydreams, she always seems to return to the place I glimpsed the night I found her in the woods: that beautiful, improbable, monumental city of glass towers. Unlike the world around us, which often fades into abstractions in her mind, this city seems entirely solid and real to her. It's so real to her that if I don't resist, I'm drawn in after her.

There's a beauty to this strange other world in her mind —an order and a scale and an energy quite unlike the woods and fields and shorelines where I've spent my life. I marvel at the tall buildings, at the crush of people and their strange machines, at the many languages and peculiar sounds and smells of this place. When we fly over the city from a great height or pass through the streets at speed, there's a grandeur to it unlike anything else I've ever experienced.

But when Ava moves through the city of glass towers more slowly, my impressions are more complicated. I feel the complete absence of wilderness and wild creatures, which makes this place feel untethered from the land beneath it. I see human filth that turns my stomach. I'm horrified by the sight of all the sick and infirm tucked in doorways and alleys, untended and unnoticed. I'm puzzled by the people drifting past one another in the streets like they don't see each other. And everywhere, eyes are covered in strange masks, locked on glowing tablets, turned inward. The people in this world are blind to their surroundings in the same way that Ava often seems blind to hers. As I look into all these unseeing eyes, I can't help feeling sorry for them.

And yet, despite all the flaws of this world, I envy the men living here. Everywhere I see them doing forbidden things: wearing bright colors, reading books, playing instruments, caring for children, commanding women. Some of them clearly hold as much power as initiate Mohirai, perhaps even more.

Ava's daydreams inspire my own, and I often find myself unconsciously modifying what I've seen in her mind, preserving what's beautiful about the city, removing what seems broken, adding what seems missing. I can lose myself in reimagining like I lose myself in sketching. When I listen, the city of glass towers calls to me, revealing its proper form and scale. Streets grow wider and greener, people and machines move more slowly, masks disappear from eyes.

I'm not sure how long I've been wandering through these imagined streets one morning when Ava murmurs, "Beautiful."

"Hmm?" I blink, and my daydream fades away. I'm surprised to see the sun's almost directly overhead. The caravan stands stopped at a crossroads, and the girls ahead are dismounting. Somehow half the day has slipped by in what felt like an instant.

"The way you imagine the city," says Ava. "It looks so beautiful."

"You could see that?" I ask. I'm pleased by Ava's praise, but self-conscious at the realization she's been observing me at work this whole time.

"Sorry for peeking. You just seemed so focused—I didn't want to interrupt. But Arkhi says we need to water the horses quickly now, before the windstorm."

"Windstorm?" I say.

Ava laughs. "Spirits, you really drifted off, didn't you? Arkhi said there's a windstorm coming. We need to make camp and take shelter before it hits."

I dismount, and Ava hops off after me. She doesn't take my hand, so I know she wants to practice separation while we're out of the saddle. I follow as she leads Eridu toward the small pool by the crossroads where the other girls are gathering. The horses crowd along the cracked mud banks in the shade of a few scraggly trees, drinking deep from water that looks decidedly unappealing to me. Whorls of sand skitter around our boots and between the horses' hooves, following the breeze.

"Where are we?" I say. Ahead, a dusty plain stretches as far as I can see—golden sand and clumps of tenacious silver-grey scrub beneath a cloudless blue sky. The sight of this barren landscape devoid of trees unsettles me. The familiar ache of separation from Ava rebuilds in my chest, adding to my uneasiness.

"The Subartu Desert," says Ava, wiping the dust from her face with her shirtsleeve. "Not my favorite place."

"You've been here before?" I say, wondering why anyone

would come here by choice.

Ava nods, squinting against a gust of gritty wind. "It's not an easy crossing," she says. "But we should be on the other side of it in a few days, if this windstorm isn't too bad."

A few days? I don't like the sound of that. I shade my eyes and look toward the eastern horizon. So much of my energy has been consumed in helping Ava practice unbinding that the days have started to run together. I've lost my sense of where we are on the route. But I vaguely recall Arkhi's description of the desert, and of the Purattu river that runs down its middle. Ava said the Purattu marks the boundary of the temple lands of Velkanos, though the temple city itself is another half moon's journey eastward from the river crossing.

No amount of Arkhi's description of the desert could have prepared me for the actual sight of it, though. I'm alarmed to see nothing green east of here beyond the few blades of grass growing in the shade around this murky pool. "What will we do for water until we reach the Purattu?" I ask, struggling to suppress my growing anxiety.

△▽△

I'm squinting at the eastern horizon, looking for signs of Arkhi's predicted windstorm, when Dom says, "What will we do for water until we reach the Purattu?"

My stomach twists strangely. It's not the prickling or stabbing chest pain that's become so familiar since my amanitai overdose. There is a little bit of that pain, too, but it's so familiar now that I hardly notice it. No, the feeling I'm noticing is anxious apprehension of the road ahead, a sense of foreboding.

Usually I trust intuitive feelings like this one. Intuition has saved me from many mishaps. But I've crossed this part of the Subartu Desert a few times with my mother. The road isn't difficult, and although some of the watering holes will be dry at this time of year, there should still be plenty between here and the Purattu. It's really only the wind we need to worry about. Even on a relatively easy crossing, the wind is a formidable opponent, and a major windstorm can be dangerous without shelter. However, if there's one thing I've learned to trust on this journey, it's the remarkable accuracy of Arkhi's predictions. If she says we'll be able to weather this particular windstorm at camp, I'm not going to worry about it. I have plenty to worry about already.

I turn back toward Dom, who looks out at the desert with a troubled expression. Ah. This is not some anxious intuition of mine. This is his anxiety I'm feeling, even though we're not touching.

I'd wondered whether this might happen. It's been clear to me almost from the start that the bond between me and Dom works at a distance. How else could he feel my pain when we're not touching? But until recently, the severity of my pain while we're separated has been so intense that it drowns out my awareness of anything but the pain itself. After nearly half a moon of practice, though, I'm growing more adept at managing the pain that comes when I hear the Voice. Perhaps as that pain lessens, it creates more space in my awareness for what Dom's feeling.

Until this moment, I'd allowed myself to hope that as my awareness of the Voice became less painful, my awareness of

Dom would lessen, too. But that was wishful thinking. Arkhi's warning at the start of the journey was pretty clear. *You and Dom have already formed a far deeper bond than any initiate would create by choice, and the more you use the bond between you, the stronger it will become.*

Of course the only alternative to using the bond with Dom is to use the unbinding pharmaka from Serapen, and that's not much of an alternative. What's the point of freeing myself from the Voice with unbinding pharmaka if it makes me forget who I am and where I need to go?

My amplified sense of Dom's anxiety, although unwanted, is definitely better than memory loss or mind-obliterating pain from the Voice. This is a feeling I can handle without any special arts.

I take Dom's hands in mine and say, "Don't worry. There's water in the desert, if you know where to look, and the Mohirai know where to find it. You're safe with them."

Dom and I smile at each other, and gratitude floods through me, unusually strong because it's a mutual feeling. Dom's grateful for my words of comfort, and I'm grateful for the chance to return a small bit of the comfort he's given me on every step of this journey. I wish there was more I could give him before I have to go.

Dom's smile fades. I bite my lip when I realize I let my guard down long enough for him to overhear that.

Dom's grip on my hand tightens. "You're planning to go soon, then?" he asks quietly.

Of course it's no secret between us that I'm leaving. Every day is full of my preparations for departure, most of which I can't hide from Dom. Still, I've avoided sharing specifics about my plan, and Dom hasn't pressed me for details, which I appreciate. I do trust Dom, and it means a lot that he's offered to help me, but there are already so many unknowns in my plan without the added risk that Dom might—wittingly or unwittingly—give away my plan to the Mohirai.

I can't see any point in denying what he already knows, though. So I say, "Yes."

Dom's head and shoulders drop together, a resigned posture that reminds me of his obedient deference to the Mohirai. Some essential part of him withdraws behind that lowered gaze. I hate to see him looking like this, especially knowing I'm the cause. Am I just as bad as any other Mohira, using Dom while it's convenient for me, casting him off when he's served his purpose, making him feel invisible? My guilt at this thought is unbearable.

"Listen," I say, and his eyes meet mine again. I reach up and smooth away the worried crease between his brows with my thumb. "My offer from Calling Day still stands. If you want to come, just tell me. I'll take you with me. I promise."

I'd hoped this reminder would make Dom feel … I'm not sure what, exactly. Better, somehow. Less like I'm abandoning him. But instead, he's unhappier. "What's wrong?" I ask, dismayed that I've done the opposite of what I'd intended.

He studies my face. "Do you want me to come with you?" he says.

"I want you to decide for yourself what you want, Dom," I say. "I can't decide for you."

He continues to struggle with something, until finally he says, "Would you feel like I'd trapped you again, if I came with you?"

I chuckle, hearing in this question how well Dom knows me. I say, "Maybe I would sometimes. Spirits, especially when you're looking at me with those awful worried eyes! But if you really wanted to come with me, I'd never leave you behind."

His expression brightens. At last, it seems I've managed to say the right thing. I don't want to give away too much, but I also want to make sure I've been clear, so I add, "You need to decide soon, though, Dom. Can you do that?"

"How soon?" he asks.

My gaze drifts eastward as I say, "The sooner, the better."

△▽△

I've grown accustomed to exhausting days and rough nights over the first part of our journey. There's been the ongoing struggle to manage Ava's pain, cold, and weakness; her grueling practice sessions with the Voice morning and evening; the effort required to minimize shared thoughts while riding; the strange glimpses of each other's dreams that disturb our sleep. But the cumulative exhaustion of all that is nothing compared to the delirium brought on by our caravan's grinding march across the windswept Subartu Desert.

I might have expected a flat, straight road to make for easy riding after so many days on steep, winding, crumbling roads through the hills. Unfortunately, though the windstorm Arkhi predicted passes quickly over us the night we camp at the edge of the desert, there's no reprieve on the vast plain from the ceaseless shifting winds.

At the start of the desert crossing, Arkhi shows us how to tie cloths over our noses and mouths, how to wrap scarves around our heads and shoulders to protect our skin from the scouring wind. She gives us devices to protect our eyes, which she calls eye glasses. I examine the glasses Arkhi hands me with confusion, but Ava seems to know already how they work, and she shows me how to position the glass discs over my eyes and secure the leather straps behind my head. It takes me half a day to grow accustomed to looking at the world through this strange green darkness, and I never grow entirely accustomed to the bizarre appearance of Ava or the other girls when they're wearing these glasses. Still, wearing the glasses is much better than squinting through dust clouds as we travel through the dazzling expanse of sun-bleached desert.

Despite these protections, the wind drives dust, grit, and sand into the eyes, mouths, and noses of every horse and rider, until at last even relentlessly high-spirited Thalia is subdued. The desert works its way into every crevice of our clothing, saddlebags, and bedrolls. It's impossible to wash anything, even when we do encounter the little watering holes Ava promised we'd find, because the windblown sand immediately adheres to any clean surface. We resign ourselves to a weary cycle of chafing riding, gritty eating, and itchy sleeping. To my relief, Ava reluctantly decides we should stop our morning and evening practice sessions, at least until the wind subsides.

The discomfort wears us down, making it harder for me and Ava to shield each other from sharing sensations, which amplifies the discomfort for us both. After the first half day of riding in these miserable conditions, I propose riding in front on Eridu. Ava's too small to shield me from the wind, but I could shield her from it if she'd let me, and then at least one of us would be a bit more comfortable. She humbly agrees to ride behind me, and this turns out to be an even greater improvement than either of us expects, because Ava quickly discovers that by focusing on her own comparative sense of well-being, she can share it with me, too. She also discovers a new use for her vivid daydreams: sharing them distracts both of us from our present circumstances.

So I'm riding in front on the early afternoon of our third day crossing the desert. I've been hunched into a headwind for some time, and I lift my head for a moment to roll my shoulders and stretch my aching neck. Ahead, I notice something new on the horizon for the first time in days. I push the tinted glasses back on my forehead and squint through the dust. I'm not imagining it—there's a dark green line in the distance.

Ava? I think. At Ava's insistence, I've given up speaking while riding. Shouting over the wind is difficult, and my throat is raw and sore from breathing in so much dust. *Is that a forest?* She can't easily see around me, so I share what I'm seeing with her. My skin tingles where her hand rests on my hip.

She straightens up. "That's the west bank of the Purattu!" she exclaims, squeezing me around the middle with such excitement that I start to laugh, which immediately turns into dusty coughing.

THE GREAT PURATTU

As soon as Dom shows me his first glimpse of the Purattu, all I want is to gallop the rest of the way to the river's edge. But that would be cruel to both Dom and Eridu, who've borne the brunt of the terrible wind for almost three days. So I wait as patiently as I can, and the caravan plods on at a pace that's even more excruciating now that relief's in sight.

What's the river like? Dom wonders, offering a distraction for me as much as for himself.

My face is completely covered by my headscarf, my cheek nestled in the space between Dom's shoulder blades, so I don't bother trying to answer him aloud. Instead, I remember the last time I crossed the Purattu with my mother. What stands out in my memory most clearly is how I pretended to clumsily spill an entire waterskin down the back of the helpful man who thought he was transporting a Mohira and a novice across the ford on his skiff. How my mother pretended to chastise me as she helped him dry the water off with a bright blue cloth. How the expression in his eyes grew distant as my mother slowly erased his memory of us and of our crossing with a series of subtle touches. But I suppose none of that answers Dom's question about what the river is like.

I close my eyes and try to focus on what Dom might have noticed, had he been with me that day. He observes so much form and movement, color and texture, sound and scent when he looks at the world. So I think of the long shoreline hugged by cool, shady groves of rustling willows. The scents of fresh water and river weeds. The sparkling blue current carving smooth hollows in steep stone cliffs and curving languidly around sandy grey beaches. The luff of a patched canvas sail above me, and the dip and splash of oars beside me. The indignant calls of *krek krek krek* from an enormous floating flock of ducks, their comical faces striped amber and emerald. My sudden exhilaration as the entire flock takes flight around me, a whirlwind of wings ascending into the blue sky. Even now, this memory makes me smile.

Dom wants to linger in that moment, so I do, and he steps inside it with me. The harsh desert wind recedes from our awareness. We sit together instead at the bow of the little skiff, and I grin up at the birds, pleased that I've remembered something that pleases him. I glance at him, and my pulse quickens at the expression in his eyes, which I've seen once before, but not on this boyish face. My memory falters, and the whirlwind of wings slips away.

Unsettled, I think, *Sorry. I ... I guess I'm so tired that it's hard to hold the memory steady. You'll love it, though. The river's magnificent.*

It's late afternoon by the time the caravan reaches the outermost stands of oak and pistachio that line the river. The choking clouds of dust subside as the road descends toward the water's edge. Dom and I push back our hoods, remove our filthy headscarves, and let our glasses hang loose around our necks. By the time the road reaches its end at the river's edge, all that remains of the wearying wind is a gentle breeze off the sparkling water.

"We'll make camp downriver, not much farther," Arkhi

calls back to me and Dom. I pass the message down the line behind us. Arkhi turns south onto a narrow, well-worn trail that weaves through the enormous willows along the water's edge.

When Eridu unexpectedly prances forward, cutting ahead of Arkhi, I grip Dom tight around the waist to catch my balance. "Where are you going?" I say.

"It's not me!" he says, bewildered.

I cast a suspicious look at Arkhi as we pass her. She chuckles and says, "It's not me, either. But don't worry, Eridu's not going far." She nudges Khaos to a trot and follows close at our heels.

I peer around Dom's shoulder to see where Eridu's taking us. We emerge from the willows onto a wide stretch of lush grass that edges a sandy beach. The beach is enclosed on three sides by short, tawny cliffs. Atop the cliffs stands a small stone house with whitewashed walls, a blue door, and two little windows that look out across the river. A staircase carved into the cliffside descends from the house to the beach.

A sandbar divides the broad, clear shallows near the beach from the darker blue current beyond, and a long wooden dock spans the distance from the beach to the deep water. A boat with a high, curving bow and a low, flat stern is secured to the dock by two heavy ropes.

On the raised platform at the bow of the boat, a man sits on a little stool. He mends a section of canvas sail that flaps around him in the breeze. The man looks up at our approach, and a broad smile spreads across his deeply lined face.

"Urshanabi!" Arkhi calls, waving excitedly at the

ferryman.

Eridu prances up to the dock and whinnies at Urshanabi, who promptly rolls up the sail he was mending and jumps over the side of the boat onto the dock. He offers Eridu a small apple from his pocket and presses his forehead to the white star on Eridu's. "Hello, old friend," he says. He turns with open arms toward Arkhi, who has already dismounted and rushes up to embrace him. "How goes the journey, Ark?" he says.

It's hard for me to reconcile the harmless-looking little man before me with the mental picture I had of the ferryman my mother said must not be trusted. I study Urshanabi as he and Arkhi exchange their news—his of the river, hers of the road. He's at least a head shorter than Arkhi, perfectly bald, barechested, and barefoot. His trimmed white beard forms a bright contrast to his brown skin, which gleams like a polished acorn shell in the sun. A dark tattoo of some intricate pattern, like tree roots, winds around the left side of his sinewy torso. He wears loose, knee-length, bright white breeches secured at the waist by a worn leather belt.

Dom and I dismount and stand behind Arkhi on the dock. Urshanabi turns toward us, and I expect Arkhi to introduce us now, but instead she looks from us to Urshanabi with an inscrutable smile. "Hmmmm," he says, tapping the side of his nose with one long finger, the wrinkles around his eyes deepening as he examines us. "My, my, my, how the time slips by, swift as the river herself. How are you, Dom? And you, Ava?"

Arkhi and Urshanabi smile at each other as if they've shared a joke. Dom and I glance at each other, confused. I'm too perturbed by all the questions this greeting raises to figure out how to respond. Has Arkhi told him our names somehow that we couldn't hear? Has this man met us before, but we can't remember him? Who is this man, exactly?

"Sorry ... how do you know our names?" asks Dom, his voice still raspy with dust.

Urshanabi smiles, revealing gleaming white teeth. He settles one hand on Dom's shoulder and the other on mine, drawing our three heads together as if to share a secret. His oiled skin gives off a spicy scent of pharmaka, and his voice is merry as he says, "Every child of the new generation is a gift that I remember well."

"But we don't remember you," I say warily.

Urshanabi's expression turns more thoughtful as he looks at me. He nods as he says, "Yes, yes, yes. It's a gift sometimes to forget, as well. But I trust you'll remember me from now on."

He claps our shoulders companionably and turns to welcome Thalia and Serapen, who approach the dock with more of the novices. By way of explanation, Arkhi says to Dom, "Urshanabi's been a ferryman on the Purattu since the time of kings. Every child takes his ferry on the westward route to the Children's Temple, and he takes great pride in his long memory."

Urshanabi repeats his trick several times, surprising one girl after another by knowing her name. I wonder how many times Urshanabi has done this before. Spirits, it would be countless times if he's really been ferryman since the time of kings. That would make him as old as Serapen. I've never heard of a man living for so many centuries.

After a while, Arkhi raises her voice over the noise of all the greetings and says, "I'm sorry to cut this short, but we should make camp before the rain so everyone will have time to prepare for the feast."

This is the first I'm hearing of a feast. Clearly it's intended as a pleasant surprise, and the news elicits a delighted response from the other girls. It's not such a pleasant surprise for me, but I try not to let it show. There's no such thing as a job without complications, and I imagine this will be the first of many. I'll have to make it work.

"Quite right, quite right, quite right," says Urshanabi. "All is ready on my end, but of course you must refresh yourselves after the desert crossing. I look forward to the pleasure of your company tonight."

Thalia clasps Urshanabi's hand and says, "Our revels make this journey worth the trouble, dear brother."

"You are the essential ingredient, sweet Muse," Urshanabi says, inclining his head.

"Careful, brother," Arkhi says dryly. "Flattery will get you everywhere with her."

For the first time in several days, Thalia's bright laugh rings out. She drops a kiss on Urshanabi's shiny bald head and says with a wink, "Until tonight."

Arkhi calls us to follow her to the campsite. I take Eridu by the lead and Dom by the hand, and we walk with the rest of the girls from the dock toward a row of shallow alcoves worn into the base of the cliffs. The alcoves look like they should offer good shelter from the predicted rain. Arkhi points out where we should unload the gear and where each trio should set up their tent.

"What was Arkhi saying before?" Dom asks as we unload Eridu. "Urshanabi's been ferryman since the time of what?"

"The time of kings," I say. I remember first learning about the ages of Dulai from the Mohirai in the Children's Temple, and my mother continued instructing me in historia after she took me away from the sisters. Of course Dom wouldn't have learned any of this, since historia is kept among the mysteries for boys. I thought it was kept as a mystery from men, too. But based on what the Mohirai have said so far about the Artifexi, and especially now that Arkhi has mentioned the time of kings to Dom, I suppose he'll be permitted to learn some of the mysteries that are withheld from other men.

"What does kings mean?" Dom asks as he unbuckles our saddlebags.

"The kings," I say, removing Eridu's bridle, "were men who ruled all the lands and peoples of Dulai, before the destruction."

"Men ruled?" Dom says, looking astonished. "The way the Mohirai do?"

"Well," I say uncertainly, "my mother always says the Voice rules Dulai, so maybe the kings were more like the Voice in all. In any case, whatever the kings commanded, the people had to do. So the people were slaves of the kings back then the way people are slaves of the Voice now."

Dom says, "Have people always been slaves, then?"

"Most people, I guess," I say with a shrug, "except for the ones who manage to escape."

Dom unsaddles Eridu, and we carry our tack and saddlebags into one of the alcoves. All our practice of walking apart for short distances makes this easier; we've been able to work independently for longer stretches every day. It's still nerve-wracking to lose sight of each other, though, because we sometimes need to reach each other quickly if pain comes on unexpectedly.

I'm still not feeling any significant pain in my chest, though, so we take advantage of having four free hands. We grab two currycombs and give Eridu a thorough rub down, his first in three days. Clouds of dust come out of his coat, tail, and mane, and by the end he looks like a new horse. He nuzzles our shoulders gratefully before we turn him loose on the grassy bank beside the willows with the rest of the horses.

With Eridu settled, we set to work raising our tent. Hanu and Eumelia rejoin us and help finish the job.

"Anyone else ready for a bath?" I say. I don't think I can wait a moment longer to strip every scrap of this itchy, sandy clothing off my body.

Hanu makes a sound somewhere between a sigh and a moan of pleasure. "Yes, please, yes. I haven't seen my skin in three days."

The four of us make our way eagerly to the sandbar. We peel off our boots and socks, glasses and headscarves, riding clothes and underclothes, leaving them in little heaps at the river's edge. As I stand looking out across the water with my bare toes in the wet sand, I feel a bit like my old self. It's almost possible to forget what's happened, to forget my tether to Dom, to forget where I'm headed and what I'm leaving behind. Embracing this rare sensation of freedom, I close my eyes, dive into the dark blue current, and let myself sink into the cool depths.

For the first time in a long time, I seem to be completely

alone with my thoughts. It's so pleasant here beneath the surface. I linger, spreading my arms as the current picks me up, like I'm flying underwater. How far would the river carry me, if I let it?

I've grown used to all the strange ways the Voice can find me, so I'm not surprised to hear it now within the liquid rush and chortle of the great river, saying, *Together you shall seek us, find us, know us.*

My awareness flows out of me, racing ahead through the current at an impossible speed.

Together you shall amplify us.

The shape of the river draped over the landscape feels as familiar as the shape of my own body, which drifts somewhere far behind me. I yearn to join the sea.

Together you shall weave us through the many worlds.

I spill out into the oceans, spreading out in all directions.

The familiar needling ache in my heart returns, tugging me back toward my body. I ignore it, even as the sensation grows more insistent, because I'm searching for the city of glass towers. I can sense it there, so close now that I—

A rush of Dom's anxiety pulls me back into my body with force.

Ava? he calls from somewhere deep inside me. *Where are you?*

My heart pounds frantically against my ribs, and I realize I need to breathe. I kick back up to the surface and fill my lungs. Despite the pain in my chest, I'm exhilarated. My entire body tingles with my residual awareness of the river, that tantalizing taste of the sea, that glorious expanse of the oceans. I'm certain that the Voice would have shown me where the city of glass towers lies, if only Dom hadn't called me back. I cast a last longing look downstream.

I turn around to see Dom, Hanu, and Eumelia standing in waist-deep water off the sandbar, scanning the river some distance upstream from me. Dom looks frantic, and Hanu rests a comforting hand on his arm. Eumelia spots me, points, and says something to the others. I wave and call loudly, "Over here!" Hanu smiles and waves back. Dom's posture relaxes a little, but even from this distance it's clear that he's upset.

I swim back toward them, and Dom swims out toward me. We meet halfway. I dig my toes into the sandy river bottom to stop myself from drifting in the current, reaching for Dom's outstretched hand. He pulls me back toward shallower water, until we reach a depth where we can both stand, but where we're still out of earshot of the others.

Though I wish Dom hadn't interrupted me, I'm eager to tell him what I saw, because we've spent so much time daydreaming about the city of glass towers together on the road. But, as we usually do after longer separations like this, we have to wait to speak until the pain in my chest subsides, until I've caught my breath, until my pulse returns to its normal rhythm. As we wait, I'm surprised by my acute awareness of Dom's naked body so close to mine in the water. Usually he's the one who has thoughts like this unbidden. After so many days of near-constant contact with him, I'd expect to be blind to his body by now. He'll probably tease me about this later.

I push the pesky thought away and say, "I saw …" My eyes meet Dom's, and the words die on my lips. The exhilaration of my close encounter with the city's possible location fades. I've been so caught up in my own excitement that only now do I see how truly frightened he is.

Dom says, in a voice barely audible over the river, "I thought you'd gone."

His hands shake, and the sensations he's been holding back now flood into me: icy fear, wrenching loss. It's not my brief plunge into the river that's upset him. It's the anticipation of my departure.

"Not yet," I say softly. And I wait, listening, hoping he'll tell me what I've been waiting to hear from him for days. He must know that this is the moment to speak, if he's ever going to speak. But he doesn't speak.

I sigh. On Calling Day, I didn't know how to persuade Dom to come with me. I could definitely persuade him now, though. I've spent enough time in his mind to know where he's susceptible to pressure. There are many ways to use the bond between us, and I'm pretty sure I could force him to come with me. Of course I would never do that. That would make me no better than the Mohirai. No, I can't decide for him how he'll live his life. If he wants to be free, he has to want it for himself.

I have to let him choose, and it seems he's made his choice.

URSHANABI'S FEAST

AVA AND I SWIM back toward the sandbar, where the rest of our party has gathered at the water's edge. Novices and Mohirai in various states of undress come and go, washing sand from clothes and hair and skin, discussing the prospect of Urshanabi's feast with great anticipation. Kor sits alone at the edge of the camp near the horses, looking up into the branches of the great willows lining the riverbank, apparently enthralled by the sight of some bird. Ava joins in occasionally with the girls chattering about the feast, smiling and nodding as if nothing has happened, while I remain silent, still shaken by her sudden disappearance into the river.

I've been consumed by exhaustion for the last three days, and maybe I've used that as an excuse to put off thinking about the choice Ava set before me at the start of the desert crossing. Being on the road has changed my sense of time, and maybe I let myself pretend the journey would go on forever, so I'd never have to make a choice at all.

I consider the choice now, but I still don't know what I want. Well, I do know what I want, but what I want is impossible. I want to stay here among the Mohirai, answer my calling from the Voice, learn what it is to be an Artifex. And I want to follow Ava. For all her faults, she makes me think and feel and experience so much more than anyone else I've ever met. She exhilarates me.

Which of these things would I choose to live without? It's an impossible choice, and I'm running out of time to decide.

Eumelia sits in neck-deep water, eyes half-closed with pleasure. Hanu stands behind her, gently massaging some fragrant, foamy concoction into Eumelia's scalp. Eumelia lets Hanu lower her head into the water to rinse her hair clean.

"What's that?" says Ava, as a ribbon of suds drifts by us. "It smells so good."

"Thalia gave us some of her bathing pharmaka," says Hanu. She gestures toward the buxom Muse, who lounges naked in the shallows with Bel and Tashlu. The two girls watch me with admiring eyes, giggling with each other, trailing ribbons of white bubbles and shimmering oil into the river. I lower my naked body a little deeper into the water. Hanu continues, "She wants everyone to look pretty tonight. And Arkhi said this is our last chance for a decent bath until we reach Velkanos, so we might as well make the most of it."

Hanu lifts Eumelia back out of the water, then smiles at Ava and says, "Want me to do yours next?" Eumelia and I exchange a sidelong look over Ava's head, probably both thinking how much touching that would entail. Clearly Ava's thinking the same, because she thanks Hanu but says she'll wash her own hair. Hanu tosses a little bottle toward her, and Ava and I each take a dollop of Thalia's bathing pharmaka and set to work cleaning. It's strange to cover myself in a scent I associate so strongly with the Mohirai, but it's much better than the pungent smell of sweat and horse that's permeated every pore of my skin and scrap of clothing after so many days on the road.

By the time we've scrubbed every last bit of the desert off ourselves and our bodies are smooth with scented oil, Arkhi's promised rainclouds are closing in on us from the southwest.

Ava and I pick up our riding clothes from the sandbar and walk a little way downstream from the bathers.

Hanu and Eumelia join us, and the four of us kneel at the river's edge, scrubbing soap into our filthy clothes. Crusts of dirt dissolve into grey plumes and flow away, but no amount of washing will entirely remove the dun color of the desert from these clothes.

"If I never see another grain of sand it will be too soon," Eumelia says irritably, wringing out her riding shirt and rising to her feet. "If anyone needed convincing that the Voice's plan for men is just, that blasted desert should do it."

"Mel!" Hanu says sharply. "That's an unkind thing to say."

Before I've fully registered what Eumelia said, a hot wave of anger rushes to my head, followed by a prickle of pain in my chest. Alarmed, I look over to see Ava glowering at Eumelia. In a harshly mocking imitation of Eumelia's voice, Ava says, "If anyone needed convincing that you deserve to be breeding stock, that enlightened view should do it."

Hanu looks shocked. Eumelia's expression wavers between amusement and contrition. "Come on," Ava says, picking up the dripping pile of her clothes and holding her hand out for mine. Hastily, I gather my things and take her hand. The prickling pain in my chest subsides, but Ava's anger still burns.

"Ava!" Eumelia calls, hurrying after us. "I'm sorry, I shouldn't have said that. Dom, I wasn't talking about you." She tries to catch Ava's arm to stop her, and Ava repeatedly shakes her off. "Ava, please, I—"

Ava lets go of my hand and wheels around toward Eumelia so suddenly that Eumelia's chin slams into Ava's face, cutting off her next words. I wince, feeling a sharp echo of the painful collision. Ava and I both touch the same tender spot below our right eye, while Eumelia rubs her jaw.

Ava glares at Eumelia and squares her shoulders. Eumelia raises both of her hands in a placating gesture and takes a step back. Hanu catches up to us and looks from Ava to Eumelia in dismay. I settle my hand on Ava's shoulder, prepared to hold her back if she gives in to her almost overwhelming desire to slam her clenched fist into Eumelia's nose.

Don't do this because of me, I think.

It's not just because of you! Ava thinks, seething. *She shouldn't have said that. She shouldn't even think that. It's not right.*

"Spirits, I hate you," Ava says to Eumelia, in a low, dangerous voice. "I've always hated you."

Don't say that. You don't mean that, I think.

You think I don't?

"Ava—" Eumelia begins again.

"Shut up!" Ava exclaims. "Can't you ever just shut your damn—"

"Ava," Hanu interrupts, slipping between Ava and Eumelia. She joins hands with the two other girls and says gently to Ava, "Mel didn't really mean that. She speaks without thinking sometimes, but …" Hanu trails off, lips parted, eyes widening in startled recognition as she looks at Ava.

My fingers tingle against Ava's shoulder. For a disorienting moment, I feel Ava's fingers tingling against Hanu's palm, and Hanu's fingers tingling against Eumelia's.

I'm not sure where my body ends and Ava's body begins, or where Ava's body ends and the other girls' begin.

Spirits, what is this? Ava thinks, pulling her hand quickly out of Hanu's grasp and stepping away from me. The disorienting sensation subsides.

"Everything all right there?" Serapen's voice appears out of nowhere. Dazed, I turn to see the High Priestess emerging from a little copse of oaks carrying an armful of gathered firewood, heading back toward the tents.

Ava, Hanu, Eumelia, and I stand silent as Serapen's perceptive eyes sweep over the four of us. Hanu stares at Ava in surprise. Eumelia's jaw twitches, but for once she holds her tongue. I glance uncertainly at Ava. Ava says tightly, "Just a misunderstanding. Everything's fine now."

Serapen's eyes linger on Ava. She nods, then says, "Better get dressed, then. Thalia wants to see everyone in ceremonial silks tonight." With that, Serapen continues on her way.

△▽△

My cheek throbs painfully where Eumelia ran into me, and my mind churns with the knowledge that Hanu's remembered me. I'm relieved that Serapen departs without asking me any more questions. I'm not sure what I might have said, or whether I could have lied to the High Priestess if I'd wanted to.

As much as I want Eumelia to regret her thoughtless comment about the justice of men's subjugation by the Voice, I have no desire to tattle on her to Serapen. But another part of me wishes I'd told Serapen more; maybe she could explain what just happened when Hanu joined hands with me and Eumelia.

At first it had felt similar to what happens right before I hear the Voice in all. When I practice using my connection to the Voice, my awareness usually slips out of my body into some part of the landscape. When Hanu took my hand, I'd lost the sense of my body's boundaries, as the edges of me somehow expanded into her, Dom, and Eumelia. But when I'm connected to the Voice, this sensation of losing my body is usually followed soon afterwards by pain. Although that pain is unpleasant, and sometimes frightening, it also helps me keep track of my body, so I can return to myself. The boundary between myself and the landscape can blur and even briefly disappear when I let my awareness expand, but pain is always there to help re-establish the boundaries.

When Hanu took my hand, it wasn't painful. It was unexpectedly pleasant. But without the pain to remind me where my edges should be, I'm not sure they've all returned to their original places. Even now, after taking a step back from Hanu, Dom, and Eumelia, my awareness of them seems amplified. The three of them look more solid, more detailed, more intensely alive than they were just a moment ago. I can't tell if something about them changed, or something changed about how I see them.

Hanu's surprised recognition turns into effusive delight. "Ava! Spirits, Ava," she says. She wraps me in her warm, soft, sweetly-scented arms and kisses me on both cheeks.

Hanu was always my favorite among the girls. Even though she's treated me as kindly on this journey as she ever did when we were little, I've missed our old familiarity. Dom's constant presence at my side and his feelings about her have led me to avoid her for his sake, even though I greatly enjoy her company.

So it feels good to be remembered by her now. I hug her back for a moment. That odd blurring feeling returns, as I lose the sense of where I end and where she begins. Dom's reaction to seeing Hanu's naked body pressed against mine further complicates this embrace, so I extricate myself from Hanu before it gets worse for him.

"But why didn't you tell us who you were?" says Hanu. "Mel, Ava's our—" Hanu turns to Eumelia to explain who I am. She sees the knowing look on Eumelia's face, and on Dom's. "Wait. You knew?" Hanu touches her forehead as understanding dawns. "Both of you knew?" She looks at the three of us with a slightly hurt expression. "But why didn't any of you tell me?"

"I asked them not to," I say. "It wasn't because I wanted to exclude you, Hanu. It's because the binding pharmaka makes every connection with someone else so much harder to manage. I didn't want any more trouble."

Hanu appears more puzzled than upset by this. She gives me a sympathetic smile and says, "Well, whatever the Voice's plan is in all this, I'm just glad it's brought us back together again. We can be a proper trio now, like we were always meant to be." She presses my arm happily. My skin tingles beneath her fingertips, and Hanu's smile fades. With a sinking feeling, I realize she, like Eumelia, perceives my thoughts with even greater ease than Dom when she's touching me. Quickly, I drop a veil over my thoughts and pull away. But Hanu's already glimpsed the essential thing.

"You don't want to stay with us," she says sadly, letting me go. Briefly, I worry that Hanu might have seen some part of my plan. But I've been very careful to suppress those thoughts because of Dom, and she says nothing more, so I think my secret's safe.

Hanu, Dom, and Eumelia look at me with variations of the same expression. They want me to stay, each for different reasons. I look away, feeling guilty. But why should I feel guilty? I never promised any of them I'd stay. They were fine before I got here, and they'll be fine after I'm gone.

Spirits blast it all. This would have been so much easier if none of them had ever remembered me.

As we stand in awkward silence, the first of Arkhi's predicted rainclouds passes over us, and a shower of raindrops dissolves the desert heat. I shiver miserably as cold rainwater trickles down my naked back.

"Come on," says Dom, touching my arm to lend me some of his warmth. "Let's get ready for the feast."

The four of us run back toward the cliffs, into the stone alcove where we raised our tent. Sheltered from the rain, we hang our wet riding clothes out to dry, then head into the tent, where we rummage through saddlebags for our ceremonial clothes. Somehow, the white silks and thick woolen cloaks from our Calling Day have remained almost entirely free of dust in the bottom of our saddlebags. It feels unbelievably luxurious to pull dry clean clothes over smooth clean skin. I don't think I've been this clean since Hedi put us to bed that night in the house of boys.

Unfortunately, even after I'm dressed, I'm still freezing, and there's a throbbing ache all through the right side of my face where Eumelia collided with me. I tug the heavy folds of my wool cloak around my shivering shoulders and press my icy hand over the tender part of my face. I know Dom will give me his warm hand as soon as he works out how to tie those complicated laces on his ceremonial cloak, so I try to wait patiently. I wish I didn't have to rely on him so much for body heat.

"May I?" says Hanu, extending her hand toward me.

"May you … what?" I say, still apprehensive of her touch after my accidental sharing earlier.

"May I help you feel better?" she says.

"What do you mean?" I say.

With a wry smile, Hanu says, "Oh, you don't have to keep the mystery from me, Ava. Like Mel not-so-subtly implied …" She shoots a mildly exasperated look at Eumelia, who smirks back at her. "I've had my share of binding pharmaka. I know the basics."

I'm curious what Hanu may know about binding pharmaka that Dom and I haven't figured out already. "How can you make me feel better?" I say, holding out one hand toward Hanu. "Would you teach me how it works?"

"Of course," she says eagerly. She kneels in front of me and takes my cold fingers between both of her warm hands. Slowly, she slides one of her hands up along my forearm. I tense again, expecting that disorienting sensation of losing the edges of my body. She says, "Try to relax, Ava. I want to give you a gift. But it's much easier for me to give if you want to receive it."

It sounds like it should be easy. I'm so cold, and I would much rather be warm. My cheekbone throbs where Eumelia ran into me, and I wish it would stop. The difficulty is that I'd much rather take care of myself than accept help from Hanu. I don't want to need her for something. I don't want to owe her anything.

Hanu lightly massages my hand, my wrist, my forearm. Warmth travels from her practiced fingers up my arm a short distance before retreating back into her hand.

"Hmm," Hanu says, tilting her head to the side and studying me as her fingers continue their work. *May I show you something that might help?* she thinks.

I nod, curious. Hanu takes my awareness in hers as gently as she holds my hand in hers, and I follow its pull. Again the edges of my body blur, then disappear. It's much less alarming now than when she intervened between me and Eumelia. This time, I'm prepared for the change, and it's much calmer somehow, when it's just me and Hanu, not four awarenesses joined unexpectedly together all at once.

Hanu's awareness feels very different from my own, and from Dom's. I explore her perspective with interest. She's exquisitely sensitive to her own body, and to mine. She relates to everyone around her with such sympathy because she's fascinated by what others feel, by all the varied causes and effects of sensation. She loves to feel good and for others to feel good. She's an artist of pleasure.

She lets me see how witnessing my suffering causes her pain. The pain she feels isn't as acute or as deadly as the pain I often feel, but it's still a kind of pain. All this time, when I've been suffering, it's not just Dom who's shared my suffering. Hanu has shared it too, though she's never complained about it.

I had no idea I had this effect on her, that I could have been hurting her with my own attempts to be stoic. The realization makes me feel awful, but it also makes the solution obvious. If I can make her feel better by accepting her help, then of course I want to. By accepting Hanu's help, I'm giving her a kind of gift as well.

As soon as I think this, my arm, my shoulders, and my back all relax. I luxuriate in the delicious warmth that suffuses my core and spreads all the way out to my toes. Once my entire body feels warm, Hanu's soft fingers move to my cheek, and the ache there melts away under her palm. Clean and warm and miraculously free of discomfort, I feel completely renewed.

How did you learn to do this? I think.

Hanu lets me in on her secret, showing me all the experimentation she's done with small doses of binding pharmaka spirited away from the personal stores of Mohirai in the Children's Temple. I see Dom has been the subject of a few of these experiments, along with many other boys and girls.

I envy her experience with binding pharmaka, which has been far more pleasurable and far less complicated than my own. The memory of the awful pain I experienced that first night after my overdose returns to me unbidden. I hasten to suppress it, as I've learned to suppress so many other thoughts, but some part of my memory still spills into her. Hanu's eyes glisten with tears as she looks at me.

I had no idea binding pharmaka could feel like that, she thinks. *I wish that hadn't happened to you.*

Her deep sympathy makes it easier to let the memory

pass. I focus instead on what she's given me: this radiant warmth, this sense of well-being, and this new perspective on pain and pleasure.

There you go, Hanu thinks, pressing a kiss to my cheek. She gives my fingers a parting squeeze and lets go of my hand, looking pleased with herself.

"Thanks," I say, rubbing my two warm hands together, then touching my cheek tentatively. I can tell there will be a bruise, but the angry throbbing is gone for now. I reach for Hanu and hug her tight, for once not caring what effect this might have on Dom. "I feel so much better," I say.

"I'm glad," says Hanu, holding me until I let go.

Once we part, I again have the unsettling suspicion that the edges of my body haven't returned to their original places. I feel more anchored to my own body than I did before, and also much more aware of Hanu, of Dom, and even of Eumelia. Seeing the world through Hanu's eyes seems to have rubbed off on me.

△▽△

Hanu and Ava kneel facing each other on the far side of the tent. Hanu's hands move up Ava's arm as she demonstrates some method of sharing body heat through the binding pharmaka. I can't help wondering whether Ava and I have learned through painful trial and error what Hanu might have been able to easily teach us our first day on the road, if only Ava hadn't been so obsessed with secrecy and I hadn't been so conflicted by my feelings about Hanu.

For the first time in a very long time, I manage to look at

Hanu without a single sexual thought crossing my mind. It doesn't hurt that Hanu's now fully clothed, but what helps more than anything else is my new understanding of what I'm actually feeling when I see Hanu.

A few days ago, when Eumelia teased Hanu about her illicit use of binding pharmaka, I realized for the first time why sex with Hanu was so different from my experiences with other girls. I wish Hanu had asked me before using binding pharmaka with me. I suppose it's not surprising she didn't—the Mohirai routinely use pharmaka on all of us without our knowledge, after all—but Hanu could have saved me a lot of confusion and embarrassment if she'd told me.

Even before I knew the cause, though, I certainly noticed the effect of having used binding pharmaka with Hanu. My awareness of her body, and her awareness of mine, have been amplified since the first time we had sex. When Hanu's nearby, I can feel what she's feeling, and since she's so aware of her own body, I'm aware of it by extension. This was useful and pleasurable when I wanted to be intimate with Hanu. This is complicated while sharing a constant close connection with Ava's mind, no matter how understanding Ava might be about it.

But knowing my feelings about Hanu are amplified by binding pharmaka has made it easier for me to manage. All the techniques Ava and I practice to discipline our thoughts for each other work equally well on my thoughts about Hanu.

And for all the complications Hanu's presence has caused me on the road, I've started to appreciate how much I unwittingly learned from her that's been useful with Ava. The reason I intuited how to share thoughts with Ava using binding pharmaka was because I'd experienced a similar sort of communication with Hanu before. I think this may also be why I've been able to lend Ava strength, and warmth, and other kinds of help, when she's needed it. It's not so different from how Hanu shared sensations with me while we were intimate.

Hanu finishes her work with Ava, and the change in Ava astonishes me. Her skin looks rosy and warm. The tight lines of discomfort around her lips and eyes are gone. She moves a bit more slowly and fluidly than she usually does, like every muscle in her body has relaxed. When she turns her gaze on me, her eyes linger longer. Her normally piercing expression softens into something more receptive, a look I'm more used to seeing on Hanu's face. I swallow, wondering what lies behind that look, wondering whether—

Thalia pops her head in through our tent flap, her eyes and lips freshly painted, her musical voice full of cheer. "Come along, novices," she says. "Arkhi says this is about to turn into a proper deluge. Hoods up!"

The four of us pull up our hoods and follow Thalia out of the tent, joining the other girls and Mohirai walking up the beach. Although I haven't felt any echoes of Ava's pain in my chest for a while, out of habit I offer my hand to her as we walk. She laces her fingers through mine, and I feel not only the pleasant warmth of her skin but a new kind of warmth in her awareness. She looks up at me from under her hood and says, "I wish I'd told Hanu sooner. She knows a lot of useful things."

"Like what?" I say, a bit apprehensive of what Ava might have seen in Hanu's mind.

Ava smiles and says, "Well, at first, it seemed like most of what Hanu knows is how to have really good sex. And I'm sure that's useful. Looks fun, anyway."

"It is!" Hanu calls over her shoulder.

Ava laughs, then lowers her voice so that only I can hear her. She says, "But what's even more useful is what Hanu knows about communicating using every part of the body. She's so ... sensitive. To everything. To everyone."

We reach the base of the stone stairs carved into the cliffs and start to climb. Ava says, "She knows how to listen with the body, to figure out what's causing pain and how to make it stop, even how to turn it into pleasure. I can't help thinking that's what I need to learn how to do. There's so much pain to manage from the Voice. Maybe I can use what Hanu showed me to figure out what's causing the pain. Maybe I could make it stop for good. Or maybe it doesn't have to feel like pain at all, and I could change it into something else."

Ava stops speaking, but her thoughts race on, her face glowing with the excitement of a promising new insight, a possible solution to her problem. I should be happy for her. I am happy for her. And yet the faster Ava gets better, the sooner she'll be gone.

I keep these thoughts to myself, though, and say only, "I hope so."

We reach the top of the stairs and hurry through the rain along a pebbly garden path toward Urshanabi's little white house. The house must have a sweeping view on a clear day, but right now it's closed in on all sides by grey curtains of rain. We pause at the bottom of the steps that lead to the blue front door. Thalia knocks.

The door swings inward, and Urshanabi stands at the threshold in a clean white robe, backlit by the cheerful golden glow of candles and firelight. He beckons us in with a bright smile, saying, "Welcome, welcome, welcome."

I'm not convinced our entire party will fit inside such a small house until Ava and I squeeze inside and Urshanabi closes the door behind us.

We stand elbow to elbow in a warm and cramped single room with a cleanswept stone floor. Urshanabi shepherds us into the bench seats arranged around the long wooden table that occupies most of the room.

I examine the inside of Urshanabi's house with interest. A short wooden ladder on one wall leads up to a narrow sleeping loft with a small mattress. Clearly the ferryman lives here alone. I've lived in shared quarters with other boys for as long as I can remember, until this journey began, so I struggle to imagine what it's like to live alone in a place like this, so far from other people. But the ferryman seems to have a great deal to occupy himself. Shelves line his walls from floor to ceiling, crammed with boxes, jars, parchment scrolls, and a large collection of musical instruments. I wonder where a man could have learned to play musical instruments.

After so long eating out of doors, it feels like a luxury to sit at a table again, even one as crowded as this. Sitting around a table with women adds a degree of novelty, too. The Mohirai who ran the house of boys always dined at their own table in the meal hall, so I only ever ate with the other boys. Now, I sit between Ava and Thalia on a bench. Their warm, sweet-scented bodies press against me on both sides, and I'm quite comfortable indeed.

In the time it took us to make camp, bathe, and dress, Urshanabi has laid out an impressive feast for fourteen. I can't imagine how he did this all on his own. He must have been preparing for our arrival for days.

Urshanabi serves his exquisite food on a humble assortment of plates and bowls. We dine on tender lamb and savory rice, soft breads and ewe's cheese, roasted vegetables and stewed fruits, delicious sweets of creamy almond paste and fresh green pistachios dripping with honey.

Wine flows from a seemingly inexhaustible supply, as Urshanabi retrieves bottle after bottle from the pantry beneath his sleeping loft. The ferryman pours out each new bottle into a large painted mixing vessel at the center of the table, and Serapen stirs in crumbly pharmaka from a leather pouch she carries in her robes. Thalia wields the ladle throughout the meal, ensuring no goblet goes empty.

The mixed wine goes down easily, and the room gradually turns into a noisy, cozy blur for me. I'm not entirely sure how much I've had to drink when I notice Ava hasn't touched her goblet. This must be why her awareness has retained its sharp edge. I realize too late that by partaking in the wine I may force Ava to share the experience, whether she wants to or not.

"Would you rather I abstain?" I ask her.

She dismisses the question with a wave and a relaxed smile. "Enjoy," she says. "It's been a long journey, and we'll be here two nights, anyway. But do me a favor and drink some of this, too. I'd rather not share your headache tomorrow." She pours me a cup of clear water from a pitcher and sets it beside my wine goblet.

The party grows steadily more voluble and boisterous, and Urshanabi prompts each of the novices in turn to tell him stories of what we've seen and done on the road so far.

The eloquence of the other girls impresses me, especially given the strong effect the wine's having on me. But they've all been accustomed since childhood to hearing and reciting poetry, and feasting with Mohirai, so they use language with far greater skill than I do, even as they grow intoxicated.

Piroza describes the unique character of each forest she particularly admired along the way. Bel recalls the dramatic views afforded by some of the winding hill roads we traveled. Narua recounts her favorite origin myths of the mountains we've seen. Eumelia offers a spirited accounting of various mishaps she observed amongst the group, walking a fine line between provoking and entertaining the party. I listen with absorption, laughing at funny anecdotes, murmuring appreciatively along with the others when a girl offers a particularly evocative description of a scene on the road. Otherwise, I remain silent, and so does Ava, though she watches and listens to everything with close attention.

Are you all right? I think at one point, glancing at Ava. I haven't overheard a single thought or felt a single reaction from her in quite some time.

Fine, she thinks, giving me a small smile. Does she look a little sad? I'm tempted to ask what she's been thinking about, or even to peek into her thoughts. But after all the work we've done to make it possible for each other to have any privacy, that seems inappropriate. If she doesn't want to share, I'm not going to force her.

Plates are almost empty and bellies are almost full when there's a lull in the conversation. Urshanabi turns to me and says amiably, "What about you, Dom? How have you found the journey?"

Nothing I say could compare to the cleverness of what the other girls have said already, so I say simply, "I'm grateful to be traveling in the company of such wise and skilled Mohirai. And I'm looking forward to learning more of my calling once we reach Velkanos."

Urshanabi nods slowly and says, "What have you been told of your calling, little brother?"

Thalia falls silent on my left side, and Ava perks up with interest on my right. Across the table, Arkhi and Serapen exchange an unreadable glance.

"Muse Serapen told me I'll learn more of my calling from the Artifexi in the proper time," I say slowly, trying not to slur my words. "But she did say I've been called to the path of mysteries."

"A rare calling indeed, for a man," says Urshanabi, taking another sip of wine.

Seeing his knowing expression, it occurs to me to ask, "Are you an Artifex, brother?"

He shakes his head and says, "I was an old man long before the first Artifex was called. And yet perhaps I may still presume to welcome you as a brother on the path of mysteries. For I too have known communion with the Voice in all."

The rest of the girls fall silent as Urshanabi speaks. Rain patters gently on the roof, and a log crackles in the fireplace.

I say, "So there are other men called to the mysteries,

besides the Artifexi?"

Urshanabi leans back in his seat at the end of the long table and says, "None born in this new age. But long ago, before the destruction, the path of mysteries could be walked by all seekers, even men. The arts were widely known and practiced, even outside temple walls.

"There was a priesthood of men, in those days. And I was an initiate of that ancient brotherhood, trained in their mysteries."

I study him with interest. I've never heard of a priesthood before. "Are you a priest, then?" I ask.

"I was, but no longer," says Urshanabi. "I had the great sorrow of witnessing the end of my order. The corruption of my brotherhood eventually ran so deep that I could no longer walk the path I loved, knowing what damage my brothers were doing to mother land and her people."

"So ... what are you now?" I ask.

Urshanabi considers this question for a long time before he says, "When I abandoned my vows, I became nothing. Worse than nothing, for all men held me in contempt.

"So I sought refuge in the wilderness outside the great temple city of Velkanos. In the age before the destruction, the sisters of the unnamed priestesshood would still tolerate a hermit in their temple lands, provided he did no mischief. And one day Mohira, the last High Priestess of the age of kings, gave me this post. She said the Voice grants purpose to all, and she revealed the Voice's purpose for me. So here I remain, a humble ferryman, alive by the mercy of the sisters and the grace of the Voice in all."

"You must have seen a lot, in all that time," says Ava, her

eyes locked on Urshanabi. She speaks in a tone that cuts through the air like a blade.

"Indeed. Far more than I ever imagined might be seen in a single lifetime," he says.

"Do you miss it?" says Ava. "The rule of men? The age of kings?"

Urshanabi's gaze grows distant, as if he looks across an inconceivably vast landscape. He says, "I've never known such peace or beauty in the land as I've seen in this new age."

Ava's eyes flick to each of the three Mohirai in turn, then back to Urshanabi. She thinks, *It all worked out quite well for him, at least.*

What do you mean? I think, my wine-dulled mind struggling to keep up with hers.

Ava's eyes meet mine. She thinks, *Why would the Mohirai let this man live so long? Did he sell out his brothers before the destruction began? Did he help the Mohirai come to power?*

Arkhi says calmly, "The Voice speaks wisdom as clearly through you as through any Mohira, Urshanabi."

The ferryman's eyes shine as he looks at Arkhi and says, "That is a great kindness, sister."

How very interesting, thinks Ava.

△▽△

I hold my tongue, deciding not to risk asking the ferryman any more probing questions, as much as I'd like to. Dom and the Mohirai watch me with uncomfortably close attention, but I need to fade into the background. Fortunately, Urshanabi chooses this moment to clap three times and rise from his seat at the end of the table. He reaches for a gleaming lyre that hangs from a high hook on the wall behind him.

"It seems you all have satisfied your need for food and drink," says Urshanabi. "So may I ask you to honor us with a song, fair Muse?" He extends the instrument with both hands toward Thalia.

Thalia rises eagerly from her seat beside Dom and accepts the instrument and its small bone plectrum. Urshanabi pulls out a low carved stool for her, and Thalia settles herself there, swinging her long auburn braid behind her shoulder and cradling the turtleshell crescent of the lyre in her lap. She takes the plectrum in the fingers of her right hand and strums it across the seven strings, humming quietly to herself.

It's been many years since I was in close proximity to such a fine musical instrument. Life on the road with my mother left no room for the Mohiran arts of revelry. I know the sound of the lyre well enough, though. I even remember what it's like to hold the instrument, because I received instruction in music like all the other girls during my first year in the Children's Temple.

I remember just enough to fully appreciate that the sound of eighth summer girls plucking at strings and singing has about as much in common with Thalia's music as the rough huts of the village workmen have in common with the temples of the Mohirai.

Thalia's voice, sweet and smooth with wine, fills the room, weaving through the haunting chords she plays. My perception of the Muse of poetika as frivolous, ridiculous, even useless, changes dramatically as I witness her art for the first time. I melt a bit into the bench as I listen.

She sings a mournful ballad of a humble priestess named Shubur, a tale I've never heard before. Shubur's great joy is listening to the Voice in all, until one day the Voice is stolen from Dulai through the trickery of a powerful priestess named Kigal. Shubur sets out on a journey to recover the Voice, which leads her to cross the great ocean that rings the world. At last Shubur discovers that Kigal has taken the Voice into the land of Death and hidden it there. So Shubur makes the journey into Death, and after many strange adventures, she returns the Voice to the people of Dulai.

I'm captivated by the lyrical descriptions of the people and places Shubur encounters on her journey. Occasionally, I recognize the names of old city ruins my mother and I used as landmarks to navigate the wildernesses of Dulai. I wonder whether this could be a true story.

No one else appears to be as gripped by the tale as I am, though this is certainly no fault of Thalia's. Her performance is beyond compare. But the eyelids of the other girls around the table grow heavier and heavier as the song goes on and they succumb to bellies full of rich food and mixed wine.

Even Dom, who drank less than anyone but me, eventually nods off. His head comes to rest on my shoulder. The last three days have been exhausting, so I let him sleep. I rest my cheek against his mop of curls, which are warm and soft and smell sweetly of bathing pharmaka. I observe his sleeping awareness pulled along in the slipstream of the Muse's song.

Dom's dreaming mind reimagines Shubur's journey into

Death and back again, casting the people and places we've seen along our own journey into new roles in Thalia's tale. Even in dreams, Dom constructs worlds of breathtaking beauty. I'll be glad to have this memory of him.

A change in tempo and melody signals that the end of the song approaches. Those who nodded off begin to stir. Dom's languid sensations slowly reorder themselves into wakefulness, until he remembers where he is. His eyelashes tickle my neck as he opens his eyes, and his nose grazes my earlobe as he lifts his head from my shoulder.

"Sorry," he whispers. His voice is husky from sleep and the dusty air of the past three days.

"Don't be," I say, smiling at him. I prop my chin up on one hand and rest my other hand on his, listening to the final verses of Thalia's song. Her beautiful voice lingers, then fades into silence. I realize only now that the rain has stopped.

"Thank you, sister," Urshanabi murmurs. "You've given me a gift that will live long in my memory."

Thalia's eyes sparkle at the ferryman as she says, "And the night is still young." She reaches for her goblet and raises it first to Urshanabi, then to the other Mohirai, and last to us novices. She takes a drink, then says, "It seems the Voice has granted us a reprieve from the rain. Shall we honor it with a dance?"

I look around the room, doubting anyone has energy left for dancing. I'm surprised—even a bit envious—to discover that the other girls have emerged from their dozing with renewed energy. Thalia's proposal is accepted with great excitement. I wonder what exactly Serapen mixed into the wine.

It's not too late to find out, Dom says, gesturing toward my full goblet.

But I have other plans. As Thalia said, the night is still young.

THE DOUBLE CROSSING

ALL THE OTHER NOVICES AND DOM RISE with Thalia and spill out of the house in a laughing, singing, somewhat clumsy tangle. They're followed by Urshanabi, Arkhi, and Serapen, who carry a few instruments selected from the ferryman's collection, as well as several more bottles of wine. I hang back for a moment, making a quick survey of the abandoned table. It's a mess of nearly empty plates and goblets, except for mine. I glance at the door to make sure I'm alone, then grab two hunks of ewe's cheese and what remains of the delicious flat breads. These I wrap in a spare linen cloth I tucked inside my clothes while I was dressing.

I slip the packet of food inside my robe and turn toward the door just as Dom reappears at the threshold, his cheeks rosy, his gaze a little unfocused.

"Ah, there you are," he says happily. "Come on!"

I accept his offered hand and close the door behind us. We step out into the cool night air and walk down the garden path, which squishes slightly beneath our bare feet. The rain has washed the desert air clean, and I breathe in the damp, sweet scent of soil with gratitude after so many days of choking dust. I catch a glimpse of Dom's softly blurred perspective as he takes in the river view from atop the cliffs. The rainclouds recede eastward as the waning crescent moon rises into a glittering vault of stars.

Our noisy companions make their way to the stone stairs and descend to the beach. I hang back near the cliffs' edge, looking down at the shimmering river, marking the position of each member of our party. Half of them construct a bonfire on the sand while the other half debate who'd better play and who'd better dance. The plaintive notes of an aulos drift up to us, followed by the beat of a drum and the strum of two kitharas. The drum settles into a dancing beat. As the first flames of the bonfire catch, the dancers join hands in a ring. Dom watches with interest.

With a burst of inspiration, I say, "Do you want to join them?" This would certainly make things easier for me.

"Boys aren't allowed, remember?" Dom says ruefully.

Dom hasn't thoroughly considered all the implications of what's changed for him since he was called as Artifex. I'd guess many of the rules from the house of boys no longer apply to him. And even if the ridiculous rules haven't changed, I'd be inclined to break them. Unfortunately, that's not really Dom's style.

Fortunately, it doesn't seem like any rule-breaking will be required this time. "Look," I say, pointing down at the swirling shadows. "Urshanabi's dancing."

Surprised, Dom looks down to see the ferryman among the dancers, arm in arm with Thalia, crossing hands with Arkhi, spinning around Serapen, weaving his way through the other girls. I'm sure Dom's never seen a man dancing before. For that matter, neither have I. But seeing Urshanabi's skill as a dancer only proves to me how silly all these rules of the Mohirai are. What possible reason could there be to exclude men from these arts? Clearly they're as capable as women.

Dom's eagerness to dance feels similar to his eagerness to

ride on the first day of our journey.

"Come on," I say, pulling him by the hand. "It's fun. I'll show you." This will be a good way to say goodbye. At least for me.

The sounds of the revelry grow louder as we descend the stone stairs to the beach. The warm swirl of movement and laughter around the bonfire pulls us in, and we're absorbed quickly into the ring. It's been years since I last danced, but dancing comes to me as naturally as breathing, and the steps seem as familiar as they were when I first learned them in the halls of the Children's Temple. Dom struggles, but he covers for his inexperience with a good sense of rhythm, a lanky grace, and a quickness to laugh at himself and learn from his mistakes. His delight spills into me when our hands touch, and I can't help laughing with him. I feel the effects of the wine in him as he spins and his vision spins and the rest of the party spins around him. I wonder whether he'll remember any of this tomorrow.

When the lead kithara cues the next dance, I seize the moment. I improvise a quick series of steps to swap my position with Hanu in the ring, so she and Dom stand hand in hand. The next dance is long and intricate, requiring close attention even for an experienced dancer. Dom will probably have to look at his feet the entire time.

I step out of the ring for a moment and pretend to rest at the edge of the bonfire's glow as I survey the group. Everyone's accounted for—Eight novices, three Mohirai, Urshanabi, and Dom—all of them thoroughly intoxicated. My eyes linger on Dom. He looks at Hanu, who leans in and says something that makes him smile. He answers, and she laughs. They look happy together. Beautiful, really. I realize for the first time how ridiculous it was for me to think he might want to come with me. He must feel like the luckiest boy in Dulai, heading to Velkanos in the company of all these beautiful women for a life in service to the Voice. It's certainly far better than any life he'd ever dreamed was possible. It's not the life I want, but it's the life he wants. It's the life he's always wanted.

So I'm happy for him, though I know I'll miss him. Silently, I wish him well, then slip into the shadows.

△▽△

Hanu's eyes gleam in the firelight as she looks at me. She leans toward my ear and says, "You and Ava dance well together."

I smile and say, "As long as I stand still and she does all the dancing."

Hanu laughs and says, "That's not true. You have a good sense of the music."

I incline my head toward Hanu, then look around the ring for Ava. I've been waiting for a break in the music to pull her aside and talk to her. That moment in the river has been replaying in the back of my mind all through the feast. I'm not sure if it's my memory of that moment, or the wine, or something else, but everything seems clear to me now. I've finally made my decision. I know what it would feel like to be left behind by Ava, because that's what I felt when she disappeared into the river. I never want to feel that again. I don't know what life as an Artifex might be like, so I can't know whether I'd want that life. But I have an idea of what life with Ava might be like, and I want to see more of that life. I want to hold on to our friendship. I want to experience everything she's going to experience on the journey to freedom. And I want to listen to her laugh on the way there.

I search the shadows at the edge of the bonfire, looking for her. My stomach twists when I can't find her. Then I relax. There she is, resting in the sand a few paces behind me, just catching her breath. That's probably a good idea; my own head is spinning from all the wine. I should go talk to her now.

I'm turning to step out of the ring when the music transitions, and Hanu takes my hand. She says, "Would you like me to teach you this one? It's a little bit complicated, but I can show you a simpler version."

"Oh—" I glance back at Ava, but the dancers are moving around us now and I've lost sight of her. "All right. This is the last dance for me, though."

△▽△

I hurry back to the tent and quickly strip off the bright white ceremonial clothes I'm wearing. I've been wary of the golden threads in these clothes ever since Eumelia explained how the Mohirai control the horses. It's a shame I have to leave such fine fabric behind, since it would be such a useful barter item, but I can't risk the Mohirai using these threads to track me down.

I change into my damp riding clothes and wrap my dark wool cloak tight around me to ward off the night's chill.

Thankfully, my spare pair of wool socks are warm and dry on my feet. The desert air should suck the moisture out of everything else by sunrise.

In daylight over the last few days, whenever I could find a moment alone, I carefully examined every scrap of my riding clothes and gear, tearing little holes into cloth and leather seams, checking everywhere for gleaming threads. I found no sign of anything suspicious; as far as I can tell, everything I'm about to take with me is free of pharmaka.

Except for one thing. I double-check my leather belt before I leave the tent, ensuring that my flask of unbinding pharmaka is securely fastened. I hope I won't have to use it, but this pharmaka is the only thing standing between me and catastrophe, if I've overestimated my ability to manage the Voice without Dom.

I cut off the thought of Dom with self-discipline I've perfected only in the past few days, pulling back the part of my awareness that reaches for his. The biggest risk of this whole job is that I'll alert him to my departure inadvertently by letting him into my thoughts, and that he'll let something slip to the Mohirai with his reaction. I know eventually he'll notice I'm gone, but if everything goes according to plan it'll be too late by then for the Mohirai to track me down using Dom's connection to me.

I stuff my bedroll, my waterskin, my glasses, and the little wrapped bundle of food into my saddlebag; sling the bag over my shoulder; and slip out of the tent. I walk through the shadows beneath the cliffs, toward the alcove where we stored the horse tack. Nisaba's bridle and saddle are right where Eumelia left them, and I pick them up, leaving behind the mare's silver-threaded saddle blanket. Eumelia will have to ride with Dom the rest of the way to Velkanos, I guess. Or maybe Hanu will volunteer to take my place.

I carry the saddle and bridle toward the grassy part of the riverbank near the willows, where the horses are resting. Most of the mares lie sleeping in the grass, but Eridu stands watch over them, as he sometimes does. He looks particularly alert tonight and nickers softly at me as I approach. I offer him the little apple I pocketed at dinner. He nuzzles my shoulder insistently, suspecting I have more, but I need to keep the rest of my food for myself, so I give him only a parting kiss on the nose.

I move on toward Nisaba, who lies on the grass. In a friendly undertone, I say her name, and she raises her head to look at me. She flicks her ears a bit peevishly but nonetheless obeys my gesture to stand. As quickly as I can, I saddle and bridle the little mare, then buckle on my saddlebag. I do my best to guess the right stirrup length for myself, then mount her.

As much as I take pride in my ability to ride any horse, it's clear that I should have been riding Nisaba all along. Eridu's wonderful, but Nisaba's the perfect size for me. Sitting properly in a saddle with full control of my reins and stirrups is a welcome change. Nisaba and I will make excellent time together.

I give Nisaba a gentle nudge to trot on toward the willows, but she sidesteps, catching me off balance. Surprised, I grip the saddle pommel to steady myself.

"Wh—What are you doing?" an indignant voice slurs from the nearby shadows.

Eumelia takes a few unsteady steps away from Nisaba, into the moonlight. Spirits blast it all. How did she manage to sneak up on me like this? She stares at me in confusion as I try to think of anything to say that might salvage the situation. But all I manage to do is repeat her question. "What are *you* doing?" I say.

Eumelia's wine-hazed expression sharpens. Her eyes travel from my riding clothes to my packed saddlebag. Cautiously, she says, "I came to apologize for what I said earlier."

I curse myself. Why couldn't I have just let that go? "It's fine," I say. "Really. It's fine."

Eumelia raises an eyebrow. "What are you doing with my horse?"

"She's not your horse," I say, annoyed.

"Well, what are you doing with Nisaba, then?" she says, her voice growing louder and clearer. If I don't shut her up fast, someone might hear her. Eumelia steps forward and reaches for Nisaba's bridle, but I pull Nisaba back a few steps.

"Stay away," I say, trying to make my voice as commanding as possible while still speaking in an undertone. "I don't want you to get hurt."

Eumelia rolls her eyes and steps directly in front of Nisaba. "What, are you going to run me over?"

I glare down at her.

"Oh, spirits," says Eumelia, with an elaborate sigh. "You can't be serious, Ava. Now? You're going to try to leave *now*? In the middle of the night? In the middle of the desert? With no supplies? I thought you were smarter than that."

I open my mouth for an angry retort, then snap it shut

again. This is wasting precious time.

Think, Ava, think.

I wish I could make Eumelia forget this ever happened, the way my mother used to do when we encountered inconvenient people on our journeys. I'm sure I have more than enough unbinding pharmaka here in my flask to wipe this moment from Eumelia's memory, but I could just as easily do some major damage to her, and to myself, for that matter. I have no experience using unbinding pharmaka because my mother never trained me with it.

What I do have, though, is plenty of experience with binding pharmaka.

My awareness of Eumelia stirs like a limb waking from sleep. I remember the two times we shared thoughts before. As I focus on those memories, it's almost like I can step inside her, surveying the possibilities of this other mind. My connection with Eumelia isn't nearly as strong as my connection with Dom, or even my connection with Hanu, whom I've always liked better than Eumelia, but it's still there. I know this girl. I know what she wants.

So now I use it to my advantage.

"You know what?" I say. "You're right." I hop off Nisaba and face Eumelia.

She looks confused. "What?"

"You're right," I say again, taking a step forward. "It's crazy for me to try to escape here, now, like this. But ... what do you think I should do?"

I reach for a memory I saw in Hanu's mind this afternoon. A practiced look. I fix that look on Eumelia.

Eumelia moistens her lips with her tongue. Her voice is a

slightly higher pitch than usual when she says, "I think you shouldn't try to escape."

"No?" I say, taking another step forward. "Why not?"

Eumelia swallows. I keep channeling Hanu. Slowly, I reach up and touch Eumelia's cheek, trace the line from her earlobe, along her jaw, down her neck. I let her feel what I feel: the smooth warmth of her skin, her pulse speeding up beneath my fingertips, the elegant lines of her collarbone. I let her see that I see her beauty. It's easy. I simply look at her the way Dom looks at everything.

Slowly, I take my hand away. Eumelia's desire for me sparks across the tiny space between us. Perfect. I tip my head to the side and smile at her, the way she wants me to smile at her, a smile that's just for her. I wait. Your move, Eumelia.

Tentatively, with a look in her eyes that's almost frightened, she touches my face with both hands. Her eyelashes flutter in a wince as her fingertips trace the bruise she left on my cheekbone. Her thumb runs lightly along the edge of my lower lip. I tilt my chin up ever so slightly toward her.

She kisses me, gently at first. Her lips are so soft, and she tastes like wine and honeyed pistachios. Her hands slide down my back as she pulls me toward her, lifting me to my toes as she presses the length of my body against hers. I let her kiss me for a moment, waiting to feel in Eumelia that feeling Hanu arouses with such expertise.

There it is. Eumelia's losing control.

I return her kiss. Softly at first, then hungrily. I slide one hand into the front of her robe, running my fingers lightly over her breast. Her nipple hardens as she inhales sharply. I run my left hand over her shoulder and down her back, feeling the soft curves of her waist and hip as I untie her sash with my right hand. I draw her robe down her shoulders and let it fall at her ankles, so she stands before me in only her translucent silk tunic and leggings, trembling.

I press my advantage and swiftly unlace the ties at the back of her neck. I gather folds of silk around her waist and lift her tunic off over her head. I let myself feel through her the sensation of the smooth fabric sliding up her back, the touch of the cool night air on her very warm skin. I don't take my eyes off her, focusing on the task at hand, blocking out every other thought but her. I can't let her see anything but what I want her to see.

I take her by the hand and pull her down beside me in the damp grass at the edge of the willow grove. I push her onto her back, and she doesn't resist. I straddle her hips, stroking her body, feeling her reaction through my hands and within my awareness. She closes her eyes. I pin her hands to the ground above her head, lacing my fingers through hers, palm to palm.

This is going to be the hard part. I know it's possible, because Dom and I have shared some pretty vivid dreams and memories, but I'm not sure whether it will work so easily with Eumelia, or how long I can keep it up before she realizes what's happening. But I have to try. Better this than threatening her with my knife or trying to knock her out. She's always been stronger and faster than I am, so I might not succeed that way. I know this will be safer for both of us, but I hesitate nonetheless. Forcing myself into Eumelia's awareness doesn't seem right.

But I don't have to force anything. Eumelia wants me. Badly.

So I imagine the rest and it pours into her: everything I know Eumelia wants from me, everything I know she wants to give to me, elevated by everything Hanu showed me. I grip Eumelia's hands tightly as I let my mind play out the scene. My palms tingle against hers, and I pull Eumelia into my imagination, sharing each sensation, drawing from a well of experience that's entirely Hanu's. And, spirits, does Hanu have some potent memories. So the sex is good. Perhaps amazing. I don't have anything else to compare it to. But I can tell from the way Eumelia's reacting that she's deep in it.

Quickly, keeping one hand pressed to Eumelia's for skin contact, I use my free hand and my teeth to rip four long strips of silk from Eumelia's discarded tunic. In my imagination, I turn Eumelia over, while in reality I also turn her over, face down in the grass. She moans in pleasure as I tie her hands, and then her feet, and finally gag her. Gently, I pull her up to her knees and bind her hands tightly to her feet behind her.

I'm flushed from the effort of holding this vivid encounter with Eumelia in my mind while tying her up. Even though I know I've imagined almost all of it, I'm breathing as hard by the end as if it really happened.

Eumelia realizes too late how I've tricked her. I touch her cheek and whisper, "I'm sorry." She screams, but I've done a good job with the gag. The sound that escapes her will be impossible for anyone to hear from the bonfire, especially over the music. I'll be long gone before anyone finds her.

Eumelia thinks desperately, *Ava, wait, you*—I pull back my hand, cutting her off. I have to get out of here before anything else happens.

Quickly, I hop back on Nisaba and ride away, trying to ignore Eumelia's muffled screams. The sound of her fades quickly enough, but my amplified awareness of her persists for quite a while, until at last I manage to suppress my thoughts of her.

My heart lifts as I think, for the first time in half a moon, that I'm heading in the right direction: toward freedom.

△▽△

When the dance concludes, I let go of Hanu's hand and step out of the ring. I make my way to the place Ava was resting a moment ago, but she's not here.

I'm about to turn back to ask Arkhi whether she's seen Ava when I recognize the small footprints in the sand. The rain has smoothed the beach into an easily readable canvas, revealing that Ava headed back to our tent. Good. We can talk there in private.

I follow her footprints up to the tent and raise the flap. It's dark inside, but it's clear she isn't here. When my eyes adjust, I see what else isn't here: her saddlebag and her boots. My stomach drops.

Ava? I think, reaching out for her. *Where are you?*

She doesn't answer, and I can tell she's shutting me out. I repeat some of the colorful curses I've learned from her as I half-stagger, half-run through the darkness toward the horses. My head spins with wine and anxiety, and it's hard to keep my balance.

The dark shapes of the horses stir on the grassy bank, clearly agitated. A strange sound comes from beneath the shadows of the willows, like a bizarre combination of a kuku bird calling and a dog panting. Has one of the horses fallen ill? I've never heard a horse make a sound like that. Maybe I'm hearing things.

I search the shadows for the source of the sound, and there I discover Eumelia kneeling on the ground, half naked, hands and feet bound behind her, gagged. Eumelia must be even more drunk than I am for Ava to have overpowered her this way.

I crouch behind Eumelia, wishing I had a knife. It takes me some time to loosen the tight knot at the back of her neck. Eumelia coughs when the gag and a crumpled ball of silk finally fall out of her mouth. Her words follow in a rush. "She took Nisaba on the trail back to the road."

My hands scramble in the darkness around the intricate knot Ava tied at Eumelia's wrists. Where did she learn to tie knots like this? I can't find where it begins or ends.

"Leave me!" says Eumelia. "I can shout for the others. You have to stop Ava! You can still catch her, but you have to go now!"

"But—" I say, my wine-muddled brain struggling to keep up.

"Go!" Eumelia cuts me off with a frustrated shout, chucking her bare shoulder into mine to get me going. "There's no time!"

"All right, all right," I say, jumping to my feet.

I turn toward Eridu, who's unsaddled and unbridled and

looking at me with a puzzled expression. I've never ridden bareback before, but I suppose there's a first time for everything.

I grip Eridu's mane as gently as I can and clamber onto his back, then nudge him to a trot toward the trail through the willows. Eumelia's shouts fill the air behind me, and the music at the bonfire stops. I'm relieved she's been heard. It feels awful to leave her behind tied up like that.

It's dark in the willows, but Eridu seems to have a good sense of the trail. I push him to go as fast as I dare given my compromised balance and all the twists and turns and low-hanging branches along the way. Riding bareback is very different from riding in the saddle with Ava, and I use everything she taught me to avoid falling off Eridu as we move faster. There's no way I can ride very far like this. If I don't catch Ava before she reaches the open desert road, I'll lose her.

But to my relief, I hear Nisaba's hoofbeats up ahead. I shout, "Ava! Wait! Please, wait!"

△▽△

Dom's voice is so faint that I'm sure I've imagined it. My elation at having pulled off my escape must be going to my head, making me hear things. I thought I just heard a pair of kuku birds calling, too, which makes no sense at this time of night or this time of year.

But then I hear his voice again, a little louder. Maybe he's reaching out to me using our connection, despite all my efforts to shield my thoughts. I redouble my effort to shut out his awareness until I'm farther along the road.

"Ava! Wait! Please, wait!" he calls, so close behind me there's no way to mistake what I'm hearing. His voice stirs a dull ache in my heart, somewhere between pain and pleasure, quite different from the sharp pain that comes from hearing the Voice in all.

I pull Nisaba to a stop and look back at Dom, ghostly white in his ceremonial robe as he rides toward me through the shifting shadows of the willows. I wonder how in the world he managed to catch up with me. Only when Eridu draws closer do I see he's riding bareback and barefoot. He obviously left in even greater haste than I did. "What are you doing?" I say.

"I want to come with you," he says breathlessly. He looks pale and almost sick with worry, although that might also be motion sickness from the wine.

"You couldn't have told me that a little sooner?" I say. I'm surprised by how glad I am to see him, but I can't suppress the note of irritation. My mind races to rework my plan to include a half-drunk, bootless, saddle-less Dom and the likelihood that the Mohirai will soon be after us, if they aren't already. And, spirits, he's still wearing those blasted ceremonial silks. We'll need to ditch those as soon as possible. He might as well have run after me stark naked.

"I'm sor—" he starts to apologize, then amends it quickly to say instead, "I only just decided. But I do want to come with you. Please, Ava, will you take me with you?"

Even as I fret over my spoiled plan, Dom's words unlock a door inside me that I hadn't fully realized was there. As it swings open, I smile at him. "I promised I would," I say.

For once, the anxious worry in Dom's eyes disappears, and his expression transforms to pure happiness. He says, "I wish—"

Several things conspire to prevent me from hearing Dom's wish. A kuku bird calls directly above us. There's a sharp rustle in the leaves of the willow behind Dom. Nisaba whinnies shrilly and lurches beneath me. Eridu rears and kicks. I cry out in alarm as Dom flies off Eridu's back and through a heavy curtain of low-hanging willow branches. His body thuds to the ground somewhere unseen beneath the tree.

"Dom?" I call, hardly recognizing my own voice in this high pitch of terror. He doesn't answer, and Eridu—the traitor—turns and canters back to camp. I try to calm Nisaba so I can dismount, but she's moving beneath me as erratically as if she's stepped into a hornet's nest. I jump clear of her, landing in a crouch on the trail, then dash toward the tree where Dom fell. Nisaba's hoofbeats follow Eridu's.

I shove my way into the bower of hanging branches that ring the enormous willow trunk. Urshanabi's entire house could fit twice over in the open space beneath these branches. I peer around in the darkness, hesitant to move in case I step on or trip over Dom, who must be injured or unconscious. But I don't see him anywhere, even though the white silk he's wearing practically glows in the dark.

"Dom?" I call again, and when he still doesn't answer, I instinctively reach out for him through our bond. To my enormous relief, his awareness floods into mine, and my frantic questions start flying. *Where are you? Are you hurt? Can you hear me? What—*

In my mind, his voice rings out so loud and commanding that—for the first time—he drowns me out entirely. *GET OUT OF HERE!!!*

There's a muffled grunt, then a snap of twigs. Confused, I wheel around toward the sound and see a thrashing white blur on the ground less than ten paces ahead, moving away from me. Is that Dom? Is he ... being dragged?

A dark figure emerges at the edge of my peripheral vision, moving with a rapid but irregular gait toward me through the branches. I spring back, but a strong hand clamps down hard above my right elbow. All my instincts kick in at once, and I lunge straight toward the person who's grabbed me.

I drive my knee with all my strength into what I discover is a man's groin. He cries out in pain and drops to the ground as I dodge away from the second figure lunging at me. A hand grabs the edge of my cloak, momentarily snaring me. I yank at my collar with both hands until the laces rip open, freeing me from the cloak. I burst out through the curtain of willow branches and hit the trail at a run.

I have no idea where I'm going. Back to camp? Into the river? Out to the road? Spirits, I can't just leave Dom! I have to get help. Back to the camp, then. Fortunately, that's the direction I'm already going.

Light footsteps pursue me. Just one set, I think, but my heart pounds so loud in my ears I'm not sure. I look back over my shoulder and catch a glimpse of a tall, slim man rapidly closing the distance between us. When I face forward again, it's too late for me to swerve to avoid the massive hooded man who seems to have materialized out of nowhere into the center of the trail. His fist swings out from beneath his cloak and lands hard in my gut, knocking the wind out of me. Dazzling pain radiates from my core along every nerve of my body, and stars explode behind my eyes. I crumple to the ground at the feet of my assailant, unable to breathe.

My pursuer slows to a stop close behind me. I struggle to push myself up to my knees, but my assailant presses his heavy boot into my back and pushes me down onto my belly. I wriggle helplessly beneath his crushing weight on my spine, my cheek grinding into the damp sand, my mouth filling with grit as I try desperately to inhale. I gasp as the first tiny gulp of air returns to my lungs, and as soon as I'm able to take a single full breath I try to scream. All I manage to get out is a wounded yelp before my assailant pins his knee into my back, grips a fistful of my hair, pulls back my head, and closes a callused hand over my mouth. There's a peculiar scent on his fingers, something sharp and astringent. I can't scream. I can barely breathe. But I can still think, so I try to focus. Think, Ava, think.

A single desperate idea presents itself, and I seize it. My lips tingle against my assailant's rough palm as I imagine my tiny body overpowering this enormous man, throwing him off my back. It's so improbable, even to me, that I struggle to make the image vivid enough to feel real. His hand jerks back like I've burned him. I take another breath to scream, but his hand returns swiftly to my mouth, this time wrapped in a thick woolen rag drenched in whatever it was I smelled before on his fingers. I briefly try biting his hand through the rag, but all I manage to do is taste bitterness.

"Well, it's a feisty one, innit?" says my assailant, as if this is all very amusing. He adjusts his grip on my hair, wrenching my neck and sending a spasm of pain down my spine. I stop struggling and focus on taking minuscule breaths through my partially-covered nostrils. I'm going to black out if I don't get more air. A troubling darkness swirls around the edges of my vision.

"Spirits, I tought de boy would be de trouble," says my pursuer, panting as he catches his breath.

"Never underestimate the little ones," says a third man, who speaks in a deep, resonant voice that's a bit hoarse, as if he's in pain. There's a strange creaking sound, and then he adds, "Take it easy on her neck there, would you?"

My assailant loosens his grip on my hair, and my forehead touches the cool sand. I focus on inhaling and exhaling through the soaked cloth. The scent in my nostrils is so overpowering I want to gag. My limbs grow weak. Rough hands hoist my limp body off the ground. The swirling void around the edge of my vision consumes what's left of the moonlight, and everything goes black.

UP THE RIVER

I CLAW MY WAY OUT of the awful nightmare, back toward my waking reality. As the heavy fog of sleep slowly dissipates from my mind, I'm relieved to find myself cozily buried in my blanket, safe inside our tent, my arms wrapped around Dom's waist, my cheek nestled against his bare back. Drowsily, I hug Dom to reassure myself that everything's all right.

But when I try to let him go, I realize everything's not all right.

I can't let go of Dom because my wrists are tied in front of him. There's some kind of bag over my head, so I can't see where we are, but we're definitely not on our bedrolls in the tent. We're covered in a damp blanket, lying on a hard wooden floor that rocks and creaks. Wind rushes over us, carrying the moist green scents of the river.

Are you awake? Dom thinks.

I hope I'm not. This has to be a dream. Or another nightmare.

Unfortunately not, Dom thinks.

I open my mouth to speak but find my lips, tongue, and throat too painfully dry to make a sound.

Better stay quiet, Dom thinks quickly. *Are you hurt?*

I take a quick inventory of myself. I'm desperately thirsty. My head aches. I can't see anything through this bag, but just enough dim light penetrates the cloth to make me think that the frightening swirl of darkness in my vision has cleared. My left arm is numb where Dom's weight presses it into the floor. My stomach aches with every breath, and I remember with a wince the awful gut punch, although nothing feels like it's broken or seriously damaged inside of me. The skin around my wrists stings, chafing under the tight bindings that hold my arms around Dom.

Apart from that, everything's great. *I'm all right,* I think.

The muscles of Dom's back relax a little under my cheek. *Thank the spirits,* he thinks. *I didn't know what they did to you.*

They … I think, remembering the shadowy figures under the tree, the slim man who ran after me, the massive cloaked man who took me down. *How many of them?*

I didn't see anything before they covered my head, Dom thinks. *But there were definitely two who tied me up under the tree, and one who ran after you. They've all been pretty quiet, except for the man in charge. He's sitting right behind you.*

That sends a shiver down my spine. I notice for the first time the sound of breathing behind me, occasionally audible over the wind. And that might be the toe of his boot poking the back of my shoulder through the blanket, although it feels oddly hard and cold to be a boot.

Where are we? I think.

On a boat, Dom thinks.

Ah. The strange sounds and sensations resolve into a mental picture. A riverboat. We're lying on the deck of a riverboat. I don't hear any oars dipping in the water, though. We must be sailing. Trying not to move, I look upward through the pinprick gaps in the weave of the bag and see a bright smudge that must be the crescent moon overhead. It's near midnight, then. I haven't been unconscious for very long.

Are you hurt? I think, remembering in a horrible rush of emotion how I'd thought Dom might have been knocked out, or worse, when he fell off Eridu.

I'm fine, he thinks. *I wasn't hurt when I fell, but as soon as I hit the ground, they were on top of me, and they gagged me. I'm sorry I didn't warn you fast enough.*

I'm appalled that he's apologizing for this. I think, *If it hadn't been for me, you wouldn't have been there. None of this would have happened.*

I'm not so sure about that, Dom thinks. Before I can ask what he means, he wonders, *What did they do to you?*

I glimpse in his mind every awful thing Dom imagined they might have done. Fortunately, what actually happened to me wasn't nearly that bad. I show Dom what I remember.

He used pharmaka to knock you out? Dom thinks, surprised.

I guess so, I think.

But where would a man get pharmaka? Dom wonders.

Now that's a very good question.

△▽△

I'm relieved that Ava's awake again. Ever since they tied us up together, I've been focusing on keeping her breathing regular and keeping her body temperature up. Her mind was blank and dreamless while she was unconscious, and I'd worried they'd hit her on the head and seriously injured her. I'd worried a lot of other things as well.

But now her mind races with questions, so she seems to be returning to normal, if anything about this situation can be considered normal.

Where would men get pharmaka? Ava thinks, running with my question. *And who would have taught them how to use it? And why? It doesn't make any sense. The Mohirai would never teach pharmaka to men.*

You know what else doesn't make sense, I think. *Why did they tie us together like this? That was one of the only things I heard them talk about. The man in charge was very specific that you needed to be tied up to me, and that you needed skin contact with me.*

Ava thinks, *How could they know about the binding between us?* She flicks through possibilities in her mind, dismissing each so quickly I can't keep up. At last, she gives up and refocuses on a more urgent insight. She thinks, *Well, if they think we can't be separated, let them keep thinking that. We can use it to our advantage.*

You think being tied up like this is an advantage? I think, skeptical.

She thinks, *Well, as long as we can't see anything, I'd rather know where you are. And it seems better to stick together until we figure out what's going on.*

I think, *Do you want to keep pretending you're unconscious, too?*

No, she thinks. *I'm going to try to get them talking. Or at least get them to give us some water. I still have grit in my mouth from when the big one squashed me into the ground.* Inadvertently, she shares the feeling of her painfully dry tongue running over the sand in her teeth.

All right, I think, swallowing to clear the strange sensation out of my mouth. *I'll follow your lead.*

△▽△

I twist my head against Dom's back and say, as loudly as I can manage through my parched throat, "Please, I need water."

"She's awake," the man in charge says from right behind me. "And she's thirsty. Pick them up." I recognize the deep voice of the man who told my assailant to take it easy on my neck. I wonder who he is. He sounds close enough that I could reach out and touch him if my hands weren't tied. Maybe that's why my hands are tied.

Two sets of footsteps walk across the deck toward us. They pull the blanket off us but leave the bags over our heads as they hoist us to our feet.

The man in charge steps up behind me, so close that the warmth of his body radiates through the back of my thin riding shirt. He smells like the sea. I consider the advantages versus the risks of ramming my head into his nose while I'm tied to Dom. Before I've made a decision, the man leans down toward my ear. His thick beard brushes the exposed skin of my neck as he says softly, "Don't try anything, child. I'll knock you out again if I need to."

I shudder involuntarily, remembering the suffocating hand over my mouth and the swirling darkness that sucked me under. *I wonder how much more of that pharmaka he has,* I think.

Let's assume plenty, Dom thinks.

"Who are you?" I say over my shoulder, in the general

direction of the man in charge.

"A free man," he says.

I frown inside my bag, taken aback. Could he really be one of the free people? My mother and I have been trying to reach them for years. But the free men live across the sea. Why would this free man be here, now, in the heart of Mohiran land? And why would he take us captive?

"What do you want?" I say cautiously.

"A better world," he says.

Someone unties my wrists and pulls me backward, and Dom slips out of my arms. I wasn't exactly comfortable being tied together, but I'm frightened to be separated like this. I grit my teeth to stop myself from crying out for him. I don't want these men to think I'm weaker than they already must think I am.

Bony fingers grip my elbows, holding my arms tight behind me. These hands must belong to the slim man who chased after me. Across the distance between us, I sense a muscular grip wrenching Dom's arms painfully backward. Perhaps that's the big man who punched me.

More of Dom's sensations spill into me as his discomfort grows. He shivers as the damp, chilly night wind off the river courses over his bare skin. I realize with a rush of anger that Dom's been stripped completely naked. I guess these men knew about the pharmaka in those ceremonial clothes, too, although I have no idea how they could know such things. I can't bear that this is happening to Dom, and that it's happening because of me.

"Please," I say. "Please give Dom his clothes back. He's freezing."

No one answers. Our captors reposition me and Dom back to back, interlacing our wrists and binding them tight behind us. They lower us to a sitting position on the deck. Dom's shivers move like tremors through me. I try to share some of my warmth with him, but soon I'm shivering too. I guess I don't have as much warmth to spare as Dom usually does. To my relief, someone at last takes pity on us and wraps the damp blanket back around our shoulders, blocking some of the wind.

A peculiar sound—a combination of creaking, thumping, and footsteps—approaches me, while a normal set of footsteps approaches Dom. I sense bodies standing around us. Someone leans down over me, and again I smell the saltwater scent of the man in charge.

What's happening? Dom thinks nervously.

I let Dom feel what's happening to me so he can't imagine the worst, and he does the same for me. Gloved fingers brush my neck as someone unties the bag covering my head and pulls it partway up. Rough calluses graze Dom's chin as his bag's rolled up to his nose. I look down and glimpse one leather-clad knee kneeling in front of me on the heavily varnished, pitted wooden deck of the boat, alongside an object I don't recognize that gleams in the moonlight. The bag stays low over my eyes, so I can't see more.

Something slips under the bottom edge of my bag, and I flinch away from the sudden pressure at my lips, until I recognize it as a leather waterskin. I grab it eagerly with my teeth and suck in a huge mouthful of cool liquid. Behind me, Dom does the same. I'm just about to swallow when I catch a whiff of flowery sweetness. Dom recognizes the scent the same instant I do.

Don't! he thinks.

Spit it out! I think.

We splutter and cough, and we must have sprayed the unbinding pharmaka everywhere because I hear wordless sounds of disgust all around us. The bag falls back down over Dom's lips, and Dom gnaws on the fabric, trying to wipe the taste out of his mouth. I spit over and over, until saliva runs down my chin, dripping onto my shirt.

"Stop," a fourth voice says wearily. "Let me do it."

I'm so shocked that for a moment I forget how to breathe.

Spirits, Ava, Dom thinks, his heart racing. *Is that ... ?*

"Mama?" I say.

△▽△

"Mama?" says Ava. "How—How are you here? Who are these men? Why—"

The man in charge interjects in a low, warning tone. "Keep her quiet, Lilith, or we'll have to gag her. There could be other scouts on the river."

"Listen, Ava," Lilith says quietly, approaching us from the side. Ava falls utterly still behind me, and I feel her listening, waiting, hanging on her mother's every word. "You've done well. I'd feared the worst when I saw you last. But you've made astonishing progress. I saw you walking today and riding tonight almost as freely as if your accident never happened. That will make everything much easier for the boy."

Ava's back trembles against mine. "I don't understand," she says nervously.

Lilith says, "I'm sure you understand why I left the way I did. There was no way to take you with me the night of your overdose, and anything I told you could have been extracted from you by the Mohirai.

"When I met our boat that night, we changed course to sail east, so we could intercept you. Our scouts have been monitoring your caravan, so we knew when you'd be at the ferry crossing. We're heading upriver to rejoin our horses now, and we should make it back to the coast of the Middle Sea in less than two days."

Ava's voice quavers as she says, "Why are we tied up like this, Mama?"

Lilith says, "We weren't expecting you to leave the camp tonight on your own. I hadn't even considered that might be possible so soon after your overdose. We'd planned to take you from the camp tonight while everyone was sleeping. As it was, you took us by surprise. The whole job came off more roughly than planned. The men had to subdue you quickly so we could leave before the Mohirai came looking for you. The Mohirai must not learn the identities of the free people living among their slaves. And since the boy can see what you see, we need to keep both your heads covered until you're unbound."

Cold understanding washes over me. In my panic, I interrupt Lilith and Ava without thinking. "You don't need to unbind us," I say in a rush. "I want to come with Ava. That's why I was following her."

"It's true," says Ava. "Dom wants to be one of the free

people, Mama."

"No," says Lilith. "He wants to be with you, Ava. He's powerless to resist you. Even a skilled Mohira would have difficulty resisting a bond as strong as the one between you."

"Why does that matter?" says Ava "We're managing the bond fine on our own now. Just leave us as we are."

Lilith sighs. She says, "Ava. I've taught you that the Mohirai have many subtle ways to control the children raised among them. To undo the work they've done to this boy would be dangerous to his mind, and still he would never be trusted among free men. He can't come with us."

Ava's silent for a long time. I overhear her working through every scenario that might possibly lead us out of this situation together. One by one, possibilities dwindle, dwindle, vanish, until only one remains. She squares her shoulders against my back and says in a hard voice, "If he can't come, I don't want to come, either. So let us go. Leave me behind."

"You know far too much to be left among the Mohirai, Ava," says Lilith. "Why do you think we've made such an effort to recover you?"

A tempest brews inside of Ava. She says, "How can you do this to him, and to me? All my life, you've taught me that unbinding is the greatest crime of the Mohirai." Her voice rises, until a warning growl from the man in charge hushes her again. She concludes in a furious hiss, "If it's wrong for them to steal memories from children, why is it all right for you to steal memories from us?"

"Unbinding memories isn't right or wrong, Ava," says Lilith. "What's right or wrong is the reason for which it is done. The Mohirai unbind memories to preserve the Voice's power over the people. We unbind to free the people from the Voice."

With contempt, Ava says, "How does tying us up free the people? And what good is your freedom, if you get it by taking ours away?"

"Peace, Ava," says Lilith. "Your resistance will only make the work more difficult for the boy. It's far easier to unbind the willing."

"I'm not willing!" Ava hollers at the top of her voice. "He's not willing! You can't do this!"

"Ava—"

"Enough!" says the man in charge. "It must be done before we reach the ford. Hold them down."

"Stay back," Lilith says in the tone of command. "Forced unbindings can be catastrophic. She's of no use to anyone if she loses her mind."

"She has more than one use to me," says the man in charge.

"She's no use to you without me," says Lilith. "Don't be a fool."

"Say that again," the man in charge says dangerously.

As the argument between Lilith and the man in charge escalates, Ava thinks, *We have to get out of here, Dom.*

But how? I wonder.

We'll have to swim, she thinks.

What? I struggle to even imagine it, bound and blinded as we are. *We'll drown.*

We can't stay here, she thinks. *I don't understand what's happening, but I don't want to stick around and find out. We're both strong swimmers. We'll manage.*

I swallow. *All right,* I think. *What do we do?*

Ava's idea materializes in my mind, as clear as sight. Standing together, rushing away from the sound of Lilith and the man in charge, letting ourselves fall over the side of the boat. It's so vivid I can almost believe we've succeeded already. My confidence grows. Or perhaps that's Ava injecting some of her confidence into me.

Are you ready? Ava thinks.

Ready, I think.

△▽△

With one swift upward thrust, Dom and I drive our feet against the deck, pushing our backs together until we're standing. We've spent a lot of time maneuvering around each other's bodies over the past half moon, but this movement is still challenging, especially with our height mismatch. Despite Dom's effort to slouch, my arms are jerked backward and upward at a painful angle by our bound wrists. The damp blanket falls off us as we scuttle blindly together toward the port side of the boat.

Surprised shouts from my mother and the free men follow our sudden movement. Dom's foot tangles in a line coiled on the deck. My knee rams into some hard protrusion. His bare hip smacks into the port side railing. We're moving too fast to feel the pain of either collision yet.

"Grab them!" the man in charge shouts breathlessly.

Dom and I leap together over the rail and tumble overboard. I think we've made it, until a hand clamps hard around my ankle, trapping me upside down. My submerged head drags alongside the hull of the boat, sending stinging water rushing up my nose and down my throat. A stab of wrenching pain in Dom's shoulder echoes in my own as he's dragged through the water by our bound wrists. The bag over Dom's head, which someone left untied, slips away in the current. He kicks and struggles to lift his head above water. For a moment, I glimpse the clear night sky through his eyes before the dark current swallows him again. I can't see anything myself or get my head above water at all, so I focus on holding my breath as I drive the heel of my free foot toward the fingers clamped around my ankle.

But another hand catches my free foot just before I land a blow. Then another grabs at my knee. Eight hands in all take hold of me and Dom, and no amount of our thrashing can free us from their grasp. They haul us out of the river like a monstrous, unruly fish and drop us unceremoniously inside the boat. The side of my head and the length of Dom's naked body slam hard against the wooden deck. I cough up water while Dom shivers behind me.

It was worth a shot, Dom thinks.

Oh Dom, I think miserably, *I'm so sorry.*

Don't apologize, he says. *This isn't your fault.*

Isn't it? I think.

The strange thumping gait approaches my head, and I sense the man in charge looming over me. There's a creak as he crouches by my head, and through the wet bag now plastered over my face I catch a whiff of that astringent smell again. A soaked rag reeking of pharmaka settles loosely over my nose and mouth. I thrash my head from side to side, trying to throw it off, but the man in charge presses his hand firmly against my face to keep it there. I force myself again to stop breathing. My heart pounds and my lungs ache for air. Why is my mother letting this happen? How can we get out of here? Think, Ava, think.

It's difficult to focus while I feel what Dom's feeling and see what he's seeing. The burly man grapples with Dom's thrashing legs, his meaty palms and forearms wrapping tight around Dom's wet, slippery knees. In the moonlight, I can just make out the man's distinctive crooked nose and a quarter moon's growth of dark stubble on his square jaw. The rough, bony fingers of the slim man clamp down painfully hard around Dom's nose, forcing him to open his mouth to breathe. I glimpse the high forehead and thinning close-cropped hair of the slim man, his brow furrowed in concentration. My mother's broad-shouldered frame looms over Dom as she wedges the waterskin between his teeth, squeezing unbinding pharmaka into his mouth, her broad hand pressing back his forehead to force him to swallow. Dom chokes, coughing and spitting the liquid everywhere.

My eyes widen inside my bag as I realize what Dom's seeing and feeling: all those bare fingers, palms, and forearms pressed against his naked skin.

Let me in! I think to Dom, as I realize what I must do to protect him.

Dom doesn't resist me as I send my awareness flooding through him. The edges between us vanish as all the walls we've carefully constructed to protect ourselves from each other come crumbling down.

△▽△

Our awareness explodes outward, binding to each awareness in our path, consuming all. We're a girl and a boy, a slim man and a burly man, a powerful woman and a man in charge, joined together on a river through a desert surrounded by seas edging oceans of a single world among the many worlds.

Together you shall seek us, find us, know us, says the Voice that calls within all worlds. *Together you shall amplify us. Together you shall weave us through the many worlds.*

We glimpse a far horizon, far in every way that far can be understood. For an instant, all is known.

And then the Voice departs.

Our awareness collapses back toward us, retreating like the ebb tide of the greatest ocean, exposing what lies beneath, setting our plan in motion. A burly man and a slim man and a man in charge, their minds confused, move as one toward a powerful woman. They seize her by the arms and rush together toward the starboard side. All four tumble headlong into the great Purattu. What remains is a girl and a boy on the deck of a boat that floats on a river flowing endlessly toward the sea.

△▽△

"Spirits, Ava," Dom gasps. "What was that?"

"I—" I don't know what I just did to drive my mother and the free men away from us. Even if I did know, there are no words to explain what I saw while I was doing it. All I know is the relief of success. Dom's memories are safe. My memories are safe. We are safe.

I shake my head to toss the pungent, pharmaka-soaked rag off my face. Through the wet bag still covering my head, I gulp deep breaths of fresh air, waiting for my pulse to slow.

My heart flutters strangely, and my face feels numb. I can't feel my arms or my legs. Something's wrong. Something's seriously wrong.

"Get my knife, Dom," I say weakly, sharing a flash of an image with him. "It's in …"

Awareness lets go of my body, withdrawing into the incomprehensible vastness where it dwells. Darkness swirls around me and swallows me whole.

△▽△

I have no idea how Ava's managed to conceal her knife from me since the night I found her in the woods. But as soon as she shares her mental image of it, I notice the slight ridge pressed against my knuckles. Ava's removed her knife's handle and embedded the blade in the thick leather at the back of her belt, hiding it in plain sight. Clever.

The image vanishes into blackness as Ava loses consciousness.

Stay with me, Ava, I think. There's no response. My heart pounds in my ears. I say aloud, louder and louder, "Stay with me, Ava. Stay with me."

I try to ignore the fact that she's unresponsive to my thoughts and my voice, focusing all my remaining energy on working the blade free from her belt. It's not easy with both hands tied behind my back and my wet fingers numb with cold, but bit by bit the blade comes loose from the leather. At last it falls into my palm. The boat lines that bind our wrists are tough, but Ava keeps a sharp blade. Eventually, I slice through our bindings.

As soon as our hands are free, I turn to her. She lies curled on her side, her arms limp behind her, her head covered in a wet bag. Carefully, I untie the bag and slide it off Ava's head. Her eyes are closed. Even in the moonlight, I can tell that she's the wrong color. There's a bluish tint to her lips, her eyelids, her cheeks.

I press my hand to her heart, closing my eyes as I focus my entire awareness on her, searching for any sign of breathing, any sign of a heartbeat. There's nothing here but silence and stillness. I touch trembling fingers to her cheek, to her lips, to her neck. She's ice cold. Warmth, movement, awareness—everything that was Ava has escaped this fragile shell.

I don't recognize the voice that cries out as I draw her into my arms. My tears fall hot and fast onto her pale cheeks.

Ava, please, I think, as my breathing turns to choking sobs. *You promised you would take me with you.*

But there's no answer.

THERE AND BACK AGAIN

I CALL OUT FOR AVA until all that remains inside me is emptiness. The wind dies down, and with no one at the tiller, the boat rotates slowly in the current, the sail luffing uselessly. I don't know how long I kneel on the deck rocking Ava's body in my arms.

A hard thump against the hull startles me, throwing me off balance. Dropping one hand to the deck to steady myself, I look up.

I must be dreaming. I blink several times, but the vision persists. Across a narrow channel of calm water, beyond a strip of sandy beach, rise the low river cliffs. Atop the cliffs stands a little house, silhouetted against the dark blue pre-dawn sky, golden light flickering behind the two little windows that keep watch over the river. It's Urshanabi's house.

I cry out, but the sound is nothing but a hoarse whisper. I swallow and try again. "Help!" I call. "Please, someone, help!"

From somewhere on the beach, Eumelia shouts, "Dom! It's Dom!"

Many voices call from many places, and three figures hurry down the beach toward me, while others scatter in different directions. Running footsteps pound the planks of the dock, and in the moonlight I make out the dark cloaked figure of the High Priestess Serapen approaching, flanked by Eumelia and Hanu in their white robes.

When Hanu sees Ava's body in my arms, she stops short,

clapping both hands over her mouth. But Eumelia jumps straight into the boat beside me and throws a coil of line from the deck onto the dock. Hanu looks down at the line, dazed. Eumelia says sharply, "Hanu! Wake up, sister." Hanu nods quickly and sets to work securing the boat to the dock.

Eumelia looks down at Ava's motionless form. Her eyes gleam with tears, but her mouth sets in a determined line. "Come on," she says bracingly to me. "We're not letting her get away with this."

Carefully, Eumelia and I transfer Ava out of the boat and into the waiting arms of Hanu and Serapen. They lay Ava down on the dock, and Serapen kneels at her side. She touches Ava's forehead and cheeks, smells her mouth, presses points along her neck, wrists, and ankles. She turns to me with a grim expression and says, "Can you carry her, Dom?" I nod, and she says, "Come with me. Hurry."

I lift Ava in my arms and follow Serapen along the dock, back onto the beach. Eumelia and Hanu follow close behind me. Serapen wades into the shallows of the river and gestures for me to follow her.

In waist-deep water, Serapen turns to me and shows me where to hold Ava, supporting her neck and her lower back so she floats face up between us. She unbuckles the silver flask from Ava's belt. I'd completely forgotten the flask until this moment.

"Think carefully, Dom," says Serapen. "Think back to the last moment you remember before you were taken."

I don't have time to wonder how Serapen knows anything about how we were taken. My mind scrambles backward through my memory, from here to the boat, from the boat to Lilith and the free men, from Lilith and the free men to the dark willow grove.

"Do you remember?" says Serapen.

"Yes," I say. "Yes, I remember."

"Hold that memory," she says. "Let go of everything that happened next."

I have no idea what she means, but I do my best to obey. Serapen uncaps the flask. I close my eyes and focus on the last moment I remember before we were taken.

Ava sits tall in her saddle atop Nisaba, smiling at me in the moonlight, framed by the shifting shadows of the willows. I've told her I want to come with her, and she's agreed to take me. Whatever happens next, we'll be together. This is what I truly want. This is what I've always wanted. There's only one thing I'd change. As I hold the memory clear in my mind, I give myself time enough to tell her, "I wish I'd told you sooner."

In the cool waters of the Purattu, my hand tingles against the back of Ava's neck. I open my eyes and see Serapen holding Ava's head above the surface, trickling unbinding pharmaka through Ava's parted lips, drop by drop. I wait for what seems like an eternity, clinging to hope. But nothing happens.

My thoughts spiral. This is madness. Ava's heart and breath stopped long ago. She's cold as ice. She's gone. She's dead. The word snuffs out whatever hope remains in me, plunging me into darkness. My hands grow cold, and my mind plays tricks on me, as Ava's skin seems to grow warmer against my palms.

I blink. Is it a trick? No … there's definitely some change.

It's almost imperceptible at first, but the color slowly warms in Ava's cheeks and lips. My arms tremble, and Serapen says, "Breathe, Dom. Breathe." I take a shuddery breath, trying to steady myself.

"Good," says Serapen. She closes the flask and slips it back into Ava's belt. She grasps my shaking hands firmly beneath the water's surface, so we cradle Ava between us. "The body is ready to receive her," she says. "But the choice is yours, novice Artifex."

It takes a moment for the High Priestess' words to penetrate the numb fog that's only slowly clearing from my mind. I look at her uncertainly. She looks at me expectantly.

"What choice?" I say.

"The choice to call her back," she says.

"Back ... from where?" I say.

"From where her mind goes when it wanders," she says.

I look down at Ava, who now appears to be merely sleeping, floating peacefully in the slow current of the river. Where does her mind go when it wanders?

As soon as I wonder, I know. Of course I know. Ava's mind always wanders to the city of glass towers.

Hope rekindled rises in me along with the image of that beautiful city. I've followed Ava there so many times before. If that's where she's gone, maybe she can follow me back from there.

Worry follows close behind my hope. I wonder what Ava would choose, if the choice were hers, but I can't bear to consider this too closely. I know what I would choose. And Serapen says the choice is mine.

"Tell me how," I say.

"Listen, novice Artifex," says the High Priestess.

I close my eyes, and the reply rises within me. "I listen."

Once again I find myself standing alone in the place where the wind blows between layers of the unseen. I gaze up at an infinite darkness pierced by innumerable stars, and I listen.

I listen.

I listen.

And once again I hear.

You have asked it. We may give it. But there is a price. Do you accept it?

I feel the pull of Ava's awareness across an inconceivable distance. My longing for her drowns out all other thought. And once again I make my choice. *Yes. Yes. Yes, I do accept the price.*

△▽△

"OMG, Dom!" I say. I push the immerger glasses back on my forehead and rub my eyes. My vision refocuses on my present reality, and I look across the living room toward the kitchen.

Dom stands at the island prepping dinner as he listens to music. It's been a hot day—too hot for clothes—and there's a light sheen of sweat on his chest. He glances up from the mixing bowl where he's massaging kale with both hands. He speaks in a tone of command to the soundbar on the wall, and the volume drops. He says, "Sorry, love, music was too loud. What did you say?"

"I said: O. M. G. This scene on the Euphrates, where I died the first time. It's some of the best immersion work I've ever experienced."

"You're there already?" he says. He steps to the sink to rinse the green off his hands, dries them on a dish towel, and comes to join me in the living room.

"I cheated a little," I say. "I skimmed some of the older memories at two-x. But, anyway, this scene. The sensory resolution is incredible. Did you augment with other sensory libraries, or did it really happen like this?"

I grab Dom's immerger glasses off the coffee table and toss them to him so he can join me in his memory. He catches them in one hand but doesn't put them on. Instead, he snags my glasses off my head with his free hand.

"Hey!" I protest, reaching up for my most precious peripheral as Dom lifts it out of my reach. He gives me a look that says, *That's enough for today, little girl.* I roll my eyes and say, "Oh, fine."

Dom sets our immerger glasses back onto the coffee table and slides into his place beside me on the sofa. He wraps his long arm around me, and I tuck my feet beside me on the cushions, curling up in the familiar space at his side. Even in this late summer heat wave, I enjoy the radiant warmth of his bare skin against mine.

Dom traces slow circles on my shoulder with his fingertip. Few have earned more accolades for immersive design than I have, and yet no digital signal I've ever crafted comes close to conveying the connection that radiates from a single one of Dom's fingertips on my skin.

He says, "It really did happen like that."

I slip my arms around his waist and hug him tight. "I'm sorry I put you through all that," I say. "And through all this."

"Don't apologize," he says, nuzzling his cheek against the top of my head. "I'd do it all over again."

I prop my chin on his chest and look up at him, considering this. He drops a kiss on the tip of my nose. I see myself reflected in those deep-set, watchful eyes. "Would you really?" I say.

The look he gives me sends a shiver of pleasure down my spine. *As long as you'll have me,* he thinks.

Oh, I'll have you, old man, I think, hopping up from the sofa. He laughs as I pull him to his feet and lead him into our bedroom.

Outside our window, the sun sinks behind the San Francisco skyline across the bay, casting rosy light into the bedroom. I turn to Dom expectantly. He takes my right hand in both of his and tugs each one of my fingertips. My silver-threaded immerger glove slides slowly off, and he sets it down on the bedside table. With equal care, he undresses my left hand, setting the second glove atop the first. Now there's nothing left between us.

I take his hands in mine and study them for a moment, savoring the tingling anticipation that flows between our palms. His hands seem to have little in common with mine in this life. His are strong, perceptive, peaceful. Mine are swift, expressive, restless. And yet within these outer forms—his so constant, mine ever changing—we feel so much the same. I raise his hands to my lips, kissing his knuckles one by one, turning them over to kiss his palms.

When I release his hands, he lays me down on our bed. His fingers and mouth move over me, gentle at first, with growing fervor as I respond. We give and receive in turns.

I've spent enough time in Dom's mind in my brief life to rediscover what he likes, and I use the element of surprise to good effect, but he maintains an insurmountable advantage of experience. I gasp with the pleasure of every point of contact between us as his sensations multiply mine and mine multiply his. My pulse races, triggering the all-too-familiar needling pain around my heart.

I try to suppress the gasp of pain that follows, but Dom misses nothing. He pauses. *Are you all right?* he thinks.

Yes, I think, refusing to let the pain steal this moment, when we have so little time remaining.

Dom's hand lingers protectively over my heart. *Do you want to keep going?* he thinks.

Yes, I think urgently, moving his hand from my heart to my breast, willing him to forget my pain, kissing him deeply. *Do you?*

Oh yes, he thinks.

He lifts me up astride his hips, arranging me around him in the precise and practiced way he does everything. His right hand anchors my lower back while his left roams further afield. I see myself through his eyes, fully present here with him in this moment, radiant with my desire for him and his for me. *Spirits, you're beautiful,* he thinks, looking at me as only he can look at me.

The hunger I feel in him amplifies the hunger in me. *I want you,* I think. *I want you.*

Now? he thinks.

"Now, yes, now," I say.

I grip his hands in mine, palm to palm, fingers entwined. My awareness slips into his, and his into mine. I'm within him, around him, beneath him. He's within me, around me, beneath me. Edges blur and disappear as we're swept into motion together, until we're only one, riding the long crest of a wave together until we crash ashore.

We're gone a while. After we've returned, I smile down at him, smooth back the curls from his forehead, and drop a kiss between his brows. He draws me down beside him. I stretch luxuriously from my toes to my fingertips and drape myself over his warm body, completely spent.

"And how was it for you?" he says.

"I think you know," I say.

"Tell me anyway," he says.

No words of mine will do him justice, so I steal the words I need. In a language that died millennia ago, I say, "Our revels make this journey worth the trouble, dear brother."

He smiles. In his mother tongue, he says, "You are the essential ingredient, sweet Muse."

"Not a Muse," I say.

"Still friends, though?" he says.

I laugh. "Best friends," I say.

We lie in a tangle of bedsheets, bodies entwined. I nestle at Dom's side, my cheek on his chest, my hand on his belly. His breath deepens and slows as he sinks into sleep. The last of the sunlight fades outside the window. As the darkness gathers cozily around us, I let my relaxed awareness melt into his, and I glimpse his dream.

He stands alone on a rocky promontory surrounded by a deep blue sea. A ladder of scarlet rope hangs before him, close enough to touch. The ladder stretches endlessly upward into a cloudless blue sky. He faces the dilemma of the ladder with a mixture of awe and wariness. Should he stay on the ground or start the climb?

It's strangely soothing to watch this dream, which I've seen so many times before. I linger unseen behind him on the promontory as he reaches for the ladder. My eyes begin to close as I drift into sleep.

A shadow in the bedroom corner moves, startling me back to full alertness. I sit up, staring wide-eyed into the darkness. There's nothing there, but the rush of adrenaline sets my heart pounding, and the wearisome pain in my chest flares, sharper now than before.

I exhale slowly to calm myself, massaging my eyes. Dom's right. I need to cut down on my immerger time. Those glasses must be messing with my vision.

△▽△

I've been standing in a dark corner of the bedroom for some time when the naked woman in the bed sits up and looks straight at me. Until this moment, she seemed to be a complete stranger, but there's something familiar about her pained expression. I stare back at her in surprise. "Can you see me?" I say.

She doesn't answer. Instead, she sighs, rubs her eyes, and settles back down beside her companion.

I wonder what I should do. Before the man fell asleep, I heard them exchange a few words I understood, which gave me hope that I might be able to communicate with them. But I've been completely unable to catch their attention. They haven't reacted in any way to my speaking, shouting, or waving at them. All I've been able to do is follow them from room to room, listening as they speak their strangely unmusical language to each other, studying the strangely shiny clothes and devices they pass between them, marveling at all the strange lights and furnishings and materials in their house. Their lovemaking is the only thing that seems entirely natural about them.

The soft sound of the woman's breathing deepens and slows. I approach the bedside, looking down at the sleeping couple, the woman wrapped in the man's embrace. In the stillness of the room, I feel the familiar pull of Ava's awareness, the pull that somehow forms a bridge between this world and the world where I stand with Ava's body in the Purattu. Ava's here, somewhere. All I need to do is lead her back across this bridge, back to the place where she belongs.

I reach out to touch the woman's cheek, and I'm overjoyed by the sensation of Ava's awareness swirling into mine.

Hello, old friend, she thinks.

I sense a change between us without knowing its cause, so confusion dims my joy.

I thought I'd lost you, I think.

It's not too late to let me go, she thinks. *We can both be free of this forever.*

Her longing for this freedom terrifies me. *I don't want to be free*, I think. *I want to be with you.*

How long? she thinks.

Always, I think, pouring my certainty into her, pulling her awareness into mine, holding her with me through our bond. She doesn't resist, but though I feel her pleasure in returning to me, I also glimpse unfathomable depths of sorrow as she lets go of her companion.

The man's eyes snap open, startling me. His arms tighten protectively around the woman. For an instant, I'm certain he sees me, but his eyes slide over me as he looks toward the woman. His face contorts in an expression of pain so intense I feel it within myself. He sits up, cradling the woman against his chest, burying his face in her hair. "No, no, no," he moans, rocking her slowly in his arms. "My love, my love."

I try not to hear my voice inside the man's as he calls out for what I've stolen from him. I slip out the way I came.

△▽△

It's almost midday when I wake to the sound of Hanu and Eumelia's hushed voices outside the tent. Dom stirs behind me, but he's so exhausted that he doesn't resurface from sleep.

"Should we wake them?" whispers Hanu.

"Let's just leave these here," Eumelia whispers back.

There's a rustle at the tent flap, followed by soft footsteps departing through sand.

Carefully, I turn over in Dom's arms to face him, trying not to wake him. My aching body protests each movement. When I regained consciousness last night—floating in the river in Dom's arms, the sweet taste of unbinding pharmaka on my tongue—it was immediately obvious that something had gone horribly wrong with my escape plan, but I still don't know what happened. All these new cuts and bruises on my body and Dom's face suggest it's quite a story, but the last thing I remember for myself was my joy at seeing Dom in the willow grove.

Out of habit, I want to blame the Mohirai for the memories I've lost, though I suspect I have only myself to blame this time. I should be grateful I lost only half a night. I should be grateful Dom was there. I have so many questions that only he can answer, and he promised to explain everything this morning.

As I wait for Dom to wake, I study his sleeping form the way he often studies me: with full attention, without turning away. I'm not sure whether the change is in him or in me, but the longer I look, the more I see in him. Somehow he is at once the child who played beside me in the cedar forest by the sea, the boy who set out with me on the road to Velkanos, the man who waits for me somewhere far from here. Somehow I've known them all, and I know them all, and I will know them all again. And somehow they've all known me and know me and will know me. Despite my uncertainty about what lies ahead, I find comfort in these thoughts. To know and be known by someone else is perhaps the only comfort in this world of unknowable things.

The tenderness I felt for Dom when he found me in the willows returns in a rush. *I want to come with you,* he'd said. Whatever else may have happened last night, I'm glad I heard him say that. I want him with me, too.

"That's a relief," says Dom.

Spirits. How much of that did he overhear?

He opens his eyes and looks at me with a hint of a teasing smile. "All of it," he says.

With mock indignation, I say, "We need a rule about eavesdropping."

He says, "First we need a rule about thinking so loud while other people are trying to sleep."

I chuckle. "Fine," I say, extricating myself from his drowsy embrace. "Go back to sleep. I'll take my noisy mind outside."

I sit by the tent flap, sorting through the folded stack of clean, dry, mended riding clothes Hanu and Eumelia left for us. A pang of guilt accompanies the thought that Eumelia might have washed and mended my clothes after what I did to her. I separate my clothes from Dom's and set his down beside him, then push open the tent flap to go outside and dress myself.

The blankets rustle as Dom sits up behind me. "Please stay," he says. "I need to show you what happened last night."

There's a strained note in his voice. I look back at him, and my curiosity turns to apprehension when I see his grim expression. I let the tent flap fall closed and sit at the foot of Dom's bedroll, facing him. He extends his hand toward me, and I take it hesitantly.

His palm tingles against my fingers, and a tempest of Dom's fear, grief, and guilt sweeps through me. My heart aches in sympathy. It seems cruel for me to ask him to revisit whatever memories caused such pain. I remember Urshanabi saying, *It's a gift sometimes to forget.* Maybe the ferryman's right. Maybe Serapen did me a kindness by freeing me from these memories.

I reach out and smooth away the deep furrow between Dom's brows with my thumb. His emotions aren't the only thing hurting him. Despite all the healing pharmaka Serapen gave us last night, his body aches as much as my own. The scrapes and bruises on the side of his face sting where my fingertips brush his skin. I'm about to withdraw my hand, concerned that I'm making the pain worse, but Dom reaches up and keeps my fingers pressed to his cheek. I remember what Hanu taught me, and I focus on Dom's sensations, doing my best to draw out the pain from his bruises, to draw out the pain of his emotions, to let my own sense of well-being pour into him. He closes his eyes, and the clenched muscles of his jaw relax against my palm. I say softly, "We don't have to do this now. I can wait."

"I can't," he says.

He draws me back down beside him on the blankets. We lie facing each other, his left hand covering my right. I close my eyes as his mind returns to the willow grove, the last moment we both remember. His memory picks up where mine leaves off. I see myself on Nisaba and hear Dom's voice saying, "I wish—" The world tilts as Eridu rears, and Dom falls into the shadows beneath the willows. With a mixture of horror and fascination, I witness the dark figures converge in Dom's peripheral vision before he's bound, gagged, blindfolded, and stripped. His impressions unfold rapidly, compressing into the space of heartbeats what took place over half the night, expanding to fill the gaps in my own memory.

When it's over, I open my eyes. Dom watches me, and I feel his awareness in mine, listening silently as I sort through all my conflicting emotions. I'm elated again by Dom's unexpected decision to come with me. I'm profoundly disturbed by all the questions raised by my mother's words and actions on the boat with the free men. I'm mystified by whatever I did to free us from our captors, and by whatever Dom did to revive me afterwards.

Most of all I'm stunned by the change in Dom. I've spent enough time in his mind over the last half moon that I thought I knew his nature: trusting and deferential, hopeful and sweet. But the wrenching anguish Dom felt as he held my lifeless body in his arms has changed him. He's glimpsed a darkness that once seen can never be entirely unseen.

He's quiet for a long time before he says, "Last night, when I knew you were ..." I realize he can't bring himself to say I was dead. I understand; it's too confusing. If I was dead before, what does that make me now?

He can't find words, but he doesn't have to. As he remembers, I feel it all: wave after crushing wave of anger and despair. I reach for him, cradling his head against my heart. His arms wrap tight around me. He says, "I'm sorry."

I say, "Why?"

He says, "I couldn't let you go, but I know how much it hurts you to stay."

I close my eyes, stroking his hair, drawing his awareness gently into mine to calm him. I have no idea yet what to think about the last memory he showed me, of the woman and the man he left behind in that other world.

At last I say, "Don't be sorry. I never meant to leave you like that. We're going to find our way out of here together. I promise."

We lie in stillness for a long time. Beneath the soft sounds of our breathing, I hear the Voice. Usually its awareness pulls mine so hard that I lose my sense of self, but with Dom in my arms, I find to my surprise that I remain anchored in my own body. I listen, and Dom listens through me as the Voice says,

> *We are the bridge joining light to darkness.*
> *We are the wheel turning season to season.*
> *We are the threads binding realm to realm.*
> *We are creator, preserver, destroyer of worlds.*
>
> *Together you shall seek us, find us, know us.*
> *Together you shall amplify us.*
> *Together you shall weave us through the many worlds.*
> *Together you shall answer our call.*

The words repeat endlessly, until at last Dom says, "What do you think it means?"

It's impossible for me to answer Dom without remembering all my mother's warnings. She taught me that the Voice wants to control all, that it enslaves its servants by making them powerless to resist its commands. But how can I trust anything my mother taught me, after what she tried to do to us last night?

I remember Dom's words at the start of our journey. *The Mohirai teach that the Voice works toward its own purposes, in its own time. If the Mohirai are right, shouldn't you try to understand what the Voice wants? Maybe you can work with the Voice, rather than fight against it.* Could Dom be right? Maybe I should try listening to him more.

But there's an awful lot Dom still doesn't know. Maybe the best I can do for now is listen and draw my own conclusions.

So I listen. And as I listen to the Voice for myself, I hear not only its command but its promise. The Voice promises knowledge—and not only knowledge, but companionship on the path to knowledge. For the Voice commands us to answer its call *together*.

Perhaps I'm a fool to trust the Voice's promises or obey its commands. But it seems to me that the Voice has already fulfilled one of its promises. The Voice led me to Dom and Dom to me, so we can answer its call together.

I'm grateful for this gift of companionship, and in my gratitude I find myself truly open to the Voice's call for the first time. I'm not sure whether it's me or the Voice speaking through me when I answer Dom's question.

I say, "The Voice wants to be heard in every world."

Dom considers this uncertainly. He says, "But what does it want from us?"

I'm not quite certain, but I hazard a guess. "Maybe it wants us to find those other worlds," I say, unable to suppress the excitement I always feel at the start of a new job.

Dom gives me a knowing look. "Or maybe that's what *you* want," he says.

I laugh. "So what if it is?" I say. "Two things can be true."

"Fair enough," he says. "But maybe sometimes you could try wanting something a little easier."

I consider him for a long moment. I think, *There is one thing I want that might be a little easier.*

I look at him. He looks at me.

Interesting, he thinks. *Very interesting.*

I decide to lead, knowing he'll follow. *May I touch you?* I think.

He can't help laughing, and neither can I. He thinks, *I thought you'd never ask.*

Tentatively, I reach for Dom's hands. The emotion that flows between us in this moment is warm and bright as sunlight. It's the first time I've let myself share this kind of love with anyone, and it's exhilarating. Each sense awakens fully, amplified by the potent mix of pharmaka and desire.

Dom's fingertips trace the lines of my brow, my cheek, my neck. I close my eyes, feeling what he feels as he memorizes me by touch. He takes gentle hold of my hips and draws me closer. I wind my arms around his neck and draw him closer.

As we kiss, my awareness slips inside of his, and his inside of mine. We glimpse what lies ahead, but it's enough for now to savor this moment, finding the perfect fit between us for the first time, losing our selves together.

START BOOK TWO

Spirits, you've finished Book One!

Book Two continues now at
audreyauden.com

Onward,

ACKNOWLEDGMENTS

FIRST AND FOREMOST, to my existence friend. Our twenty years together have been rich with the adventures and learnings that inspired this story. I know it's not easy to share a life with someone whose mind often wanders from this world; you're my reason for always coming back. Thank you for your thoughtful critique and high standards for this story, and for the excellent title and series name. You make everything you touch more beautiful.

To my editor, Tanner Perkes. Your comprehensive feedback transformed my storytelling. Thank you for helping me, Dom, and Ava find our voices.

To my old friends and dear family who embraced *Realms Unreel* in 2011 and kindly continued asking about the sequel for eleven years. Thank you Robbie Auray, Barbara Hampden, Ed Hampden, Mac Hampden, Madison Hampden, Natilee Harren, Sophie Steplowski, and Christian Waugh. Special thanks to Ian Steplowski and our one hundred and forty-six generous Kickstarter backers who made the illustrated version of *Realms Unreel* a reality. Your collective enthusiasm for my first book made me dare to write another.

To my new friends from the North Country, for your good company throughout the writing of this book. Our friendship has been the silver lining in these tumultuous times. Thank you Tendai Gomo, Emily Meacham, Doug Morin, and Manali Patel.

And to Tanya Tellman, for the gift of sanctuary. Living in the home you and Dave created and continuing your work of land stewardship is a blessing and a privilege. The peace I find here has made it possible for me to write again. When I listen, I hear the Voice in these woods.